DEAL BREAKER

A HAL AND KRISTINA NOLAN LEGAL THRILLER

LARRY A. WINTERS

E-book ISBN: 979-8-9914997-4-3

Paperback ISBN: 979-8-9914997-5-0

Hardcover ISBN: 979-8-9914997-6-7

For Ryan,
Keep kicking butt, kid. Nothing can stop you.

1

"Oh, that's incredible...." If Hal Nolan had ever questioned the five-star reputation of Bistro Cannata, the paper-thin slice of raw bluefin melting on his tongue dispelled all doubts.

Across the table, Kristina sipped her wine, her eyes fixed on a point over Hal's left shoulder. "Glad you're enjoying yourself, but let's not forget why we're here."

To anyone else in Bistro Cannata, she would have looked like a woman enjoying a leisurely lunch with her husband. Hal knew better. The barely perceptible crease above the bridge of her nose, the way her fingers tensed around the stem of her wine glass—she was completely focused on their objective.

"Well?" Hal said.

"We're running out of time," Kristina said, her gaze still fixed over his shoulder. "They just wrapped up dessert."

Hal resisted the urge to turn around. Instead, he picked up his own wine glass, catching a glimpse of the corner table behind him in the curved surface. Even in the warped reflection, Hal could tell the men were fixated on Gavin Brantley, billionaire hedge fund manager.

A waiter walked past Hal's table with a tray of sizzling dishes.

"Is that the Wagyu ribeye? Suddenly I'm experiencing food envy."

"This is serious, Hal. Brantley's finishing his power lunch. We need to figure out our move."

"Give it a little more time. I'm sure some opportunity will present itself. Besides," he said, leaning toward her, "we should be savoring this moment. I mean, look at us, eating at Bistro Cannata like a couple of big shots."

That made her laugh. "It *is* nice." Her smile softened, some of the intensity fading from her eyes. "This place has an old-world charm."

"Is it charm or pretentiousness?" Hal said. "I haven't decided."

"Can't it be both?"

They clinked glasses, and Hal felt a surge of warmth as he met Kristina's gaze. It was a toast to their resilience, and to the Paige Hess trial, which had pulled them back from the brink of financial ruin. Sure, Hal still woke up some nights in a cold sweat, but a victory was a victory. Because of the Hess verdict, they were attracting paying clients, they could once again afford decent office space, and they could even splurge on lunch at Bistro Cannata.

But they weren't in the clear yet. *Far from it.*

Hal's attention drifted back to Brantley's table, where the men were now laughing while Brantley regaled them with some joke or war story. *We need another high-profile trial*, he thought. *We need Gavin Brantley.*

"What's our approach?" Kristina said.

"Just give it another minute." Hal put down his wine glass and risked an actual glance behind him. Brantley was in his early sixties, silver-haired and square-jawed. He wasn't exactly handsome, but something about his easy smile and total self-assurance gave him an undeniable magnetism. He'd look great between them at the defense table, and even better on the news.

"What's going to happen in a minute?" Kristina said.

"Trust me."

As if on cue, the waiter approached Brantley's table and leaned down to speak into the man's ear. Brantley's gaze swept the room, settling on Hal and Kristina with a curious expression.

"Hal?" Kristina said.

Hal gave her a wink. "Showtime." He wiped his mouth with a napkin and stood, then turned to Brantley with a warm smile.

"What did you do?" Kristina's voice held a note of warning as she stood beside him.

He maintained his smile while speaking under his breath. "I told the waiter to put Brantley's bill on our tab."

"You *what*?" Kristina said, but it was too late. Brantley's lunch companions were already saying their goodbyes, leaving the hedge fund manager alone at the table.

"We needed an approach," Hal said. "This is it."

"It's a bribe," she said through clenched teeth.

"Can't it be both?"

"We're going to talk about this later."

Brantley stood as they neared his table, curiosity and a hint of suspicion playing across his features. *Too late to turn back now,* Hal thought.

"Great to see you again, Gavin," Hal said, extending his hand. "It's been too long."

He waited for Brantley to do what most people did in this situation—clasp his outstretched hand and pretend they recognized him.

Brantley didn't move. His blue eyes locked onto Hal's. "We've never met."

"Sure we have." Hal's smile didn't waver, but his mouth felt dry. "You probably forgot. It was at the—"

Brantley made a point of looking at his watch—a Patek Philippe—and said, "I appreciate your hustle but I don't have all day. Who are you?"

Hal hesitated, but only for a second. "Hal Nolan. This is Kristina Nolan, my law partner."

Brantley's expression darkened. "I'm not in the market for legal representation...."

"Of course not," Kristina interjected smoothly. "We wouldn't presume. But we'd love just a moment of your time, Mr. Brantley. We think we could be helpful."

Brantley arched an eyebrow, glancing between them. After a beat, he gestured at two empty chairs. "Don't make me regret this," Brantley said, checking his watch again. "You have five minutes."

They sat, Kristina smoothing her skirt as Hal leaned back in his chair, trying to project an ease he didn't feel.

"Well?" Brantley said. "How exactly do you think you can help me?"

They exchanged a quick glance. Kristina took the lead. "We've been following your career, Mr. Brantley. It's pretty impressive how you keep beating the market year after year. But we couldn't help noticing some ... increased scrutiny in your direction lately."

"Scrutiny?"

Hal leaned forward, his voice low. "Gavin, we believe you might be facing a situation that requires a different kind of expertise than what you're used to."

"You're talking about the SEC investigation." Brantley looked surprised, and maybe slightly impressed. "How do you know about that?"

"We're well-connected," Hal said, choosing not to elaborate on the small network of janitors, valets, and clerks happy to provide The Nolan Law Firm with potential client leads in exchange for hard cash.

"It must be stressful," Kristina said, her sympathetic voice redirecting Brantley's attention.

"Not really," Brantley said. "I have good lawyers. The best money can buy." He paused, seeming to study them. *Come on,* Hal thought, *give us an opening.* Brantley hesitated a moment longer, then leaned forward. "What makes you think your expertise would be any more valuable?"

And there it is. Hal barely managed to keep the grin off his face.

"You have two excellent white-shoe law firms on retainer," Hal said. "And those firms are great for structuring deals, advising on regulations—even handling the occasional dispute. But this case the SEC has been quietly building against you? We're talking about market manipulation, insider trading, fraudulent accounting practices. These are serious allegations, Gavin—the kind that could tear down your reputation and your life's work. You don't want lawyers who've been to Yale. You want lawyers who've been in the trenches."

"Lawyers like you two, I suppose." Brantley's tone was dry.

"We did just win the Paige Hess trial," Kristina pointed out. "Maybe you heard about it."

"I did read about that trial," Brantley said. "But that was murder. Hardly the same thing."

"They're not as different as you might think," Hal said. "Whether it's a criminal trial or an SEC enforcement action, the burden still falls on the government to prove its case. And Kristina and I are very good at finding the weaknesses in the government's evidence, no matter which agency we're up against."

Hal watched Brantley's expression shift from dismissive to intrigued. "You make some compelling arguments. But—"

Whatever Brantley was about to say was cut off by the arrival of their waiter. "Excuse me, Mr. Nolan? There seems to be a problem with your credit card."

Hal felt his stomach drop, but he managed to keep his expression confident. "I'm sure it's just a glitch," he said. "Please run it again."

The waiter looked uncomfortable. "We did, sir. Three times. It's been declined."

Hal forced a laugh, aware of Brantley's eyes on him.

"Here, try mine." Kristina handed another card to the waiter.

The waiter returned a moment later, his expression grim. "I'm sorry, ma'am. This one's been declined as well."

Kristina's smile was brittle. "That's impossible. There must be some mistake."

Hal's mind raced. He was sure he'd made the minimum monthly payment on their firm's credit card. And even if he'd somehow missed a payment, their personal cards wouldn't be affected. It made no sense. Unless....

Oh, God.

He couldn't let Brantley see his panic. Couldn't show weakness. Not now.

"You know what?" Hal said, pulling out his wallet. "Let's just use cash. How much do we owe?"

The waiter cleared his throat. "Including Mr. Brantley's table? It comes to $1,346.81."

Hal felt the blood drain from his face.

Brantley sighed, his earlier interest replaced by annoyance as he handed a platinum card to the waiter. "Just put everything on my card. Hal, Kristina, thank you for the ... interesting conversation. I'll be sticking with my current legal team."

"Gavin, wait—" Kristina started, but he was already walking away from the table.

"Well," Hal said, once they were alone. "That could have gone better."

Kristina didn't answer. She was staring at her phone, tapping its screen, her lips pressed tightly together.

"What is it?" Hal said.

"It's not just our cards." She looked up at him, her eyes wide. "Our bank accounts are empty. All of them."

Hal felt the floor shift beneath his feet. The restaurant seemed to blur around him, the noise fading to a distant hum. He'd thought they'd hit rock bottom before, but this was a whole new level of screwed.

"Looks like our hacker friend is back," Kristina said.

Hal pulled out his own phone. "We need to talk to Cooley. Now."

He waited while his call connected to the FBI.

2

HAL STOOD at the window of their new office, staring at the street, watching for Cooley's car.

The lease was so new, he could still smell the paint on the walls. It wasn't much—a ground-floor storefront in the Old City neighborhood of Philly—but at least here, they could each have their own room again, the air didn't smell like an overflowing Dumpster, and they could walk to their car without fearing for their lives.

Even so, it was hard to celebrate the upgrade. The space was still cramped, still furnished with mismatched, secondhand desks and chairs, and the view—while a slight improvement over their prior trash-strewn location—was a far cry from the gleaming skyline their Center City office had overlooked before the first cyberattack had wiped them out.

Hal focused on the view now, a quaint cobblestone street close enough to the criminal courthouse to serve as their new headquarters, and far enough to be a bargain.

Not for the first time, he felt a sharp ache of loss for what they once had. Floor-to-ceiling windows overlooking the Philadelphia skyline, sleek modern décor, state of the art technology that had made even the most jaded clients do a double-take. The Nolan Law Firm had ascended to the top.

Now, instead of clawing their way back to those heights, they seemed to be barely clinging to the edge of a cliff, legs dangling over a plummet that looked bottomless.

Yesterday, he'd been joking with Kristina that with any luck, they'd be breaking their new lease and upgrading again within a few months. Now, he was worried about their next rent payment.

All because of one woman.

Kristina entered the small reception area from her office. "I can't believe this is happening again."

"I'm guessing your call to the bank went as well as mine?"

"All our accounts are frozen."

Hal's stomach churned. The embarrassment of their credit cards being declined at Bistro Cannata still burned. Worse was the realization that Gavin Brantley had slipped through their fingers.

"Where the hell is Cooley?" he muttered.

Kristina's gaze went past him to the window. A black sedan was parallel parking in front of the building. "That's him."

A moment later, the reception door opened and Special Agent Charles Cooley entered, looking as put-together and unflappable as ever in his crisp suit. Hal felt a flare of irrational resentment. *Must be nice to have a steady government paycheck.*

"Hal, Kristina," Cooley nodded to each of them. "I came as soon as I could."

"Thanks, Charles," Kristina said.

The FBI agent's piercing gaze took in the office. "Nice upgrade."

Hal forced a smile. "Enjoy it while you can. At this rate, we won't have it for long."

Cooley frowned. "Is there somewhere we can sit?"

Hal led Kristina and Cooley into his office. The space was small, dominated by a battered desk and a wobbly chair. He indicated two equally unsteady chairs that faced the desk. Cooley settled in one.

Rather than sit beside Cooley, Kristina dragged the second visitor's chair around to position it next to Hal. Hal had to suppress a smile. Cooley might be their ally right now, but he was still law enforcement. Old habits died hard.

If Cooley was offended by the seating, he didn't show it. "Tell me again what happened at the restaurant." His tone was maddeningly neutral.

Hal scoffed. "Seriously?"

"I understand you're upset, but I need the facts."

Hal sighed, then recounted their lunch fiasco and subsequent discovery of financial disaster. As he spoke, he watched Cooley's face, searching for any hint of ... well, anything. The man was a stone wall.

Hal leaned forward, struggling to keep the desperation out of his voice. "Why the hell haven't you arrested her, locked her up where she can't do this?"

Cooley's expression didn't change. "You're referring to Olivia Hazenberg, I assume."

"You said yourself she's the most likely suspect. She's obviously determined to destroy us."

"We've been over this, Hal. We need evidence before we can make an arrest."

Hal's fist clenched. "Evidence? How about the smoking crater where our bank accounts used to be?"

Kristina placed a hand on his shoulder. "What's the latest on the investigation? You must have made some progress?"

"We're pursuing several leads."

"That's it?" Hal was incredulous. "We just had our finances

wiped out for the second time, and all you can offer is bureaucratic bullshit?"

"Hal," Kristina said quietly, though her eyes reflected the same frustration.

"We're the victims here, Charles. Again. But you're still treating us like defense attorneys." Hal was glad when Cooley flinched at that. "We need something concrete. Something that tells us the FBI is actually taking this seriously."

Cooley's jaw tightened. He sat back in his chair, silent for a long moment. "This isn't standard procedure."

"We lost everything once and thought we were on our way back," Kristina said. "Now it's happening again. We need to know there's an end in sight."

Cooley sighed. "What I'm about to show you doesn't leave this room. Technically, I shouldn't be sharing this—with victims *or* attorneys."

"Yeah, we get it," Hal said. "Our lips are sealed."

Cooley studied them both for another moment, still not convinced, but then he reached into his jacket and pulled out a small tablet. "We brought Hazenberg in for questioning last week. I'll show you a portion of the interview—just so you understand what we're dealing with."

He tapped the screen, and a video began to play. It showed a sterile interrogation room, all gray walls and a single metal table. Sitting at the table was a woman Hal had never seen before, but whose face sent a chill of recognition down his spine. Her brother Oscar had been a nondescript, ordinary-looking man—hardly the type you would suspect of torture and murder. Olivia was similarly unremarkable in appearance, a young woman with her dark hair pulled back in a ponytail and oversized glasses that gave her an innocent, almost nerdy appearance. But the eyes behind the lenses told a different story. Like her brother's, they were cold, calculating, filled with an almost alien intensity that made him want to look away.

In the video, she sat across from Cooley and another agent. She looked bored and vaguely amused. The smug look on her face, so similar to the one Oscar Hazenberg had worn during their awful meetings with him, made Hal's blood pressure spike.

Hal was so focused on Olivia Hazenberg that he almost didn't notice the man sitting next to her. Mid-forties, hair shellacked into submission with enough product to violate EPA regulations, suit that was as expensive as it was tacky, teeth so white they threw off the video's contrast. Hal's vision went red. "Is that Ricky Sawyer?"

Cooley paused the video. "You know him?"

"He's one of our ... competitors," Kristina said. She glanced at Hal, hesitating. "We don't really get along."

"He's a grade-A asshole," Hal bit out.

Cooley made a face. "Showing you this was probably a mistake." He reached for the tablet.

"No, wait." Kristina's hand shot out, stopping just short of grabbing Cooley's wrist. "We appreciate your trust in showing us this. We know it's not protocol. Please ... keep going."

Cooley tapped the screen to resume the playback.

In the video, Cooley spoke. "Ms. Hazenberg, we'd like to ask you a few questions about your brother's death."

Olivia's face remained impassive. "It was years ago. I've moved on."

"Have you?" Cooley placed a photograph on the table in front of Olivia. Even on the small tablet screen, Hal recognized the image—he'd seen it blaze across every screen in their Center City office. The timer counting down, the skull and crossbones, the words *GO TO HELL HAL*.

Olivia looked down at the photo.

"I don't know what that is," she said. Her smirk made Hal's

blood run cold. "But it looks like someone really doesn't like this Hal person."

"As if she doesn't know who I am," Hal said. Kristina touched his arm again, quieting him.

"Ms. Hazenberg," Cooley's voice again, from the tablet's speaker. "We have reason to believe you may have been involved in a cyberattack against The Nolan Law Firm. The same firm that represented your brother at his trial."

Before Olivia could respond, Ricky Sawyer leaned forward. "That's quite an accusation, Agent Cooley. Do you have any proof?"

"We know about your client's history with cybercrime," Cooley said. "Her involvement in the DDoS attack that landed her in prison. And now, just months after her release, we have a sophisticated ransomware attack targeting the very lawyers who defended her brother."

"Still not hearing any proof." Sawyer leaned back in his chair, the picture of relaxed confidence.

Olivia did not share her lawyer's calm. Her face twisted. "*Defended* my brother? Is that what you call what happened?"

"Olivia, stop talking," Sawyer said.

Olivia followed her lawyer's advice, but even on the video, Hal could see the memories flashing behind her eyes. He felt Kristina's grip on his arm tighten as she no doubt experienced the same memories. The chaos. The gunshots. Hal had almost died that day. Oscar Hazenberg *had* died.

"So you think this is what?" Olivia glared at Cooley with an intensity that made Hal's skin crawl. "Revenge for my brother's murder?"

"Your brother wasn't murdered." Cooley's voice remained calm. "He attempted to kill Hal Nolan in open court. The deputies had no choice but to use lethal force."

"I believe this interview is over," Sawyer said, placing a hand on Olivia's shoulder. "My client has cooperated fully, and unless you're planning to charge her with something, we'll be leaving now."

Cooley ignored the lawyer. "Olivia, the ransomware attack displayed a level of sophistication that matches your known skills. And the timing, so soon after your release from prison...."

Sawyer stood, pulling Olivia up from her chair as well. "I said we're done here."

In their office, Cooley stopped the video, looking up at Hal and Kristina. "We had to let her go—not enough evidence to hold her."

"That's it?" Hal's nails dug into his palms. "You brought her in and then you let that smug bastard Sawyer walk her right back out? You realize she probably went straight from your field office to her computer to empty our bank accounts, right?"

"We didn't have enough to hold her, Hal." Cooley's expression remained impassive.

"When has that ever stopped the FBI? Arrest her and find the evidence later! Isn't that the Bureau's speciality?"

"Hal," Kristina said in a quiet voice, "this isn't helping."

He took a deep breath, forcing himself to calm down. "So how does this work, exactly? You just let her keep attacking us until there's nothing left to attack?"

"We're continuing to build our case against her. In the meantime, we've arranged for a safe bank account for you to use temporarily. She won't be able to compromise it."

Hal barked a laugh. "Now you're asking me to put my faith in a magical government bank account?"

"I'm asking you to put your faith in the Federal Bureau of Investigation." Cooley sighed. His voice softened. "These things take time, Hal. You need to remain patient."

"No, I need to remain solvent." He rubbed a hand over his face.

Cooley stood, straightening his jacket. "I'll keep you updated on any developments. Try to stay calm. We'll get her."

"Sure," Hal muttered.

He offered a half-hearted nod and walked the FBI agent to the exit. As the door closed behind him, Hal stood there a moment, feeling the weight of their situation settle onto his shoulders.

When he returned, he found Kristina in the common room, straightening one of their framed law degrees on the wall. The gold embossing caught the light.

"You know what's really depressing?" Hal said, standing beside her. "After the Hess trial, I actually thought we were on the rebound."

"We are." Kristina adjusted the frame one final time.

"Kind of hard to practice law with an empty bank account. What's our next move? Sell a kidney?"

Kristina checked her watch. "We should probably go home and start getting ready for the charity dinner."

Hal stared at her, waiting for the punchline. When it didn't come, he realized she was serious. "Kristina, we just got hacked—again—by the sister of a man who almost killed me. You want to go to some black-tie circle jerk?"

"Gavin Brantley will be there."

"Just what I want to do. Spend the evening begging for work from a man we just humiliated ourselves in front of."

"Still beats selling a kidney, right?" Kristina arched an eyebrow. "Come on, Hal. Do you want to wallow in self-pity? Or do you want to start filling up that magical bank account?"

3

———————

Samantha Klein muttered a string of expletives as she navigated the hallways of the Philadelphia District Attorney's Office. As she passed a group of her colleagues huddled around the coffee machine, all conversation hushed and she felt their stares. Her jaw clenched. She quickened her pace. Three years as the office pariah had thickened her skin, but not enough.

To hell with them. She hadn't become a prosecutor to make friends.

She flexed her empty hand, missing the reassuring weight of the Morris case file she'd managed to cajole from a friend in the police department. But bringing it to Burke's office would've been too obvious, too desperate. Besides, she'd already memorized it.

"Morning, Sam," a voice broke her reverie and stopped her short. Derek Perry, one of the senior prosecutors in the Homicide Unit, leaned against the wall outside his office. His gaze lingered a bit too long on her chest, as it always did. "Did you hear? Brady Morris was arrested last night. Gonna be a hell of a trial."

Samantha forced a tight smile. Derek was the only prosecutor who talked to her, a fact that might have been welcome if it weren't for his obvious ulterior motive of trying to get into her pants. "Yeah, I've been following the investigation pretty closely."

"I bet you have." He gave her a knowing look.

"Actually, I'm on my way to talk to Burke about it now."

Derek's eyebrows shot up. "Good luck with that."

"Thanks." She'd heard the sarcasm in Derek's voice, but why acknowledge it and give him the satisfaction?

She stepped around him, suppressing an eye roll as she felt his gaze follow her.

Focus, Sam. Derek Perry didn't matter. The Morris case did. She needed the Morris trial, needed it like she needed air. She would have to be strong. Unyielding.

As she approached Burke's office, she took a deep breath and steeled herself for a confrontation.

Because it would be a confrontation. Of that, she had no doubt.

She paused outside Burke's door, her hand hovering over the knob. She didn't hear any voices inside, which meant he was alone. Good. She knocked twice and entered without waiting for a response.

"Aldo." She flashed a confident smile that she hoped looked more real than it felt. "Please tell me you haven't assigned a prosecutor to the Morris case yet."

Burke looked up from his computer screen, his bushy eyebrows furrowing. "I'm doing great, Sam. And how are you?"

She resisted the instinct to flinch at his sarcastic tone. Instead, she met his gaze. *Be strong. Unyielding.* "Is that really what you want? To make small talk with me?"

He leaned back in his chair, sizing her up. "No, not really."

"Assign me the Morris case."

Burke shook his head. "I'm giving it to Parrish. He's got the experience."

"Parrish? He's a good prosecutor, obviously, but his plate is full. I've got room on my docket, and I haven't had a decent case in months." She hated the hint of desperation that crept into her voice, but she couldn't help it. "I'm ready for this. I've been ready."

Burke fixed her with a scrutinizing gaze. "This isn't some run-of-the-mill homicide. The media will be all over it. And after what happened with the *Orozco* case—"

It always came back to the *Orozco* case.

"*Orozco* was three years ago," she snapped. Burke's eyes narrowed and she immediately regretted interrupting him. She forced herself to soften her tone. "I learned from that mistake. I do good work." Her phone buzzed in her pocket. She ignored it. "You know I do good work. How long are you going to ... exile me?"

"No one is exiling you, Sam."

"It sure feels like you are."

Burke sighed, rubbing his forehead. "Look, maybe you're capable. But this case.... It's just too high-profile. We can't afford any mistakes."

The unspoken words hung in the air—we can't afford any of *your* mistakes.

Sam's phone buzzed again. She resisted the urge to check it, keeping her eyes locked on Burke. Inside, she was seething. Three years of impeccable work, of late nights and sacrificed weekends, and still, she was defined by one mistake. *Orozco.* The injustice of it burned in her chest.

"Aldo, please," she said, fighting to keep her voice level. "I'm drowning in plea bargains and public defenders. I can handle more complex matters. I'm a good lawyer." She hated groveling to this arrogant jerk, but if that's what it took, she would do it. "I *need* this. Please."

For a moment, she thought she saw a flicker of sympathy in Burke's eyes. But it vanished as quickly as it appeared. "The answer's no, Sam."

Her phone buzzed a third time, seeming somehow more insistent than before. She clenched her fists, feeling the familiar tightness in her chest. She forced it down, years of practice allowing her to maintain her composure despite the frustration and resentment and humiliation.

"Will you at least think about it?"

"Nothing to think about." Burke turned back to his screen. "Close the door on your way out."

Sam slammed the door shut, the bang echoing through the office. The force of it surprised even her, but did nothing to alleviate the hollow ache in her stomach. She leaned against the wall, closing her eyes and taking deep breaths.

Finally, she pulled out her phone. Three missed calls from Emily's school. Her heart dropped.

The drive to the school passed in a blur of worry. Sam hurried into the nurse's office, her eyes immediately finding her daughter. Emily sat hunched on the edge of a cot, her small frame looking even tinier than usual, her face pale. The nurse, a woman in her fifties, looked up as Sam entered.

"Ms. Klein." There was no mistaking the note of reproach in the nurse's voice. "It took over an hour to reach you."

Sam felt a fresh wave of guilt wash over her. "I'm sorry. I was in a meeting. I'm here now."

The nurse's expression softened, but only slightly. "I understand it must be difficult juggling everything, but we need to be able to reach you."

Sam nodded, swallowing hard. "Of course. I'll make sure it doesn't happen again. How's Emily doing?"

As the nurse explained about Emily's fever and stomach

ache, Sam knelt in front of her daughter. "Mommy," Emily said weakly, reaching out her arms.

Sam gathered her daughter into her arms. "I'm here, baby." She looked up at the nurse. "Thank you for taking care of her. I'll take her home now."

The drive home was quiet, Emily dozing in the backseat. As they neared their apartment building, Emily stirred slightly. Her eyes still closed, her voice barely above a whisper, she mumbled, "I'm sorry, Mommy."

Sam's hands tightened on the steering wheel. "Sorry for what, sweetheart?"

"For being sick," Emily murmured, her words slurring with exhaustion. "I know how important work is." Her small body curled into the car seat and she drifted back to sleep.

Sam felt her chest constrict. Her vision blurred with sudden tears. With shaking hands, she signaled and pulled over to the side of the road, barely managing to put the car in park before the first sob escaped.

She leaned forward, burying her face in her arms. Her body shook. Silent tears streamed down her face and soaked into the sleeves of her crisp work blazer.

When had things gotten this bad?

As her sobs subsided, Sam straightened in her seat. She took a deep, shuddering breath. Wiped her eyes. A strange mix of emptiness and determination settled over her.

She couldn't keep going like this. Something had to change.

4

DRESS LIKE YOU BELONG, and no one will question you.

Hal Nolan's father's words echoed in his head as he adjusted his bow tie, staring at his reflection in the spotless mirror of the Ritz-Carlton's restroom. His tux was a beautiful, bespoke Armani that he couldn't look at now without thinking of the firm's empty bank balance. *It's a sunk cost,* he reminded himself. *May as well put it to use.*

Outside in the grand ballroom, Philadelphia's elite were congratulating themselves on being awesome, while sipping champagne and nibbling caviar on toast points—all for the greater good, of course. And somewhere in that sea of black ties and designer gowns was Gavin Brantley, future client of The Nolan Law Firm.

He splashed some water on his face and gave himself a wink in the mirror. *Lookin' good, baby.*

He took a deep breath, straightened his shoulders, and strode out of the bathroom with the smile of a man who didn't bounce checks or dodge calls from the landlord.

As he navigated the hotel corridor, the muffled sounds of clinking glasses and polite laughter grew louder.

The charity dinner was in full swing when Hal emerged into the ballroom. Crystal chandeliers bathed the room in a warm glow that made everyone glitter and gleam. He scanned the crowd, searching for Kristina.

A hand brushed his elbow, and Kristina materialized beside him, offering a flute of champagne. "Here," she said, pressing it into his hand. Her gaze swept over him, a hint of mischief in her arched eyebrow. "You look *good.*"

"Not next to you," Hal said. And he meant it. Her deep blue gown—as much a work of art as his tux—clung to her curves. Her auburn hair was swept up in an updo that revealed the soft curve of her neck.

She smiled and bumped his hip with hers. "Just remember why we're here."

"For a second chance to make a first impression." Hal took a sip of champaign. "What could go wrong?"

"Shall we?"

They waded into the crowd, exchanging pleasantries with politicians, CEOs, old-money socialites, even a few professional athletes. Hal plastered on a smile, but the sole purpose of each interaction was only to move them closer to Brantley, who stood on the far side of the ballroom holding court with a group of admiring executives. By the time he and Kristina extracted themselves from a mind-numbing conversation with a judge old enough to be his grandfather, Hal's cheeks ached from all the forced smiling.

Just as Brantley came within range, Hal's gaze landed on a far less welcome sight.

Ricky Sawyer.

The lawyer stood near the bar, chatting with a council-woman. His tux looked every bit as elegant as Hal's, his blond hair slicked into place.

"Son of a bitch," Hal muttered.

He felt Kristina tense beside him. "Hal, now is not the time."

But Hal's feet were already moving, powered by pure, seething hatred. He shouldered past people, a dull roar of blood in his ears.

When Sawyer spotted him coming, his mega-watt smile lit up a few extra notches. "Nolan! What a surprise. Did you sneak in through the service entrance?"

Hal was in no mood for banter. "Representing the woman who tried to destroy my firm?" His voice sounded low and dangerous, even to him. "The sister of the man who shot me? That's a new low, Ricky. Even for you."

The councilwoman at Sawyer's side shifted uncomfortably, then slipped away. Sawyer frowned at Hal. "That's not personal. I'm just doing my job."

"Bullshit."

Sawyer's smile returned. "Okay, maybe it's a little personal. That's part of the fun, right?"

"You think this is fun?" Hal felt his fist clench around the stem of his champaign flute. He was dimly aware of Kristina hovering anxiously nearby. "She's trying to destroy everything Kristina and I have built."

"Oh, come on," Sawyer said. "I mean, did you really build that much?"

Hal stepped closer. "You smug—"

"Hal!" Kristina's sharp voice cut through the haze of his anger. "That's enough."

But it was too late. Heads were turning, conversations falling silent as people noticed the juicy drama unfolding before them. Hal felt his face flush with anger and embarrassment.

"Is this how you do business?" Hal said. "Screwing over your colleagues, defending people who don't deserve it?"

"*Everyone* deserves a defense, Hal. I believe they teach that in law schools—even the one you went to. But maybe you slept through that class. It would explain a lot." Hal could feel Kristina tugging at his arm now, hear her urgent whispers. But he couldn't turn away from Sawyer's malicious grin. "Face it, Hal. You're a has-been. No, scratch that. You're a never-was. You and your wife—"

Something snapped inside Hal. Before he knew what was happening, his fist was flying toward Sawyer's face. But Sawyer, despite the scotch on his breath, was as slippery as ever. He dodged, and Hal's punch connected with the shoulder of a waiter balancing a tray of champagne flutes.

The man's yelp and the crash of breaking glass cut through the din of the party. Sawyer glided away, and suddenly, all eyes were on Hal. The fight drained out of him instantly, replaced by a cold, sinking feeling in the pit of his stomach. A few beefy-looking security guards regarded him from the corner. Hal caught a glimpse of Gavin Brantley, watching with disdain.

Kristina gripped his arm. "Act like nothing happened and walk with me. We're leaving. *Now*."

As she steered him toward the exit, he caught snippets of conversation from the crowd. A lot of it was about them. None of it was positive.

The cool night air hit Hal like a slap to the face as they burst out of the Ritz-Carlton and onto the Avenue of the Arts. Kristina rounded on him, her eyes flashing with a fury that made him want to throw himself in front of a passing bus.

"What the hell? We had a shot at landing Brantley in there, and you lost control? That's not like you!"

The streetlights caught the shimmer of Kristina's dress. Even furious, she was breathtaking. It was almost enough to make him forget the monumental screw-up he'd just committed. Almost.

"I'm sorry. I just ... when I saw Sawyer there, so smug, knowing he's representing Oscar Hazenberg—"

"*Olivia* Hazenberg." Kristina's gaze softened as she seemed to study him with concern. "Oscar Hazenberg is dead, Hal. Dead and burning in hell where he belongs."

Hal ran a hand through his hair. "Maybe it's not as bad as we think. I could go back in, apologize...."

Kristina let out a humorless laugh. "We're going home."

He knew she was right. No amount of smooth talking could salvage this train wreck—not tonight, anyway. The smart play was to cut their losses, retreat to lick their wounds, and pray inspiration for Plan B struck before the creditors did.

"Nolan!"

Hal turned, surprised to see Gavin Brantley emerge from the hotel's entrance. He felt a flicker of hope. Maybe all wasn't lost after all.

"Gavin," he said, meeting the man with what he hoped was a winning smile. "Sorry about that ... professional disagreement in there. If we could just have a moment to discuss your situation—"

Brantley held up a hand, silencing him. "I'm not here to talk about the SEC. I have a different proposition for you."

Hal shot a quick glance at Kristina. "We're listening," he said cautiously.

Brantley stepped closer, the scent of expensive cologne wafting over Hal. "Not here. Meet me at my office tomorrow morning, 8 AM sharp."

"Why?" Kristina said. There was suspicion in her voice. "If you're not interested in our services—"

"I have a friend with a problem," Brantley said.

Hal frowned. None of this was sounding good, but neither did bankruptcy. "What kind of problem?"

Brantley's expression was cold, inscrutable. "Your kind."

5

THE OFFICES of Brantley Capital occupied the top six floors of a downtown high-rise that put even their former Center City office building to shame. As Kristina stepped out of the elevator onto the 35th floor, the view made her heart skip—a panoramic vista, Philadelphia bathed in the soft glow of morning.

A receptionist ushered them into Brantley's corner office. He rose from his chair to greet them. "Right on time. I appreciate punctuality."

"Nice place you've got here," Hal said, turning in a slow circle.

Brantley's lips curved into what might have been a smile. "You haven't seen anything yet."

"There's more?"

"Follow me."

He led them to a door at the back of his office. Kristina shot Hal a look, but he just shrugged and stepped in after Brantley.

They emerged into a full-sized basketball court, complete with polished hardwood floors and professional-grade backboards—and glass walls displaying a sweeping view of the city below.

"Welcome to my inner sanctum," Brantley said.

"I would've pegged you as more of a golf guy," Hal said.

Brantley smirked, grabbing a basketball from a rack. "You play?"

"Some pickup games in college," Hal said.

"How about you, Kristina?"

"I'm not really into sports." The closest she'd come to basketball was a sports law elective she'd taken in law school.

"How about a friendly game of HORSE?" Brantley stripped off his suit jacket and rolled up his sleeves, revealing arms that were surprisingly muscular. "We can discuss business while we play."

Kristina glanced at her heels. *Screw it.* She kicked them off and stood barefoot on the hardwood. "I'm game."

"Really?" Hal's eyebrows shot up.

She shrugged, unable to suppress a grin. "Why not?" It was worth agreeing to this ridiculous game just to see that stunned look on his face.

"That's the spirit." Brantley bounced her the ball. "Ladies first."

The last time she'd touched a basketball was probably middle school gym class. She walked to the free throw line, bounced the ball twice like she'd seen on TV, and shot.

The ball arced through the air and swished through the net.

All three of them stared in silence.

"Not really into sports, huh?" Brantley said. "You're up," he said to Hal, passing him the ball.

Hal took Kristina's place at the free throw line and squared up before releasing his shot. It clanged off the rim. "H," he muttered.

Brantley laughed, then sank his shot easily. "Tell me why you think you're here."

Kristina took the ball from him. "We're hoping it's because

you've reconsidered our offer to represent you in the SEC investigation." Another shot, and, to her surprise, another swish.

Hal said, "Who are you and what have you done with my wife?"

She grinned at him. "Beginner's luck."

"Right." Hal grabbed the ball, lobbed it up, missed. "This is starting to be embarrassing."

Brantley copied her shot perfectly, sinking the ball. "This isn't about the SEC. It's a murder case."

"A murder case?" Hal turned with obvious interest.

"One of my employees was arrested yesterday. I actually learned about it during the charity event. Nico Ramirez. Twenty-six years old, Mexican kid."

"I didn't think finance bros were that violent," Hal said.

"He's not an analyst. He's actually ... well, he's a janitor." Brantley tossed the ball to Kristina. "You're up."

Kristina moved to the three-point line. The ball left her fingers and dropped through the net without touching the rim.

"Oh, come on," Hal said. "*Seriously?*"

She was starting to enjoy this.

Hal gave her a look, loosened his tie, and took a deep breath. Carefully, he aimed his shot.

Not even close.

"H-O-R." She couldn't hold back a grin.

"Well?" Brantley said.

Kristina turned to look at him. "Why would a hedge fund manager hire lawyers to defend a janitor?"

"Because I believe he's innocent." Brantley matched her three-pointer casually. "And because I take care of my people."

"Really?" Maybe the competition was making her bolder, but she didn't bother hiding the skepticism in her voice. She took a position to the right of the hoop, almost directly under it. The ball went in.

Hal took her spot, pitched the ball up, missed and cursed loudly.

But Brantley seemed to have lost interest in the competition. His gaze was on Kristina. "You don't believe me?"

"That you're worried about the murder charge? No. I think you're worried about what Ramirez might tell the Feds to save his own skin."

Now Brantley's smile disappeared completely.

"He cleaned your offices, right?" Kristina said. "Moving in the background, invisible while everyone talked freely around him. And you're thinking maybe he witnessed things he shouldn't have. Maybe he overheard conversations. Saw documents that weren't meant for a janitor's eyes. The kind of information the SEC would love to get their hands on."

Brantley retrieved the ball from the floor, but instead of taking his shot, he shoved it roughly into its place on the rack. Apparently, the game was over.

"You have a cynical worldview."

"You haven't denied it."

Brantley's face hardened. "*You* came to *me*. Did you forget that? Desperate, practically on your knees. Your firm is one missed payment away from bankruptcy. I can smell it on you."

She flinched, suddenly feeling tiny in his vast, personal basketball court, an insignificant peon with whom he'd condescended to share his toys. But then Hal's shoulder pressed against hers, a warm, solid presence.

"No one's on their knees, Gavin," he said, his voice firm.

"You asked me for a case. I'm offering you one."

"Not the one we wanted," Kristina said.

"Money is money."

"And in return for that money?"

Brantley shrugged. "All you have to do is make sure Ramirez's defense stays focused on the murder charge. Keep him away from any deals involving ... other matters." He pulled an envelope from his pocket and held it out. "Consider this a retainer."

Hal seemed to hesitate, then took the envelope, opened it. Kristina didn't look. She didn't want to be tempted. But she heard Hal's sharp intake of breath.

"We'll need to discuss this," she said, before Hal could speak.

"Understandable. But don't take too long. If you're not interested, I'm sure Ricky Sawyer would be."

From the corner of her eye, she saw Hal's face go red. She knew exactly what he was thinking. Ricky Sawyer, who was already representing the hacker who'd attacked their firm. Who'd humiliated Hal at the charity dinner. Who'd probably love nothing more than to steal a client from them.

In the elevator, Hal couldn't seem to meet her eyes. "Did you have to be so confrontational? Brantley's right—we *did* ask him for a case, and he *is* giving us one. You threw it back in his face."

"He's using us, Hal."

"He's retaining us for a murder trial."

The elevator glided silently downward.

"We can't take money from Brantley to represent Ramirez," she said.

"I disagree."

Now they faced each other, and she could see in his eyes that he'd already made up his mind that they should take Brantley's deal. She shook her head, exasperated that he could be so willfully blind to the ethical implications.

"If Ramirez has evidence about Brantley that he could trade to the authorities, then his interests are directly opposed to Brantley's. What if the prosecution offers Ramirez a deal? Immunity in exchange for testimony against Brantley? What then?"

"Then we advise Ramirez of his options and let him decide."

"While taking money from the man he'd be testifying

against?" Her hands clenched at her sides. "Hal, we need to go back, apologize, and tell Brantley we can't take this case. The rules exist for a reason."

"The rules?" Hal pulled out Brantley's envelope and held it open in front of her. "Look at the number, Kristina."

She tried not to look, but couldn't help herself. The figure written on the check made her throat go dry. "That doesn't change anything." But even as she said it, she could feel her resolve wavering. She thought of their ransacked bank accounts, the declined credit cards, the unpaid bills.... Her hands trembled.

"One case," Hal said. "We take one case that requires a ... flexible interpretation of the rules. And then we're back on our feet." He met her gaze. "Trust me."

Kristina watched the envelope vanish into his suit pocket. This time, she didn't argue.

6

———

THE INTERVIEW ROOM at Riverside Correctional Facility hadn't changed since its days as a women's prison—same institutional beige walls, same migraine-inducing fluorescent lights, same metal furniture bolted to the floor. It had been at least thirty minutes since a correctional officer, Juan Gomez, had brought them here to wait for their new client. They always made defense attorneys wait—it was basically a tradition, and promptness would only have awakened Hal's suspicions. He usually didn't mind waiting, was used to it, but thirty minutes of pretending not to notice Kristina's angry looks was becoming more challenging by the second.

Finally they heard sounds from the other side of the door. Gomez's keys working the lock.

"Remember," Kristina said in his ear, "we're here as Ramirez's lawyers, not Brantley's."

Before he could respond, the door opened. He and Kristina stood as Officer Gomez stepped inside the room with a lean, compact man in an orange jumpsuit. Nico Ramirez, the man whose freedom they'd been paid to safeguard. *Or sacrifice,* Hal thought, *depending on how you look at it.*

Most inmates hunched and shuffled. Not Ramirez. He moved with surprising composure, chin level and back straight. Gomez placed a hand on his back in a gesture that almost looked friendly, steering rather than shoving him into the room.

Ramirez's gaze lingered on Hal and Kristina for a moment before turning to Gomez. "*Has visto a estos payasos antes?*"

Gomez smirked. "Careful. That one understands." He nodded at Kristina. "Isn't that right, *chica?*"

"It's *Señora Nolan* to you." Kristina turned to Hal. "He asked if we're clowns."

Hal laughed and shook his head. "Answer him, Gomez."

Gomez's eyes narrowed. "The Nolans are ... more than they appear." He guided Ramirez to one of the metal chairs. "Annoying, *si*. But effective."

"Wow, Gomez, thanks. I'm going to have that printed on billboards."

He and Kristina sat at the table and waited while Gomez went through the routine of securing Ramirez to the furniture. Hal noted an absence of Gomez's usual roughness—replaced by an almost paternal demeanor as he placed the younger man's hands on the table and fed the chain through the loop. And it wasn't Mexican solidarity—he'd seen Gomez bounce plenty of Latino heads against this room's walls. No, Ramirez had somehow managed to make Gomez like him, which was no easy feat.

Interesting.

He waited until the door clanged shut behind Gomez, then leaned forward. "My name is Hal Nolan. This is my partner, Kristina Nolan. Gavin Brantley arranged for us to represent you —assuming you agree."

"I'm innocent. I didn't kill Natalia." Ramirez's voice caught on the name, which Hal recognized as his wife's from the minimal information they knew about Ramirez's alleged crime.

"Why do the police think otherwise?" Hal said, trying to keep his voice gentle.

Ramirez shook his head. His hands curled into fists. The chain between them jingled against the table's metal loop. "I loved her."

Hal exchanged a quick glance with Kristina. She leaned in. "Tell us about her."

"We met in high school." His scowl softened. "Been together ever since." He traced a pattern on the metal table with his finger. "Natalia was smart—way smarter than me. She was getting her nursing degree. Taking night classes while working days at the hospital to help pay for tuition. She was going to be a great nurse."

"With schedules like that, you must have barely seen each other," Kristina said. "That must have been hard. A strain on your relationship."

"Not for us." Ramirez shook his head firmly. "We made it work. I'd drive her to class most nights. Sometimes we'd squeeze in a quick dinner." A ghost of a smile touched his lips. "And every Sunday was just for us—no work, no studying. We were happy."

"What about the night she died?" Hal said.

Nico took a shuddering breath. "I got home late that night. Later than usual. One of Brantley's analysts had spilled coffee everywhere right before I was supposed to leave. By the time I got home...." His voice cracked. "She was strangled. With a ... a USB cable from her laptop."

The image that flashed through Hal's mind was not pleasant.

"I called the police right away," Ramirez said. "911. They were supposed to help but...."

"But they took you into custody instead," Hal finished. "They always think it's the husband."

"The public defender said I should take a plea deal. He's

already talking to the DA." His eyes grew wet. "That's why I need *real* lawyers. Someone murdered Natalia and I need to find out who. You can get me out of here, right?"

"We're very good at winning murder trials," Hal said. He placed their retainer letter on the table in front of Ramirez, along with a pen. "If you'll sign—"

Kristina cleared her throat. "Before we formalize our relationship, Mr. Ramirez, there's something we need to discuss."

"Nico," he said, meeting her gaze. "Call me Nico."

"Okay, Nico. Hal mentioned that Gavin Brantley is paying our fees."

Hal tensed. He knew what was coming.

"Yes," Nico said. "It's generous of him."

Kristina's expression tightened. "It is generous. But it also creates what we call a potential conflict of interest. So before we proceed, we need you to understand that Gavin Brantley may have ulterior motives for paying your legal fees. He may be hoping to influence your defense strategy in ways that protect him rather than serve your best interests."

"What kind of ulterior motives?"

"He may be concerned about information you might have gained while cleaning his offices. Information that could interest federal investigators."

Hal cringed, holding his breath.

But instead of recoiling from this revelation, Nico visibly relaxed. "You don't need to worry about that."

"We do, actually," Kristina said. "As members of the bar, we're bound by certain rules of ethics—"

"No, I mean it's not a problem." Nico leaned forward, lowering his voice. "When they arrested me—threw me in here —I made a few calls. Enough to get the rumors started, you know? I knew word would get back to Brantley." His eyes flickered between them. "And I knew what he'd think."

"Wait a second." Hal blinked. *"You're playing him?"* A laugh burst from his throat before he could stop it.

Nico straightened in his chair. His voice hardened. "I didn't kill Natalia, and I can't afford a good lawyer. Brantley makes millions, paying me minimum wage to clean his toilets." His chains rattled as his hands clenched into fists. "I never heard anything, never saw anything incriminating. But Brantley doesn't know that. He just knows I might have."

"Hey, I'm not judging," Hal said. "But you understand what you just told us can't ever leave this room, right? If Brantley discovers you've been ... misleading him, the money will stop."

"But you're my lawyers now, right?"

"Absolutely." Hal tapped the retainer agreement. "Once you sign this."

"Okay," Kristina said. Hal couldn't tell if Nico's revelation had relieved her ethical concerns or increased them, but she pulled out a legal pad. "Tell us everything. Start from the beginning."

7

———

Samantha Klein stared at the autopsy photographs spread across her desk, trying to focus on the dead woman's face. But her thoughts kept circling back to Emily's whispered "I'm sorry, Mommy" in the car ride home from the nurse's office. Sorry for being sick. Sorry for interrupting her very important career. The memory twisted in Sam's gut like a knife.

What career? The endless parade of plea bargains and minor cases under which Aldo Burke intended to bury her? Sleepless nights, missed school events, frozen dinners eaten alone while Emily slept? What was she doing with her life?

"Hey, you with me, Sam?"

She blinked and looked up at Dan Coffey. The homicide detective filled one of the visitor chairs facing her desk, his broad shoulders blocking her view of the door. Despite being well into his fifties, with a face lined by decades of hard cases, he still looked as invested as ever—while she felt burnt out at thirty-four.

"Sorry." She shuffled the crime scene photos into a neat stack. "Just thinking about the case."

"Uh-huh."

"What?" she said, a note of challenge in her voice.

His weathered face held an uncharacteristic expression of concern—but also skepticism. "What's the victim's name?"

Sam shook her head. "Dan—"

"Natalia Ramirez," Coffey said. He leaned forward. "Sam, you look like hell."

"Thanks. You look great, too."

"I'm serious."

"I know the case," she said, even as some of the facts miraculously came back to her. "The husband killed her. Strangled her with a power cord from a laptop—"

"A USB cable."

"Right." Samantha looked at the photos again. *Natalia Ramirez.* The autopsy slab was never flattering, and the harsh lighting made the young woman's high cheekbones appear gaunt, made her long dark hair, splayed across the metal surface, seem spidery. A pale, grooved line circled her throat, bordered on both sides by ugly reddish-purple bruising. Where the cable had crossed over itself, the bruising was darker, deeper. Crescent-shaped scratches showed where her fingernails had raked at her own skin in desperation.

"This is the killer." Coffey reached forward to slide a different sheet in front of her—the defendant's booking photo. "Nico Ramirez."

A normal-looking young guy. They were always normal-looking, especially the wife-killers. Why had he done it? Jealousy? Drunken anger? Some sex kink? After years working cases like this one, Sam had learned not to expect answers. Answers came at trial. But when the accused couldn't afford a lawyer and one was appointed to him from the Public Defender's Office, a plea deal was the expected result.

She glanced at her watch. Ramirez's public defender was twenty minutes late.

Is this what I went to law school for? She jotted down a few notes, solely for Coffey's benefit. Cases like this one didn't need a prosecutor—they needed a rubber stamp. And apparently that was all Burke thought she was.

"The ME noted petechial hemorrhaging and a fractured hyoid bone," Coffey said. "This wasn't quick. She suffered."

"And?" Sam met the detective's stare. It amazed her that after decades on the job, he could still get personally invested—that he could still care. "We'll offer to knock the charge down to third-degree murder. It's not like we have evidence of premeditation anyway. Jerry will say yes, because he's got three-hundred other cases on his docket and no time or resources to fight this one. Ramirez goes to a maximum security prison for forty years. We move onto the next dead woman of color."

"Jesus, Sam. Listen to yourself. It's not healthy to be this jaded. Is there someone, maybe, you can talk to?"

Her phone vibrated on her desk. She swept it up, grateful for the interruption, then frowned at the display. "It's Jerry."

"About time," Coffey said. "Put him on speaker."

She did. "You're late."

"I meant to call earlier, but you know how it is." The public defender's voice filled her small office. He sounded harried, frantic—but Jerry Newman always sounded that way. "Listen, sorry about the confusion, but I'm not representing Ramirez anymore."

"What?" Sam sat up straighter.

"He's got new counsel. Hal and Kristina Nolan. You know them?"

Everyone in this building knew the Nolans. "When did this happen?"

"They visited him at the jail yesterday, apparently. Anyway, you'll need to coordinate with them on the plea discussions. Talk soon."

The call ended. Samantha stared at her phone, mind racing.

Coffey whistled low. "Donovan almost lost his job over the Paige Hess trial. Burke hates the Nolans—has some personal grudge. He's going to explode when he hears this."

She leaned back in her chair, thoughtful. "Do me a favor, Dan. Keep this between us. Just for now."

He peered at her. "Sam, you have to tell Burke...."

"Why?" She let out a harsh laugh. "He'll just say the case is too important for me to handle. He'll give it to Parrish or Perry."

"He runs the Homicide Unit. He's your boss."

"So?" She gestured at her cramped office, her cluttered desk, the stack of plea agreements waiting for her signature. "I followed all his rules. Kept my head down. Smiled and nodded while he buried me under busywork. None of it matters. One mistake—*one mistake*—three years ago, and he treats me like I'm radioactive."

Coffey's eyes widened, apparently taken aback by the bitterness in her voice. She didn't care. It felt good to finally say it all out loud.

Coffey studied her for a long moment. "How long do you think you can hide this from him?"

"Let me worry about that." Her gaze drifted down to the photos again—Natalia and Nico Ramirez. "Why would the Nolans take a case like this? There's no money in it. No publicity. What's their angle?"

"I can poke around. See what I can find out."

The comment caught her off-guard. "You'd do that?"

Coffey shrugged it off with typical cop nonchalance. "Hey, this is our case, right?" He pushed himself up and headed for the door. Sam was turning her attention to the case file when he paused. "Sam?"

She looked up.

"The Nolans didn't get where they are by losing trials."

She smiled, and this time it felt genuine. "Time to change that."

8

————

HAL GRIPPED the steering wheel of their battered Camry while Kristina sat beside him, both surveying The Sharp End's parking lot. Nothing but gleaming Audis, BMWs, and even a Cybertruck—apparently axe-throwing was how Philly's young professionals got in touch with their inner lumberjack these days.

"When did Lena become a hipster?"

"I think she's here on a job," Kristina said.

"Then she doesn't need us." Hal gave her a look. "Kristina, with Brantley's money there's no limit anymore. We could engage Monarch Investigations, have them put a whole team on this. Former FBI agents, forensics experts—"

"We've been over this." Kristina turned toward him, her lips tightening into a line that said this was non-negotiable. "Lena helped us rebuild after the ransomware attack. When we needed her, she worked for nothing. Now that we have money, we can finally pay her what she deserves."

"*Brantley's* money," Hal reminded her. "I thought you were uncomfortable with that."

Kristina turned away, gazing toward the trendy bar entrance

as a group of laughing twentysomethings filed in. "Might as well put it to good use. Besides, Lena is good at what she does."

"She is." Hal drummed his fingers on the steering wheel. "But she's also rigid as hell. You really want someone with her ... principles ... poking around a case where our client is conning a crooked hedge fund manager into paying his legal bills?"

"Yes." Kristina met his gaze with a determined stare. "That's *specifically* why I want her."

Hal sighed and turned off the engine. He could keep arguing, but he knew his wife well enough to sense when her patience was wearing thin. "Let's do it."

They crossed the parking lot and pushed through a heavy door emblazoned with a crossed-axes logo. Immediately, Hal felt out of place.

The Sharp End's interior was an assault on his senses. The mix of hipster aesthetics with actual danger did not sit well with him, nor did the waiver they were required to sign at the door— longer than most mortgage documents.

As a lawyer, he couldn't help wondering how well the clause *Customer assumes all risk of dismemberment* would hold up in a courtroom.

"There she is," Kristina said, gesturing across the crowded space.

Kristina's cousin sat ramrod straight at a high-top table, her back to the wall. Her clothes were way too practical for a bar this trendy—dark pants, button-up shirt, shoes you could actually run in—but Hal kept that opinion to himself. As he and Kristina approached the table, Lena gestured for them to take the stools opposite her.

As he slid onto his barstool, Hal noticed that Lena was holding her phone low to the table, inconspicuously aiming its camera toward a group of women gathered behind him in one of the throwing lanes.

"Are you ... using us for cover?" he said.

Lena's gaze did not move from the group of women. "I'm less conspicuous if I'm not here alone. I didn't think you'd mind."

Hal risked a glance behind him. The women wore matching tank-tops emblazoned with the words *BRIDE TRIBE*. A cheer went up as one of them—she wore a tiara, so Hal figured she was the bride in question—managed to embed her axe in the target. All of the women did a victory dance.

Hal felt a moment of concern for the groom.

"Worker's comp case," Lena explained. "My client is very interested in how someone with a supposedly devastating back injury manages to go out seven nights a week to party."

"Ah," Hal said, understanding. "So they're paying you to be the party-pooper."

Lena's eyes narrowed. "Do you know the impact of worker's comp fraud on the economy?"

"Can't say that I do."

Lena tucked her phone away, apparently having captured the footage she needed. "This is important work, Hal."

"And I would never disparage it," Hal said, even as he suppressed half a dozen jokes about *workplace axe-idents*. Even after knowing her all these years, Hal found Lena hard to read. Sure, she might laugh at a pun. Or she might use one of those axes on him.

"Why did you want to meet?" Lena said.

"We have a case," Hal said. "A man accused of killing his wife. But if you're too busy, we understand—"

"His name is Nico Ramirez," Kristina said, cutting him off with a look. "We'd really like you to work this one with us, Lena."

"A new murder case? That's great, right? That's what you wanted."

"I mean, it's not high-profile or anything," Hal said, hoping to deflate her enthusiasm. "He's a janitor—"

"A janitor? And he can afford your fees?"

"His employer is paying," Kristina said. She shifted awkwardly on her stool. "It's complicated."

"Un-complicate it."

Hal ground his teeth. Lena's dedication to ethics and transparency was exactly the reason he'd hoped to pursue this matter with a different investigator.

"The employer is Gavin Brantley," Kristina said. "He runs a hedge fund where Nico works as a janitor. Brantley is ... concerned about what Nico might have overheard while cleaning the offices."

"So Brantley's buying his silence?"

"That's what Brantley thinks," Hal said. "But Nico told us he never actually saw or overheard anything incriminating. He just let Brantley believe he did so Brantley would pay for his legal defense. Genius, right? This needs to stay between us, by the way."

"Let me get this straight." Lena leaned back, arms crossed. "Your client is manipulating his employer into paying his legal fees by implying he has dirt on him. And you want me involved in this?"

One of us does.

But Kristina kicked him under the table, so he blurted, "Of course we want you involved."

"Why?"

"Because you're a great PI. And, you know, we're trying to save an innocent man."

"With a guilty man's money."

"The allegations against Brantley haven't been proven," Kristina said.

Lena's face hardened. "This sounds shady. You know I don't do shady."

"Oh, that is a shame." Hal turned to Kristina. "Guess we'll have to go with our second choice."

As in, the top-rated investigative outfit in the whole state.

"Hold on," Kristina said. She leaned forward. "Lena, I know how it sounds. But this isn't about some rich guy. It's about a twenty-six-year-old janitor who worked his butt off so his wife could attend nursing school. He came home from work and found his wife's body, and when he called the police for help, they arrested him. Probably on the shakiest of evidence. His public defender was ready to hand him a forty-year-prison sentence and sell it as a better deal than a lethal injection. Normally, a guy like Nico Ramirez has no chance at justice. But because of his quick-thinking, he has us."

"So you approve of this guy basically conning a man?"

Kristina stiffened. "I didn't say I approve. Just—"

"Did he kill his wife?" Lena studied them both with her unsettling stare.

"He claims he didn't," Kristina said. She shrugged. "For what it's worth, I found him convincing."

Lena's face turned pensive as she seemed to consider. Another axe thudded into a target behind them, followed by squeals of laughter.

"If I'm going to do this," Lena said after a moment, "I need ground rules."

"Of course." Hal struggled not to roll his eyes.

Lena counted off on her fingers. "One—no false pretenses. Don't ask me to deceive anyone, especially innocent bystanders. Two—no cherry-picking. Whatever evidence I find, you need to deal with it, even if it implicates your client. And three—do not ask me to break the law." Her gaze fixed on Hal, making clear exactly who she was talking to. "I'm going to need your word."

Hal forced a smile. "You have it."

9

————

Kristina checked her watch as she strode into the preliminary arraignment courtroom, Hal trailing behind her. They had one simple goal—get bail set for Nico Ramirez. With Brantley's hedge fund millions backing them, the amount wasn't a concern. But the very real possibility of Magistrate Judge Clementine Peck denying bail altogether definitely was.

The basement courtroom hummed with its usual grim efficiency. She and Hal stood together in the gallery, waiting for their turn. On the video screen, a young black man in an orange jumpsuit waited as Peck reviewed his file, her steel-gray hair pulled back so tightly it seemed to stretch her face into a permanent expression of disapproval.

"Your Honor," the man's defense attorney said, "my client has three young children at home who depend on his income. He has no criminal record and—"

Peck cut him off with a dismissive wave. "Bail is set at seventy-five thousand dollars." The man's shoulders slumped as the video feed cut out.

Seventy-five thousand for simple possession. She glanced at Hal. "You're doing that thing with your jaw."

"What thing?" Hal said. "I don't have a thing."

"You do. It's a clenching thing. It means you're concerned."

"Concerned that Peck's a racist and our client has brown skin? Yeah, I'm concerned."

"You can't just throw around words like that." Now Kristina was the one clenching her jaw. "She might have some unconscious biases."

"She might have a white hood in her chambers."

The clerk cut off their conversation, calling, "*Commonwealth v. Nico Ramirez.*"

The video feed flickered back to life. This time, Nico appeared on screen. He sat straight-backed, his dark eyes alert and watchful. Even through the grainy feed, Kristina could see him taking in the details of the courtroom with the same quiet observation she'd noticed during their jail visit.

"Representing the Commonwealth?" Peck's gaze swept the courtroom.

The woman who stepped forward looked familiar—mid-thirties, red hair, slightly harried—but Kristina couldn't place her at first. "Samantha Klein for the Commonwealth, Your Honor."

Samantha Klein. Now Kristina remembered. The assistant DA infamous for burying exculpatory evidence three years ago, almost condemning an innocent man to a life sentence or worse. Kristina was surprised the woman still had a law license.

"And for the defendant?"

Kristina stepped closer to the judge's bench. "The Nolan Law Firm, Kristina Nolan on behalf of Mr. Ramirez, Your Honor."

"Very well." Peck's mouth tightened at Nico's image on the screen. "Mr. Ramirez, you are charged with criminal homicide in the death of Natalia Ramirez. Do you understand these charges?"

"Yes, Your Honor."

Peck regarded him skeptically for a moment, then turned her gaze on Kristina. "I assume you believe bail is warranted in this case, Ms. Nolan?"

"Yes, Your Honor. We believe a bail amount reasonably sufficient to secure Mr. Ramirez's appearance at trial is appropriate here."

"Your Honor, the Commonwealth strongly opposes any consideration of bail in this case," Klein cut in. "This man is accused of a premeditated domestic homicide—he wrapped a cable around his wife's neck, viciously strangling her—"

"Objection." Kristina cut her off. "Ms. Klein is attempting to introduce unproven evidence. There hasn't even been a preliminary hearing."

"Sustained." Peck frowned at Klein. "Confine your argument to bail considerations."

"But given the severity of the charges—" A muscle twitched in Klein's jaw. She smoothed her skirt with a hand that trembled slightly. There was something desperate in her eyes as she looked from Peck to Nico and back to Peck. She hesitated for just a moment, then pressed on, her voice losing some of its conviction. "Your Honor, we also need to consider the defendant's ties to Mexico."

Kristina shot a look at Klein. She had a sinking feeling about where this was headed.

"Is this true?" Peck peered at the monitor. "Are you Mexican, Mr. Rodriguez?"

"Your Honor, my client's name is Ramirez, not Rodriguez. And I have to object again." Kristina fought to keep her voice level. Klein stared at her hands, a flush creeping up her neck.

"Are you in this country legally?" Peck said.

"He was born here, Your Honor."

"I'm asking the defendant. You do speak English, I hope."

"Yes, Your Honor," Nico said. "I speak English. I'm a United States citizen."

"I see." But Peck's tone suggested she saw no distinction.

"He could have family across the border." Klein shuffled her feet uneasily. "You know these people are a flight risk—"

"These people?" Kristina glared at Klein. *Was she serious? Appealing so transparently to Peck's prejudices?* The sheer cynicism of it was shocking even to Kristina—and thanks to Hal, she was familiar with just about every dirty lawyer trick in the book. She fought to keep her composure. "Do you hear yourself? You know you're on the record, right?" Kristina shook her head in disgust. Turned back to the magistrate judge. "Your Honor, Mr. Ramirez has lived in Philadelphia his entire life. He graduated from Northeast High. He has stable employment. He has no prior criminal record."

"The nature of the crime suggests he's a danger to the community," Peck said. "And as Ms. Klein noted, his ties to Mexico make him a flight risk."

"*What* ties to Mexico?" She felt Hal's hand touch her elbow —a warning gesture. She reined herself in. "Your Honor, my client deserves the opportunity to assist in his own defense from outside a jail cell."

But Peck had already made up her mind. "Bail is denied. The defendant will remain in custody. Let's move along, please."

On the screen, Nico's eyes widened in the split-second before the feed was cut.

Kristina couldn't even summon a perfunctory *Thank you, Your Honor*. She felt a sinking in her stomach as she stepped out of the well of the courtroom with Hal. Behind her, the clerk called the next case.

As she walked with Hal out of the courtroom, he said, "Just some minor unconscious biases, huh?"

"Not now, Hal."

A body pushed past them—Samantha Klein making a hasty exit. Kristina headed her off. "Are you proud of yourself?" she said, cornering the woman. "What you did in there was disgusting. Winning a hearing by stoking a judge's bigotry."

Klein turned to face her. "I won the hearing because your client is a violent killer."

For a moment, neither woman looked away. The courthouse hallway seemed to recede, the bustle of lawyers and clients fading to background noise as they locked eyes. Klein didn't flinch, didn't lower her gaze. The woman had no shame.

Hal stepped between them. "Samantha Klein, right? Let's start over." He extended his hand. "I'm Hal Nolan. This is my partner, Kristina."

Klein ignored his hand for a beat too long before taking it. She turned to Kristina, the gesture more challenge than courtesy. Kristina shook her hand, matching Klein's grip exactly.

Klein dropped their handshake first. "Your reputation precedes you."

"So does yours," Kristina said.

Klein's face darkened. "I hope you prepared your client for what's coming, because this case is airtight."

"Like *Orozco*?" The name hung in the air between them. Kristina found a grim satisfaction in the pain she saw in Klein's eyes. "We'll see who's standing when this is over."

Before Klein could respond, a commotion at the courtroom doors drew their attention. A group of people pushed into the hallway—a middle-aged couple and three younger men, all with the same deep brown eyes and high cheekbones. The woman's face seemed hollowed by grief, her eyes red-rimmed. The men flanked her protectively. Kristina didn't need to be told they were Natalia's family. They headed straight for Klein.

"Where is my daughter's body?" the older man said. "It's

been a week. She needs a proper Catholic burial, not to be cut up in some basement."

The three brothers moved closer to Klein, surrounding her. Compared to them, she was tiny. Hal moved to intervene, but Kristina caught his arm, held him back. She wanted to see how this played out.

"Your daughter's body is still at the morgue."

"Then get her out!"

Klein met the man's gaze steadily. "Mr. Molina, every new detail we uncover, every test we run, brings us closer to bringing Ramirez to justice. I know you want to bury Natalia, but right now her body is evidence."

Molina seemed to waver, his anger giving way to grief. "How much longer? We need to ... to say goodbye."

Klein turned to the mother. "I'll make sure you're notified the moment she's released. I promise." The woman responded with a grateful nod. The brothers' attention shifted from Klein to their mother, moving to comfort her.

Watching Klein manage the family, Kristina felt a chill. The woman was good—better than her reputation had led Kristina to believe.

The father's arm circled his wife's shoulders as their sons led them away. Klein followed with her phone already out. Kristina watched them go, then turned to Hal.

He let out a low whistle. "I like her."

10

———————

"Come on, Kristina. You know what they say about bail hearings." Hal signaled the bartender for another round. "They're like blind dates. You dress up nice, make your best pitch, and still end up going home alone."

"Nobody says that about bail hearings," Kristina said.

They sat at Habeas Corkus, an upscale bar three blocks from the courthouse that had been serving Philadelphia's finest legal minds their liquid lunches for generations. The kind of place where day-drinking wasn't just tolerated, but practically endorsed by the Bar Association. The wood of the bar gleamed, wine goblets and martini glasses interspersed with briefcases and legal briefs.

"Well, somebody should. You made all the right arguments. Nico got screwed anyway."

"Because of Samantha Klein's racist dogwhistles."

"Look at the bright side. Now we know she plays dirty."

The bartender slid their drinks across the polished bar. Hal hesitated before reaching for his wallet, the memory of his declined cards at Bistro Cannata still fresh. He pulled out cash instead, noting with concern how thin the stack of bills had become.

On the stool next to him, Kristina absently swirled the ice in her glass. Hal recognized the slight tension in her jaw and the flicker of pain behind her eyes.

"Hey," he added, squeezing her arm, "It's a minor setback. We'll win this."

Kristina nodded, then looked toward the door. "Oh, great."

Ricky Sawyer strode in, thousand-dollar shoes and too much hair product. His usual look-at-me entrance.

"Hal and Kristina!" Sawyer called out, loud enough to turn heads. "Drowning your sorrows after that bail hearing?"

It was too late for Hal to throw a briefcase onto the leather-upholstered stool next to him, and he groaned as Sawyer slid onto it.

"How do you know about the hearing?" Hal said, not bothering to hide his annoyance.

"You didn't see me there? I had a client further down the docket." He flagged the bartender with a casual flick of his wrist. "My hearing went significantly better than yours, by the way. ROR. Total win."

Released on recognizance. Meaning Sawyer's client strolled out of jail without even having to pay bail, while Nico remained in a cell.

"Well at least you have the class not to brag about it, Ricky."

Sawyer snorted a laugh. "And at least you have the grace to lose with dignity, right?"

"We haven't lost," Kristina snapped. "We've barely gotten started."

"Ooh, did I touch a nerve?" The bartender brought Sawyer his martini. He raised the glass. "Cheers."

Hal left his drink on the bar. Beside him, Kristina checked

her watch. Sawyer shrugged and sipped his drink, then smacked his lips with satisfaction.

"You're a decent lawyer, Hal, but your networking skills could use some work."

"If you think we're drinking buddies, you're even more delusional than I thought."

"We don't need to be drinking buddies to be civil."

"I'll take that under consideration. How's Olivia Hazenberg, by the way?"

"Still annoyed about that?"

"You're representing the hacker who destroyed our firm. I—" Hal bit back the rest. Getting into it with Sawyer in public, *again*, wouldn't help anything. He swallowed the rest of his drink. "It's been great catching up, but Kristina and I need to run."

Hal was halfway off his stool when three men entered the bar. Kristina's breath caught audibly.

Natalia Ramirez's brothers.

They blocked the doorway like a wall of muscle. The smallest one was barely shorter than the door frame, and he spotted Hal and Kristina first. His face twisted. "There they are. The lawyers."

Well, this is not good.

The brothers advanced. At the sight of them, the afternoon crowd of lawyers began to quietly gather their belongings. A gray-haired trial veteran at the end of the bar signaled frantically for his check.

Sawyer was already easing off his stool, martini abandoned. "Been fun," he murmured. "Good luck with ... whatever this is."

Coward.

Within seconds, the place emptied, leaving only Hal, Kristina, and the bartender, frozen behind his polished counter. And the Molina brothers.

"The Molinas, right?" Hal stood. The brothers did not

respond. Only glared at him. He positioned himself between them and Kristina. "Listen, I know you're upset."

"Upset? Our sister is dead."

"I understand. And what happened was a tragedy. But Nico Ramirez is innocent until proven guilty. That's how our justice system works."

"Justice?" The largest of the brothers stepped into Hal's space. He rolled his neck, cracking the joints. A vein pulsed at his temple. "You think that's what this is—you helping my sister's killer with your fancy words?"

Hal sighed. His words *were* fancy, to be fair, but....

The man's fist caught him square in the jaw and sent him spinning against the bar. The metallic taste of blood filled his mouth. His eyes refused to focus on the grain of the wood.

"Hal!"

A second blow nailed him in the ribs. Pain exploded through his side. Out of the corner of his eye, he saw the smaller Molina brother reach for Kristina.

Hal grabbed his whiskey glass and hurled it at Kristina's attacker. The glass banged against the man's shoulder, liquor spraying across his face. The momentary distraction gave Kristina an opening, and she took it, stomping down on the guy's foot and slapping him across the face.

Suddenly the bartender was there, swinging a Louisville Slugger.

The rest was chaos.

Someone knocked over a table. Glasses and bottles crashed to the floor. A lawyer had left a case file behind—now its pages flew through the air.

"*Enough!*"

The commanding voice cut through the mayhem. Everyone froze.

In the doorway stood the elder Molina—Natalia's father. He

was still wearing his ill-fitting suit from the courthouse, salt-and-pepper hair slicked back from his face.

"Is this how you honor your sister's memory?" Anger radiated from his face. His three sons shrunk from him. "Fighting in a bar like common *nacos*?"

The men backed away, chastened. The father turned to Hal and Kristina.

"I apologize for my sons' behavior. They are ... confused by grief." His voice was gentle now, although the anger in his eyes had not faded completely. "I hope there is no need to involve the police?"

"Who needs the police?" Hal touched his aching jaw, made sure all of his teeth were still there.

Molina studied him for a moment, seemed satisfied. "My name is Gabriel Molina."

"Hal Nolan. This is Kristina."

They shook hands, causing Gabriel Molina's sleeve to ride up slightly. Hal caught a glimpse of blue-black ink on his wrist. A familiar-looking tattoo.

Now that's interesting.

"Come," Molina said to his sons. They followed him out, casting vicious glares at Hal and Kristina behind their father's back.

The moment the door closed, Hal went to his wife. "Are you okay?"

She nodded, brushing hair from her face. "Yeah. Are you?"

"Yeah." He winced. "Mostly."

The bartender's throat-clearing broke the moment. "Someone's paying for all this damage." Only then did Hal fully take in the carnage—shattered crystal, an overturned bottle of scotch that was probably older than him, a broken table. "You said your name is Nolan?"

11

———

HAL WINCED as Kristina dabbed antiseptic onto a cut on his cheek. "Hold still. Unless you'd prefer to explain your injuries to an urgent care doctor."

"Right after we explain why we don't have health insurance?"

Kristina smirked. "Hence the Walgreens first aid kit."

They sat in the common room between their offices, the sun setting on the cobblestone street outside the window. Lena sat in a chair tilted against the wall, watching them. She looked amused.

"So let me get this straight," Lena said. "You two ... got into a *bar fight?*"

"Why is this so funny to you?" Hal said.

Lena's smile widened. "Just trying to picture it. Did you cite legal precedent before throwing the first punch?"

"Ha ha."

"Did you beat them into submission with a strongly-worded motion?"

"Are you done?"

Lena turned to Kristina. "Please tell me you at least picked up a chair."

"Hal threw a scotch glass to defend my honor." Kristina gave him a wink. "It was kinda sexy."

"Okay, now that's too much information." Lena grinned.

"Can we focus?" Hal said. "Believe it or not, I actually learned something during this unfortunate incident. Something that might be useful."

"Besides the fact that you can't fight?" Lena deadpanned.

Hal ignored that. "The father—Gabriel Molina. He has a tattoo on his wrist. I'm pretty sure I've seen it before, when Kristina and I defended a gangbanger a few years ago."

Lena's smile faded. "What gang?"

Hal shook his head. "I don't know, but it wasn't the chess club."

Lena's expression turned thoughtful. "Even if you're right, it could be an old tattoo. You said this guy broke up the fight. Apologized to you for his sons' behavior. People change."

"Who cares if he changed?" Hal realized he'd spoken too harshly. He waved an arm, wincing again as the movement pulled at his bruised ribs. "Look, all we need is something to make the jury think he's suspicious. Dig up whatever you can."

"He's the victim's father." Disapproval flashed across Lena's features.

Kristina gathered up the antiseptic wipes and turned to her cousin. "You know how this works, Lena. Samantha Klein is going to tell the jury that Nico killed his wife in cold blood. We'll need to provide an alternative theory. If her father has a violent past as a gang member, that could go a long way in establishing reasonable doubt."

"Going after a grieving father feels wrong."

Hal and Kristina exchanged a glance. Lena was a great investigator, only held back by her rigid moral code—a flaw Hal hoped she could overcome. "You know what else feels wrong?" he said. "An innocent man going to death row."

Lena's jaw flexed as she seemed to consider his words. Finally, she rose from the chair. "I'll look into Molina. But if I don't find anything suspicious, we drop this angle. Remember our ground rules."

Hal sighed. "How could I forget?"

After Lena left, Kristina lifted Hal's shirt and moved a hand gently over his ribs. He sucked in a breath, gritting his teeth.

"This looks serious," she said.

"I'll survive." He moved her hand away and stood. "I need to call Brantley."

Her eyes narrowed. "Why?"

"Someone has to pay for the damage to that bar."

"Hal...."

He pulled out his phone. Brantley answered on the first ring.

"Brantley." The hedge fund manager's voice was gruff.

"We need to talk about the case."

"Now?"

Hal could hear the sounds of people behind Brantley's voice. Chatter and the clink of glasses. He checked his watch. 5:32 PM. "It's important."

"Hold on." The noise level dropped—Brantley moving somewhere private. "Make it quick."

"There's been a development."

"What kind of development?"

"We had an encounter with the victim's family tonight. Things got heated. There was ... property damage."

"What does that have to do with me?" Irritation crept into Brantley's voice. Hal sensed he was about to hang up.

"If we don't make it right, the owner might file a police report. That would put Kristina and me in a difficult situation—taking our attention off of Nico's defense."

"I was under the impression you could handle difficult situations."

"With the right resources, sure." Hal hesitated, then went for broke. "Nico's been approached by the Feds. They want to make a deal. They were very persuasive. His freedom for yours."

Kristina's eyes widened. She shook her head and made a slashing motion across her throat, silently demanding he stop.

Hal turned his back on her and pressed on. "We managed to talk him out of it, but if he doesn't believe we're one-hundred percent focused on defending him, things could spiral. Dealing with this bar is a distraction we don't need right now."

There was a long silence.

"Gavin?" Hal said.

"How much?"

Hal let out a silent breath and named the figure.

"Fine. I'll have my assistant wire it in the morning. But Hal? You better get results."

"That's what you're paying us for—"

The line went dead.

Hal looked at Kristina and sighed. "Problem solved."

"Are we con artists now?" Her arms crossed tightly against her chest, the pulse at her throat visibly quickening.

"I'm trying to prevent an innocent man from going to death row."

"That line might have worked on Lena. Not me." Her eyes burned with barely contained fury. "You deliberately played on Brantley's fears about Nico having evidence—evidence we *know* he doesn't have. You *lied* to him."

Hal blinked, taken aback by the intensity in her voice. "Weren't we already doing that?"

"There's a line between lying by omission and outright deception. You know there's been no offer from the Feds."

"Not yet."

"You crossed an ethical line and ... and you *ignored* me."

"Kristina—"

"You turned your back on me."

"Only so I could focus on Brantley. We're in survival mode. Do you really want to get involved in a dispute with Habeas Corkus on top of everything else? I'm working with what we have. Why do you have to question every move I make?"

"I question moves that risk our law licenses!"

He tried a smile. "Can we just rewind to when you said I was sexy?"

"No, we can't." She glared at him, then gathered her things. Through the window, he watched her walk down the cobblestone street toward their parking spot. Their battered Camry pulled away from the curb.

Guess I'm Ubering home tonight.

He sat at his desk, alone in their crappy little office. His ribs and jaw throbbed. Had he crossed a line? Maybe. *Probably.* But he didn't see any alternatives. Not if they wanted to survive.

12

———

Samantha sat in a metal folding chair in the Ben Franklin Community Center's multipurpose room. Emily's group wouldn't perform for another twenty minutes, but Sam had promised to watch the entire recital—the whole endless, interminable, torturous thing. "The other parents always do," Emily had insisted that morning. "It's not fair when people only watch their own kid."

So she was here at 5:30 on a Tuesday. *As if every parent can just ditch work.* She forced herself not to grind her teeth.

Someone had strung crepe paper streamers across the fluorescent lights, casting rainbow shadows on the linoleum floor. On the makeshift stage—really just a cleared area marked off with blue painter's tape—a group of seven-year-olds in slightly crooked tutus twirled to a Taylor Swift song Sam vaguely recognized. Their dance instructor crouched at the edge of the "stage," making frantic gestures trying to keep them in sync. Sam had to shift her head every few seconds to see around the raised arms of proud parents wielding smartphones with all the zeal—and annoyance—of paparazzi.

Sam's own phone was in her bag. She could feel it vibrate through the leather. Again.

Don't answer it.

The phone buzzed. Sam's fingers twitched.

What if it's important?

Another group of girls took the stage—star-covered leotards, this time. An upbeat Olivia Rodrigo song played from the sound system. The mother next to her was recording every second, phone held high, elbow inches from Sam's face.

Sam's phone went silent. Then immediately started buzzing again.

Screw it.

She dug out her phone, angling the screen away from her neighbors. Five missed calls from Dan Coffey.

Sam tapped a message back: *At dance recital. Urgent?*

The response came instantly: *Address? Only need 5 min.*

Samantha sighed. She scanned the program—a double-sided photocopy on pink paper. Three more groups before Emily's. Maybe if she was quick....

She texted Coffey the community center's address, then gathered her bag and whispered "excuse me" as she squeezed past the other parents in her row of folding chairs. Several shot her dirty looks.

She waited in the hallway, straining to hear any change in the music to make sure she didn't miss Emily's performance. Coffey arrived after about five minutes.

"That was fast," she said.

"I was in the neighborhood." He glanced around. "How's the recital going? Is Emily—"

"I don't really have time for small talk, Dan." They walked together down a hallway that smelled like old gym socks, the sound of music and occasional applause diminishing behind them.

"How much time do we have?" Coffey said.

"Ten minutes max."

Coffey nodded. "Okay, first thing—I may have found out why the Nolans took the Ramirez case."

That got Sam's attention. She stopped walking and turned to face him. "I'm listening."

"The day before they started representing Ramirez, they were seen meeting at a restaurant with Gavin Brantley." Coffey pulled out his notepad, flipping to a page with scribbled details.

Sam leaned against the wall, trying to remember why the name seemed familiar. "The hedge fund guy?"

"The hedge fund guy who also happens to be Ramirez's employer."

Holy shit.

"You think Brantley's bankrolling the defense? That would explain the Nolans' interest. But why would a billionaire care about his janitor's murder case?"

"I don't know yet, but I intend to find out." Coffey paused. She could see the uneasiness in his expression. "Sam, you should talk to Burke about this. If Ramirez has unlimited funds for his defense, this case could blow up in our faces."

"No." Sam's voice echoed in the empty hallway.

"Sam—"

"I said no. I can handle it." A burst of applause echoed from the multipurpose room, followed by the musical notes of a new song. She checked her watch. "I should get back to my seat."

"Hold on." Coffey caught her arm. "There's something else. We sent the lab the USB cable and samples from the victim's neck collected during the autopsy. There's ... an inconsistency."

"What do you mean?"

"The lab found...." She shifted impatiently from one foot to another as he flipped a few pages in his notebook, the paper rustling loudly in the quiet hallway. "Metal particles, embedded in Natalia's tissue sample. They don't match the cable's composition. I took another look at the autopsy report, and the ME noted unusual abrasion patterns. I'm thinking this could mean—"

"Hold on." Sam held up her hand. "Stop. Drop this. Now."

"What? What if it leads to important evidence?"

"What if that evidence hurts us?"

He looked perplexed at first, then angry. "Sam, are you forgetting what happened with *Orozco*?"

As if she would ever forget that case. "*Orozco* is exactly why I'm being careful now." She kept her voice steady, reasonable. "The less we dig into this, the less we might have to tell the defense."

Music swelled from the multipurpose room—the song Emily was performing to. Sam's heart rate spiked.

"I need to go," she said. "My daughter—" Sam met his gaze, lowering her voice. "Please don't do anything about the USB cable until I give you the green light. Okay?"

Coffey's jaw tightened. "You're not my boss, Sam."

"I know that."

They stared at each other. Sam could hear children's voices from down the hall. Emily would be walking onto that stage any second.

"Fine," Coffey said finally. "I'll back-burner this. For now."

"Thank you, Dan." She was already moving, her footsteps echoing in the hallway as she jogged back to the multipurpose room. She slipped inside just as Emily's group took their positions.

There was her daughter, third from the left, her face set in fierce concentration as she waited for her cue. It was an expression Sam recognized with a mixture of pride and dread—an expression she recognized from the mirror.

Then the music started, and the girls began to move.

Sam tried to focus on Emily, tried to be present. But her

mind kept drifting to metal particles and abrasion patterns, to the mistake she'd made in *Orozco* that still haunted her career three years later.

This isn't the same, she told herself. *I'm not hiding evidence. I'm just ... being strategic about the investigation.*

Emily executed a wobbly pirouette. Her eyes met Sam's, and Sam forced herself to smile and nod encouragingly. But inside, her thoughts spun.

Gavin Brantley funding the defense. Unexpected lab results on the murder weapon.

On stage, Emily beamed as she hit her final pose. The crowd of parents burst into enthusiastic applause. Sam clapped until her hands hurt, trying to focus, to force away the thoughts crowding her mind.

Emily chattered the whole way home about her performance, about Miss Katie's praise, about the next recital in three months. Sam nodded along, making the right noises at the right moments. But in her mind, she was fighting a rising dread— wondering how long she had before the Nolans found out about the lab results and, using Brantley's money, transformed those metal particles into reasonable doubt.

Wondering how long she had before everything came crashing down.

Again.

13

———

HAL STARED at the wall of their living room, where he'd taped photos and documents relating to the Ramirez case. In the center was a photo of Gabriel Molina he'd found in a news article about Natalia's death. The man's gaze seemed to meet Hal's eyes, cold and deadly.

"Ladies and gentlemen of the jury, ask yourselves which is more likely—that Natalia was murdered by her loving husband, violently strangled to death by a man with whom she'd never had a cross word, or that she was actually killed by her father, a gang member with a violent past?"

Behind him, Kristina emerged from their bedroom. He heard her stop in the hallway.

"Really, Hal? You turned our living room into a crazy wall?"

"It helps me think."

She came closer, her bare feet silent on the hardwood floor. "And what profound thoughts has this produced?"

He turned to face her. She wore yoga pants and a faded law school tee-shirt. Her hair was still damp from the shower. No makeup.

"Come here," he said, reaching for her, "and I'll show you what the sight of you in those yoga pants produced."

She sidestepped his hands, shaking her head. "I'm still mad at you."

"About the Brantley thing?"

"Yes, Hal. About the Brantley thing." She enunciated each word through clenched teeth.

He forced a laugh. "I manipulated a manipulator."

"You lied to a man to pressure him to give us money."

"To give *a bar* money. And it's only a lie temporarily. The Feds will reach out to Nico. It's only a matter of time."

She crossed her arms tight against her chest, her eyes narrowing to slits. *Okay, maybe not the best time to try getting lucky.*

"You should have asked me first," she said.

"Is that what this is really about? Kristina, by now you should know that I know what I'm doing."

She shot a meaningful look at the wall—which, he had to admit, did appear like the work of a slightly crazy person. All it needed was some red string.

A knock at the door saved him from whatever cutting observation she was about to make. "That must be Lena," he said. "See how crazy you think I am once she gives us the lowdown on Gabriel Molina."

He opened the door. Lena brushed past him without a greeting, her messenger bag slamming against his hip. Apparently, she was still pissed off at him for sending her to investigate the victim's grieving father. He wasn't winning any popularity contests in this room.

Lena took in the wall of photos and documents with a quick scan, made no comment.

Hal trailed her into the room as she pulled a folder from the bag. Hal was encouraged by its thickness, at least.

"You found something on Molina?"

"I sure did."

Hal rubbed his hands together. This was going to be good. He sat with Kristina on the couch. "Let's hear it."

Lena handed him a drawing—a dagger, blade pointing down, with the shorter line of the hilt turning the image into a cross. It was the full tattoo, half of which he'd glimpsed on Molina's wrist. "Nasty! Great work, Lena!"

"What does it mean?" Kristina said, taking the sheet of paper from him.

"It's the symbol of the Iron Keepers."

Hal frowned. "I haven't heard of that gang. Nazis?"

"It's a faction in a tabletop war game called *Starborn Cataclysm*." Lena pulled several photographs from the folder and handed them to him and Kristina. Hal's frown deepened as he studied each one—instead of mugshots and surveillance photos, they were pictures of Molina holding up a tiny plastic soldier with metallic paint, of he and his sons gathered around some kind of gaming table with painted terrain, of Molina holding up a small trophy.

Kristina looked up at Lena. "*Starborn Cataclysm?* Isn't that one of those tabletop war games? Like *Warhammer?*"

"Don't compare it to *Warhammer*," Lena said. "The *Starborn* players get very defensive about that. It's its own thing."

Hal's temples began to throb. "Hold on."

Lena pulled out another photo. "Here he is at last year's CataCon—it's an annual gaming convention held in Minneapolis. That's him with his sons."

The photo showed Molina in some kind of event hall, dressed in elaborate armor made of painted foam and cardboard. A plastic helmet was tucked under one arm. A cape sparkled with glitter.

"Space Guardian cosplay," Lena said. "He won third place in the contest."

Kristina looked at Hal, then burst out laughing.

"Oh, yeah, laugh it up," Hal said. "Meanwhile, our defense theory is swirling down the toilet."

"*Your* defense theory." Her voice was ice. "But I guess by now I should know that you know what you're doing, right?"

Hal turned away, unable to hold her gaze. "There has to be more, Lena. Please tell me there's more."

"Oh, there's more. When he's not commanding his Iron Keepers in tabletop battles, Gabriel Molina spends most of his time at Parroquia de San Miguel Arcángel. Heard of it?"

A Catholic church in North Philly. "That's not what I meant," he muttered.

"Maybe not, but it's the truth. Gabriel Molina leads prayer groups, organizes charity drives, counsels troubled youth. The parish priest called him one of their most devoted members. I have photos from the soup kitchen, if you want to take a look."

"No thanks." He stood up and walked to the wall, where he stared at the photo of Molina. The man seemed a lot less menacing now after seeing him in that sparkly cape. "We can still spin this. The Molinas *showed* their violent natures at Habeus Corkus."

"They showed their grief and frustration with the system," Kristina said. "Putting them front-and-center at the trial will only give Samantha Klein an opportunity to show those emotions to the jury, too."

"Damn it!" Hal paced. Lena opened her mouth, but he raised his hand. "Don't. I can't bear for this to get any worse."

Kristina's phone buzzed. She checked the screen and her eyebrows drew together. Hal heard her say, "Yes, this is Kristina Nolan." Low, serious—her lawyer voice. Then she disappeared into the bedroom.

He and Lena exchanged a glance.

When Kristina returned, her face had gone pale.

"What?" Hal said.

She glared at him. "It got worse."

14

———

It was midnight when they arrived at Riverside Correctional Facility, leaving the Camry in a near-empty parking lot. High-intensity lamps lit the jail's perimeter with harsh, institutional light that somehow managed to feel even more foreboding than the darkness it was meant to dispel.

The visitor entrance was locked. Kristina slammed her palm against the reinforced glass for the tenth time. Through the smudged surface, she could see a couple guards inside. Night duty. Neither acknowledged her.

"They can't just leave us out here," Hal said.

Kristina didn't bother to respond. They both knew the guards could absolutely do that. She continued to pound on the glass, the heel of her hand starting to go numb.

Finally, one of the guards lifted his head with weary disdain. He jabbed a button and an intercom crackled to life.

"Visiting hours ended at six."

Kristina pressed her ID against the glass. "We're Nico Ramirez's attorneys. We need to see him now."

After a long silence, a buzzer sounded and she heard the

clunk of the lock disengaging. Kristina yanked open the door before the guard could change his mind.

"That's far enough," one of the guards said. "You can't go past this point. Not at this hour."

Hal let out a sound of annoyance. "Then why let us in at all?"

Kristina gave him a look and he fell silent. She focused on the guards, straining to keep her tone patient and professional. "My name is Kristina Nolan. This is Hal Nolan. Our client, Nico Ramirez, was—"

"Your client is fine. He's in the infirmary. You can see him during normal visiting hours."

"*Fine* being a relative term for someone who just had the shit kicked out of him in a jail common room," Hal said.

The expressions on both guards' faces darkened. Kristina braced herself to be forcibly ejected from the premises. "Rough day at the office, counselors?" It was Juan Gomez, entering from a side door. The correctional officer who'd escorted them to see Nico during their first visit. His gaze lingered on Hal's swollen jaw.

"Bar fight, actually," Hal said. Did she actually hear a note of pride in his voice?

Gomez shook his head with a rueful laugh. "Visiting hours are over, even for attorneys. Come back tomorrow."

"We have a right to see him now," Kristina said. "If we have to get a judge on the line—"

Gomez exchanged a glance with the other officers.

"We understand you have protocols," Kristina said. "But Mr. Ramirez has a constitutional right to counsel. If anything happens to him tonight because we weren't allowed to see him, assess his condition, and ensure his safety, that's a civil rights violation."

One of the guards straightened. "She's threatening us."

"No. Just explaining the situation." Kristina held the man's gaze, though her heart hammered.

After what felt like minutes, Gomez said, "I'll take them back."

The usual series of security checkpoints seemed even more grim after hours, each door's electronic buzz echoing through the empty corridors. Gomez led them toward the infirmary, past darkened cells where shadows moved and voices whispered.

As they walked, Kristina studied his face in profile. "How bad?"

He glanced at her. "He'll be okay."

Prison-speak for *lucky to be alive*.

Gomez stopped in front of a thick metal door. "Five minutes. That's all I can give you."

She nodded. "We'll take it."

The infirmary was a claustrophobic room with a row of metal-framed beds with thin, industrial sheets stretched over the mattresses. The air was uncomfortably warm. About half of the beds were occupied, but there were no privacy curtains separating them—no pretense of dignity here. A man in a white coat sat at a desk near the door, watching a video on his phone.

"Ramirez's lawyers," Gomez said. "I told them they could have five minutes with him."

The man shrugged without looking up from his screen.

Nico sat up. His face was puffy and bruised, but he did not appear to have suffered any major injuries—none that she could see, anyway. One of his wrists was handcuffed to the bedrail.

"Wow," Nico said, managing a smile. "You guys really are first-class lawyers."

Kristina exchanged a glance with Hal, then moved closer to his bed. "How are you?"

"It's nothing." He shifted and winced. "Just some love taps."

"Who administered these love taps?" Hal said. "Did they give you a reason?"

Kristina touched Hal's wrist. "Better if we don't get into details right now." She tilted her head, indicating the other occupied beds—one inmate appeared to be sleeping, but another was watching them with undisguised interest. They needed to be careful what they said in here.

Nico seemed to understand. He gestured them closer with his free hand. She and Hal leaned over the bed.

"Three guys," Nico whispered. "I don't know who they are. I was watching TV in the common room and they came at me. Knocked me around. Guards pulled them off me pretty quick, but before that, one of them spoke in my ear. Told me this is a warning—and that if I open my mouth, they'd gut me."

Kristina felt her blood go cold.

"We're going to get you out of here," Hal said, "talk to the judge tomorrow—"

"That racist old lady? She'll probably be happy."

Hal shook his head. "Not Peck. She's a magistrate judge. We have a trial judge assigned now."

"Callum Harding," Kristina said.

"Is he good?"

Kristina caught Hal's gaze. The truth was, they had no idea. "He's new to the bench."

"Five minutes are up," Gomez said.

Hal looked like he was about to argue. Before he could, she said, "We should go anyway. Nico needs rest."

They said goodbye to Nico and followed Gomez back through the maze of corridors. Kristina didn't trust herself to speak during the walk back.

In the parking lot, she could feel the cold night air against her face as harsh security lights cast long shadows between the few scattered cars. She strode ahead quickly. She could hear

Hal's footsteps on the asphalt as he tried to catch up with her, but she didn't slow down.

As she reached their car, he grabbed her arm.

"Kristina, what's wrong—"

She yanked her arm free. "You did that, Hal. Nico's injuries—the threats—that's on you."

He stared at her. "What?"

"You told Brantley that the Feds reached out to Nico. Then three guys attack him and warn him not to open his mouth. You think that's a coincidence?"

"Seriously?" Hal scoffed. "I hardly think Brantley is the kind of man who would sic thugs on someone—"

"That's the problem, Hal. You *don't* think. Everything's a scheme to you. A game. Our client is in the infirmary because you had to play chicken with a billionaire, show everyone how clever you are."

He let out a dismissive laugh that only deepened her anger. "That's not what happened."

"It's exactly what happened."

The laugh died on his lips. His expression sobered. "I'll make this right."

"Just don't make it worse."

His face fell, and for a moment she felt guilty. But then she remembered Nico's swollen face. "Get in the car. I'm driving."

15

As the newest judge at the Criminal Justice Center, Judge Callum Harding had inherited both the smallest office and the heaviest caseload. His chambers were barely large enough to qualify as an office. Case files and legal texts covered every surface except a narrow strip of his desk with a half-empty coffee cup Hal knew was lukewarm just by looking at it. A single window admitted weak morning light that only made the space feel gloomier.

Hal studied the young judge as they waited. Harding looked as harried as his surroundings would suggest—suit jacket draped over his chair, tie askew, hairline a good inch higher than it had been at his swearing-in six months ago. But his eyes were sharp as he scanned Kristina's brief.

Word around the courthouse was that Harding had turned down a partnership track at Cooper Hutchinson to pursue a spot on the bench—the kind of boneheaded career move that made veteran lawyers spit out their scotch in horror. But according to Hal's contacts at the courthouse, Harding was thoughtful, smart, quick-thinking. Even better, he hadn't been around long enough for the system to grind away his belief in justice—or to develop the distrust of The Nolan Law Firm that seemed to have become standard for anyone wearing judicial robes in Philly's hallowed halls of justice.

He and Kristina sat shoulder-to-shoulder in rickety wooden chairs facing the judge's desk. Their knees almost touched his desk's edge—the room was that small. The close quarters meant that when Samantha Klein rushed in, breathing hard and muttering apologies, she had to squeeze past them to reach the remaining chair. Her shoulder brushed Hal's arm, and he caught the distinct aroma of breakfast cereal.

"*Eau de Froot Loops?*" he said.

She didn't even smile. Just greeted him and Kristina with a predatory glare.

Judge Harding placed the brief at the top of one of his stacks of paper, then ran his fingers through his hair. "*Commonwealth v. Ramirez.* You guys don't waste any time—I was just assigned this case yesterday."

"This is urgent, Your Honor," Kristina said.

"The Commonwealth disagrees," Sam cut in.

"We're here on an emergency motion to revisit Magistrate Judge Peck's denial of bail for our client."

Harding held up his hands for silence. "One at a time, okay? Ms. Nolan, I read the defense's brief in support of its motion." He picked up his coffee cup, frowned at its murky contents, and set it back down. "You allege your client was attacked in jail."

"It's more than an allegation," Hal said. "We have a correctional officer, Juan Gomez, who is prepared to testify—"

"What the defense characterizes as an attack was a routine jail altercation," Sam said. "If we're going to reverse a bail decision every time someone gets in a scuffle, we might as well install a revolving door."

Kristina glared at the prosecutor, then faced the judge. "Your

Honor, Mr. Ramirez was assaulted by multiple attackers in the jail common room."

"And the facility was perfectly capable of interceding and managing his safety. What happened is hardly a valid basis for releasing a murder suspect."

Judge Harding's gaze shifted between the three lawyers. Hal knew that look. The man was on the verge of being persuaded—but by which side?

"Your Honor," Hal said, "Officer Gomez graciously agreed to be here this morning. He witnessed the attack. Why not hear him out?"

Harding nodded, and a few minutes later Gomez was squeezing his considerable frame into the cramped room. He shot Hal and Kristina a look as he straightened his uniform. They'd pulled him off his shift for this hearing.

"Officer," Judge Harding said, "tell me about this incident."

Gomez cleared his throat. "Three inmates jumped Mr. Ramirez in the common room. Got him down, worked him over a bit. Could've been worse, but we broke it up." He shifted uncomfortably.

"Did you identify the three inmates?"

"Yes, Your Honor. All three are in administrative segregation pending disciplinary action."

Sam leaned forward. "In your experience, Officer Gomez, how common are physical altercations between inmates?"

"They happen. It's a high-tension environment."

"Was there anything unusual about this particular incident?" Judge Harding said.

Gomez hesitated. Hal held his breath.

"Well," Gomez said finally. "There was one thing...."

"Which was?" Judge Harding prompted.

"According to Nico—I mean, Mr. Ramirez—the men told him if he opened his mouth, they'd gut him."

The words hung in the air. Hal felt Kristina stiffen beside him. He kept his own face carefully neutral. They'd argued about this before the hearing—whether to tell Judge Harding about Gavin Brantley. Kristina had wanted to lay it all out. Brantley's involvement made the threats more credible. But Hal had convinced her—barely—that they had a duty to maintain Brantley's confidence.

Hal braced himself for the judge's natural question.

"Keep his mouth shut about what?"

"I don't know, Your Honor."

Sam seemed to consider Gomez with renewed interest. Hal could sense her processing this new information. Then something shifted behind her eyes and she glanced at him with a knowing, cunning look.

"Gavin Brantley was seen meeting with the Nolans shortly before they took this case," she said. "Could this supposed attack be related to that?"

How the hell did she know?

"Gavin Brantley, the hedge fund billionaire?" Judge Harding's eyebrows rose.

Hal and Kristina exchanged a look. Hal gave a minute shake of his head—knowing even as he did it that it would be ignored.

"Mr. Brantley is covering our fees as a humanitarian gesture," Kristina said carefully. "Mr. Ramirez was his employee."

"A humanitarian gesture." Skepticism laced the judge's voice.

"Brantley is currently under SEC investigation," Sam said. She was putting it all together in realtime, and there was no way to stop her.

"Your Honor," Hal cut in, "is this relevant? Why does it matter who's paying our fees?"

"Why does it matter?" Judge Harding's expression turned to stone. He looked at each of them in turn, his expression growing darker with each passing second. "Taking money from a man under federal investigation to represent his employee? You don't see the conflict of interest—"

"Oh, they see it," Sam said. "They just don't care. Maybe you haven't heard about the Nolans—"

"I have," Judge Harding said. "And I've also heard of the *Orozco* case, Ms. Klein."

Sam's face flushed.

"So here's what's going to happen," Judge Harding continued. "I'm denying the motion to revisit bail. Mr. Ramirez will be moved to administrative segregation for his protection."

"You're talking about isolation." Kristina's voice rose with panic. "Twenty-three hours a day alone in a cell. A man who is innocent until proven guilty!"

"You're the one who claims he's in danger, Ms. Nolan. Administrative segregation will protect your client without endangering the public or increasing the risk of flight."

"Your Honor—"

Harding glared at her. She fell silent.

"Listen to me now," the judge said, "all three of you. I don't know what games you—or Gavin Brantley—are used to playing. But in my courtroom, you will run the cleanest case in the history of Philadelphia jurisprudence. Because I will be watching every motion, every filing, every breath you take during this trial. Step one inch over the line, and you will regret it for the rest of your career—which will be short. Are we clear?"

They mumbled their agreement.

Outside in the hallway, Sam gave them a pointed look. "I was wondering about the connection between Brantley and your client. Thanks for filling in the blanks."

"I guess you need all the help you can get," Hal couldn't resist saying. "Still haven't found a motive for a devoted husband strangling his loving wife?"

"Not every marriage is as perfect as yours," Sam said, her gaze moving from Hal to Kristina with cruel precision.

Kristina went rigid beside him. Hal kept his eyes locked on Sam, afraid of what he'd find if he turned to face his wife. He forced a confident smirk. "The Ramirez marriage was as close as you can get."

A small smile played at Sam's lips. "That's what he told you?" She pulled a folder from her briefcase and held it out. "Here, Hal. A preview of discovery."

Hal looked at the folder as if it might be coated in poison. "What is it?"

"Statements from six different neighbors about constant, loud arguing from the Ramirez apartment. Shouting matches that went on for hours. One witness saw Natalia crying in their apartment building's lobby the day before her death."

She pushed the folder into Hal's hands and walked away, leaving them staring after her.

"Hal," Kristina said quietly. "If she gave us this...."

"I know." The familiar taste of bile rose in his throat—the same taste he got every time a client blindsided him. "It means she has something even worse."

"Nico's been lying to us."

16

Hal stood at the window of their Old City office, staring at the cobblestones of the street outside without really seeing them. Behind him, Kristina's typing echoed from her office—sharp, angry keystrokes that matched her mood. She'd barely spoken three words to him since their meeting with Judge Harding.

He knew what was bothering her—Harding's accusation that by taking Brantley's money, they were ignoring a flagrant conflict of interest. Even though Kristina tolerated—and sometimes abetted—Hal's unconventional tactics, she prided herself on knowing where the boundaries were, and respecting those boundaries. Hearing otherwise from a judge couldn't be easy for her.

At least she's still here. That was something. He couldn't afford to take an Uber home every night.

The door opened and Lena strode in, looking annoyingly put-together in pressed khakis and a crisp white button-down. She carried a thick manila folder under one arm.

"Traffic cleared up faster than expected." She paused, seeming to study him. "How'd the hearing go?"

"Not great," Hal said. "Our client was condemned to solitary confinement. Tell me you found something that will help him."

Kristina's staccato typing stopped. She appeared in her doorway. Without so much as glancing at Hal, she gestured for Lena to join her in her office. "Let's talk in here."

Persona non grata in my own firm. Hal sighed and followed them in anyway.

Kristina settled behind her desk while Lena took one of the two chairs facing it. Hal leaned against the doorframe.

"I like the natural light in here," Lena said, glancing around.

"Better than the last place," Hal said. "Remember that smell from the alley—"

"How about if we focus on the case?" Kristina cut him off. She tapped a pen against her desk, not looking up.

Lena's eyes darted between them. "Right." She smoothed her already-smooth khakis, then opened her folder. "I started with the neighbors—"

"Let me guess," Kristina cut in. "They told you about hearing Nico and Natalia having loud arguments."

Lena looked up, surprised. "How did you know that?"

"Samantha Klein. She couldn't wait to rub it in our faces after the hearing. Hal likes her, by the way. Because of course he would." Kristina glared at him.

"In fairness, I said that before I really knew her."

"Uh-huh."

Lena again looked from one of them to the other, and somehow managed not to acknowledge the tension. "Well, Mr. and Mrs. Delacruz in 2B confirmed it. Said they heard frequent arguments from the Ramirez apartment."

"Does the timing coincide with Natalia's murder?" Kristina said.

"None of the neighbors I spoke with remember an argument

happening on the night of Natalia's death, but in the weeks leading up to it, things were ... tumultuous."

"Tumultuous," Kristina echoed. Her voice was leaden.

"It's not like this is fatal to our case," Hal said. "All couples argue." He gestured between himself and Kristina. "Case in point."

The look Kristina gave him could have frozen Hell.

"The Delacruzes couldn't make out the exact words being shouted, but Mrs. Delacruz mentioned...." Lena faltered and an uncharacteristic blush rose along her cheekbones. She glanced down at her notes. "During one of the fights, Mrs. Delacruz thinks she heard Nico call Natalia a slut."

The unpleasant word hung in the air.

"There's more," Lena said.

Hal stared at her. "It gets *worse?*"

"I looked into Natalia's nursing program—the one Nico told you she was attending. She's no longer enrolled."

"What do you mean?" Kristina sat up straighter.

"She dropped out a few months ago."

Hal let out a sigh. He came off the wall and started pacing. "Nico's working his butt off as a janitor, postponing his own opportunities to put her through nursing school, and she threw it all away. I guess that explains the fights."

"And the motive," Kristina said. "No wonder Klein is so confident. She's going to paint Nico as an angry husband who strangled Natalia in a fit of rage."

"Why would he hide all of this from you?" Lena said.

Hal ran a hand through his hair. "Because all clients are liars."

"We need to talk to him," Kristina said.

Hal nodded. "I'll set up a meeting at Riverside."

17

Nico looked better than he had in the infirmary. His bruises had faded and the swelling around his eyes had gone down. Hal might have felt relief about his client's recovery, but his sympathy for the man had taken a serious hit over the past few days.

"Thanks for getting me moved to isolation," Nico said. "It's better there."

Give it time. A few more days alone in a concrete box might change your mind about that.

"How are you holding up?" Kristina asked. Her tone was gentler than Hal's would have been.

"I'm okay," Nico said. "Knowing you're out there fighting for me, it helps."

Hal had to hold back a derisive snort. "We need to talk."

"About the trial?" Nico's gaze darted between them. "Have you found anything that could help prove I didn't kill Natalia?"

"Actually, we need to talk about why you've been lying to us."

Nico's face went blank. "What?"

"We need to talk about the lies, Nico."

Not even a flicker of guilt crossed his features—only confusion. "What lies?"

"Let's start with the fights," Hal said. "Almost every night, the two of you shouting at each other. You calling her a slut."

"What? No. I would never—" Nico shook his head, his expression incredulous. "We never fought. Ask anyone."

"We did ask," Hal said. "That's the problem. Neighbors reported hearing frequent arguments between you and Natalia. Loud ones."

"Then they're lying. Or they made a mistake—heard someone else fighting. I don't know."

Kristina leaned forward. "Multiple neighbors made statements, Nico, to the police and to our investigator. They specifically said the noise was coming from your apartment. They were certain about it."

"That doesn't make sense." Nico's voice broke. The skin around his eyes tightened. "We didn't fight. Ever. We were happy."

"We've had clients lie to us before, Nico," Hal said. "It never ends well."

"I'm not lying!" Nico slammed his palm on the table. The sound echoed through the visiting room.

"What about nursing school?" Kristina said.

"What about it?"

"Natalia dropped out months ago."

"No." Nico shook his head. "She was doing well. She loved it."

Hal exchanged a look with Kristina. They'd had plenty of clients lie to them, but most of them gave it up after being caught. Nico seemed unusually stubborn. Unless....

"Maybe she didn't tell you," Hal said.

"That's impossible. I dropped her off myself. Almost every

night. We'd grab dinner near campus—this little Thai place she loved—"

"Our investigator spoke with the school directly," Kristina said. Her voice remained gentle, but firm. "Natalia withdrew from the program months ago."

"Then someone's made a mistake." But Nico's hands were trembling now, and something flickered in his eyes. Fear? "I *saw* her go to class."

"Okay." Hal rubbed his eyes, distrust and empathy battling within him. He studied Nico's face, looking for any hint of deception. "Let's try this. Walk us through a typical evening. When you'd drop Natalia off for class."

Nico took a deep breath. "I'd finish at the office around six. Pick Natalia up from our apartment. Grab dinner if there was time. Drop her at nursing school by seven."

"Every night?"

"Most nights. Sometimes she'd take the bus if I worked late."

"You *saw* her go inside?" Hal said.

"Yes I saw her. Sometimes walked her to the door." Nico's voice hardened. "What are you saying—that my wife was lying to me? Going somewhere else every night?"

Hal met Kristina's eyes. "We're just trying to understand."

"Yeah, well understand this—she wasn't sneaking around. She wouldn't do that. We loved each other."

"Did you ever run into any of her classmates or professors when you walked her to the door?" Kristina said.

Nico shifted in his chair. "No."

"What about homework?" Hal said. "Tests? Did you see her studying during the past few months?"

"She studied while I was at work. Said she couldn't focus with me around."

"That doesn't sound suspicious to you?" Hal said.

"You're *making* it sound suspicious."

"Right now, we have two very different versions of events," Hal said.

Kristina leaned forward. "Your neighbors say you fought constantly. You say you never fought. The school says Natalia dropped out months ago. You say she was attending classes right up until—"

"Until someone killed her." Nico said. "Someone who wasn't me." The conviction in his voice was absolute. "I swear to you, Natalia was in nursing school. We were happy. We didn't fight. I don't know why people are saying these things, but they're not true."

Hal nodded. "We're going to get to the bottom of this, Nico. One way or another. We always do." Even as he spoke the words, he wasn't sure if he meant them as a promise or a threat. Maybe a little of both.

They said their goodbyes and knocked for the guard. As he and Kristina walked through the series of secure doors back to the normal world, his mind churned.

"You think he's lying?" Kristina asked as they reached the car.

"Either he is, or his wife was, or everyone else is." Hal started the engine. "And the trial date's approaching fast."

"Sounds like a typical Nolan case." She smiled—the first warmth she'd shown him all day. "But like you said, we always get to the bottom of it."

"So where do we start?"

She seemed to consider. "With Natalia. If she wasn't at nursing school, we need to figure out where she really was those nights ... and why she lied to her husband about it."

"Yeah," Hal said. "And whether it got her killed."

18

———

HAL RODE the elevator to the thirty-fifth floor of the gleaming spike of a building housing Brantley Capital's offices. The hedge fund's usual bustle had subsided for the night, the hallway lights were dimmed, and most of the offices and cubicles were empty.

Because nothing says "I own you" quite like summoning a person after hours like a servant.

As if that power play weren't enough, Hal enjoyed the further indignity of being escorted to Brantley's office by a security guard, rather than the pleasant receptionist from his last visit.

Brantley waited behind his massive desk, backlit by the nighttime skyline glowing through his floor-to-ceiling windows. He didn't get up.

"Where's your partner?"

"It's just me tonight." Hal kept his voice light even as he winced inwardly. Kristina had been clear that she was done with Gavin Brantley. *You want to grovel before the throne? Go ahead. Leave me out of it.* He forced a casual shrug. "Kristina had a prior engagement she couldn't get out of."

"Sit down." Brantley's expression was unreadable. Hal pulled one of the visitor chairs out. Brantley was speaking again before he could lower his butt into it. "I don't appreciate my name appearing in official court transcripts—especially murder trials."

The hearing in Judge Harding's chambers? Hal's stomach dropped. Not even a day had passed. "You ... know about that?"

"I didn't get where I am today by missing much, Hal. What the hell were you thinking?"

Hal straightened in the visitor chair. "You didn't give us much choice in the matter."

"And what exactly is that supposed to mean?"

"It means when your client gets jumped by three guys in prison who warn him to keep his mouth shut, it kind of piques people's interest as to who might benefit from his silence."

Brantley's gaze bored into his. "And the response, 'I have no idea, Your Honor,' never crossed your brilliant legal mind?"

"Unfortunately, the prosecutor, Samantha Klein, knew about our meeting with you. She's the one who brought up your name. There was nothing we could do."

"That's quite disappointing to hear." Brantley's fancy chair creaked softly as he leaned back. He watched Hal intently.

And then something clicked in Hal's mind. Here he was, practically apologizing to Brantley, when Brantley was the one who'd put them in this position. Heat rose in his chest—anger at Brantley, but also disgust at himself for being so expertly manipulated.

"You know what? *I'm* the one who should be ripping into *you*. If you hadn't arranged for those inmates—"

Brantley's eyebrows rose slightly. "Are you accusing me of arranging the attack on Nico Ramirez?"

"Well—"

"I'm paying his legal bills. Why would I want him hurt?"

"Come on, Gavin. You got spooked when I told you Nico had

been approached by the Feds, so you had him roughed up. It's not exactly hard to figure out."

"You give yourself too much credit, Hal."

"Is that right?"

Brantley leaned forward. "If your ego would get out of the way, you'd see that your brilliant deductive reasoning is nonsense. But you and your wife seem to be under the impression that you're taking the legal world by storm." His eyes narrowed, but his voice remained eerily calm. "What you are is a joke—a couple of bottom-feeders from a third-rate law school, suffering from delusions of grandeur."

The words stung, but Hal kept his face neutral. "Why did you come to us if we're such a joke?"

Brantley's mouth twitched into a smile, his expression shifting to one of amusement. "Because I needed lawyers who were desperate enough to take whatever scraps I threw them, but not completely incompetent." He gestured at the Philadelphia skyline behind him. "How many lawyers do you think there are in Philly? Hundreds? Thousands? And yet somehow, when I needed someone to handle my ... unique dilemma ... it was *your* name that came up. Do you know why?"

"Enlighten me."

"Because you have a reputation, Hal. One you've clearly earned."

"Such a change from our friendly game of HORSE," Hal said. "At least then you pretended to be human. Are we done?"

"Almost." Brantley's voice hardened. "If you drag my name into this case again, or attempt to screw me in any way...."

"You'll cut off the money. I get it."

"Oh no." Brantley leaned forward. "I wouldn't make it that easy for you. I'll start by calling in favors. Make sure every bank in Philadelphia knows what a bad investment The Nolan Law Firm would be. I'll stir up trouble about your ethical lapses, maybe involve the state bar. And of course, the public deserves to know about your woefully incompetent data security. How can any client feel safe when your network is so easily breached? By the time I'm done, you won't be able to get a job reviewing contracts for a cheesesteak truck."

The threat hung in the air between them. Hal knew he should probably stay quiet. Brantley had all the leverage, and the smart thing to do—the prudent thing—would be to take his beating, leave, and focus on Nico's trial.

But being prudent was a skill he'd never quite mastered.

"You know what I think, Gavin?" Hal rose from his chair. "I think you're a scared little bitch."

Brantley's face flushed red. "Excuse me?"

"You know that if Nico talks to the Feds, everything you've built—your business, your reputation, your *life*—will come tumbling down. You think your tough guy act fools me? I may have gone to a third-rate law school, but I know a man who's pissing his pants when I see one."

"You're finished, Hal. You and your wife."

The mention of Kristina sent a chill down Hal's spine, but he forced himself to maintain eye contact. "You came to us because you thought we'd be good at this. And you were right. So back off and let us handle Nico's defense our way." Hal straightened up. "Otherwise, maybe in the stress of trial preparation, we accidentally subpoena the wrong security footage. Maybe we call the wrong witness. Maybe we start asking questions about what really happens in this office."

Brantley's face went very still. When he spoke, his voice was quiet. "Are *you* threatening *me*?"

"New experience, huh?" Hal turned toward the door. "You're not the only one who knows how to play games, Gavin."

He made it halfway to the door before Brantley's voice stopped him. "Hal."

He turned back. Brantley was looking at him differently now —still like he was studying an insect, but at least an exotic one.

"I hope you're this convincing at trial."

Hal smirked. "You have no idea."

He left Brantley's office, threaded his way through the maze of cubicles, and rode the elevator down to the lobby. His hands were shaking by the time he reached his car.

Inside the Camry, he pulled out his phone and saw three missed calls from Kristina. He started to call her back, then stopped. What would he tell her? That he'd just dug them in deeper? That he'd managed to make their situation even more dire?

The drive home would give him time to think of a way to spin this. To make it sound like he'd won some kind of moral victory tonight, instead of what had really happened—that he'd pushed all their chips into the center of the table without looking at his cards.

19

———————

Samantha Klein stared at the stack of cardboard boxes on the conference room table, each filled with documents she was legally required to hand over to the defense.

A mountain of paper that would look impressive to anyone unversed in litigation tactics. She'd mastered this part of discovery—drowning the defense in paperwork, thousands of pages of phone records, witness statements, even parking ticket histories. Relevant? Technically. Useful? Some of it—maybe ten percent. The real skill was in the organization, making sure that ten percent got lost in the shuffle.

Or never made it to the boxes at all.

She thought of *Orozco* and her stomach tightened painfully. She pushed the thought away. This time she knew what she was doing.

She checked her watch. The Nolans were late. Probably on purpose. *Petty.* She had better things to do with her time than wait for defense attorneys who couldn't be bothered to arrive on schedule.

Like figuring out how to explain to Aldo Burke why she'd kept him in the dark about the Nolans taking over Ramirez's defense, and the fact that the case was proceeding to trial, with her at the prosecution table.

The thought of that conversation brought another stomach clench. *Get out of your own head before you give yourself an ulcer.*

Her phone buzzed. A text from Emily's school: *Reminder: Parent-teacher conferences next Tuesday.* Sam tapped the screen and added the meeting to her calendar, already knowing she'd have to miss it. Again. Between prepping witnesses and drafting motions, she'd barely have time to keep Emily bathed and fed, much less sit down with her teacher.

The conference room door opened. Detective Dan Coffey entered, followed by the Nolans and their investigator, Lena Randall. Hal looked cocky as ever, smirking as if he'd already won the trial. Kristina was more controlled, but her tailored navy suit and measured movements radiated the same irritating confidence as her husband. And Randall.... Coffey's background check had turned up a combat tour in Afghanistan. It showed. The investigator's gaze swept the conference room like she was clearing a kill zone. Sam didn't like the idea of being her enemy.

She collected herself quickly, summoning her own smirk. "Thanks for finally gracing us with your presence."

"Sorry we're late," Hal said, not sounding sorry at all. "Traffic was murder." He grinned at his own bad pun.

"The discovery materials are all here." Sam gestured at the boxes. "Everything's properly indexed."

"I'm sure," Kristina said. Her tone suggested Sam's index was the first document they would discard.

Randall began loading the boxes onto a handcart with an efficiency that made Sam's neck prickle.

"I trust you've included *all* the relevant materials?" Kristina's emphasis on 'all' wasn't subtle. "We wouldn't want another *Orozco* situation."

"Everything's there." She bit back the word 'bitch.' "Though

I notice you haven't reciprocated with your Rule 573(C) disclosures yet. Planning to sandbag me at trial?"

Kristina's eyebrow arched—a micro-expression Sam had already grown to hate. "Our disclosures will be filed well within the deadline. We play by the rules."

Says the woman taking dirty money from a corrupt hedge fund billionaire.

"Speaking of rules," Sam said, "how is Mr. Brantley? Still paying Ramirez's bills?" She savored the flash of discomfort that crossed Kristina's face. "Judge Harding seemed very interested in your arrangement."

Randall looked up from the boxes. "There's a lot here." She placed a hand on the top of the stack, testing its steadiness.

"Just being thorough," Sam said.

"That's one word for it," Kristina said. That eyebrow arch again.

"Do you think you're being clever?" Sam stepped forward, invading Kristina's personal space. The air between them practically crackled with animosity. "I'm getting really tired of your holier-than-thou attitude. Especially coming from you."

"What's that supposed to mean?"

Coffey stepped between them. "Let's keep things professional, okay?" His tone was mild, but he shot Sam a look that said, *Don't let them bait you.*

"Of course," Hal said, giving Kristina the same kind of glance. "We're all professionals here."

"Well." Randall wheeled the cart toward the door. "If we're finished establishing dominance, I could use some help loading these boxes into the van."

Sam held her breath as the Nolans followed Randall and the cart out of the room. As soon as they were gone, she sagged against the conference table.

"You okay?" Coffey asked.

"Fine." Her hands were shaking slightly. She clasped them together to hide it. "They're sharks. And Kristina's smart. You know she's going to read every page." She let out a breath. "At least they won't find anything about the USB cable."

Coffey was quiet for a moment. "Actually, they will."

"What?"

"I added the findings to the discovery materials. The lab results about the metal particles, the ME's notes about the unusual abrasion patterns—it's all in there."

"You did *what*?"

"It's required."

"Required by what? Your conscience?" She wanted to hit him. "Do you have any idea what you've done?"

He squared his shoulders and met her gaze. "We don't need to hold anything back, Sam. We have more than enough evidence to win."

"That's *my* decision to make, not yours."

"I'm protecting you—"

"Protecting me?" The room suddenly felt too small, the air too thin to breathe. "I need this win, Dan. Taking this case to trial, going behind Burke's back—this is all or nothing. And you just sabotaged me!"

"That kind of thinking is exactly what got you into trouble with *Orozco*."

"Don't you dare lecture me—"

The conference room door opened. She spun around, ready to tear into whoever was interrupting, but found one of the building's security guards in the doorway.

"Sorry to interrupt, Ms. Klein, but there are two federal agents here insisting they need to speak with you immediately."

Coffey moved to her side as two people barged past the security guard. A man and woman, both wearing dark suits. The woman was older, with steel-gray hair and sharp features that reminded Sam of a vulture from one of Emily's cartoons. The man was younger, with the kind of earnest face that made Sam trust him even less.

Without waiting for an invitation, the woman commandeered the chair at the head of the conference table. Like she owned the place.

"Detective Coffey." The woman nodded at him, then turned her gaze on Sam. "And Assistant District Attorney Samantha Klein."

"You know us," Coffey said. "Who are you?"

"Special Agent Lilliana Ventura," the woman said. "Federal Bureau of Investigation. This is Special Agent Austin Glover."

Glover picked up Sam's legal pad from the table and flipped through it without asking.

Sam snatched her legal pad from Glover's hands. "That's privileged work product." The move felt pathetic even as she did it, but after the Nolans and now this, she couldn't stand being pushed around for one more minute.

"Ah yes, the Nico Ramirez case," Ventura said, as if she'd just remembered why they were here.

"Our jurisdiction," Coffey said. His jaw was set. "It's a homicide."

"No one's disputing that." Ventura's tone managed to be both placating and condescending. "We're here about a different matter. One that ... intersects with your homicide."

A different matter? Then it hit her.

"Gavin Brantley." She kept her voice neutral. Inside, her mind was racing. "Since when does the FBI work SEC cases? The SEC has its own enforcement staff."

"True." Ventura's thin lips curved into something approximating a smile. "We're working in conjunction with the SEC's enforcement division."

"Why?" Sam said.

"The SEC investigation relates to potential securities fraud," Glover said, sounding like he was explaining things to a child. "But we're running a parallel investigation. Money laundering, wire fraud, RICO violations."

"You're going after him personally," Coffey said. "Criminal charges."

Ventura nodded. "And we have reason to believe that Nico Ramirez has information that could help our case. That's why we're going to leverage your prosecution to ensure his cooperation."

"Absolutely not." Coffey's voice was steel. His hands gripped the back of a chair. "Ramirez murdered his wife. She died violently and brutally. I'm not letting you turn her death into a bargaining chip for some white-collar criminal case."

Glover leaned against the table. "Sorry to tell you this, Detective, but you don't have a choice."

"What?" Coffey let out a derisive snort. "Bullshit."

Ventura didn't even glance at the two men. She kept her gaze fixed on Sam. "Ms. Klein, we'll expect your full support on this matter."

Sam shook her head. Her case. Her shot at redemption. And now these Feds waltz in and try to take over? No. *Hell no.*

She matched Ventura's stare. "I'm not interested."

Ventura shrugged as if she'd expected this response. She nodded to Glover. "Do it."

"Do what?" Sam said, watching uneasily as the other agent pressed his phone to his ear.

"He's arranging to lift the restraining order against Emily's father." Ventura's voice was casual, as if discussing the weather.

"What the hell?" Coffey straightened.

The room tilted. "You're bluffing," Sam said. "You ... you can't do that. Colten's violent. He—"

Glover ended his call. "It's done."

"What's done? What does he mean?" Sam stared at Ventura. Her voice cracked. She hated the weakness in it, hated how quickly they'd reduced her to panic.

"This is just the start, Ms. Klein. Next, we look into custody arrangements. Maybe they need ... revision."

Coffey's face burned red. His fist clenched, and for a terrifying second, Sam thought he might strike one or both of the FBI agents. Sam gave him a look. *Don't make this worse.*

Ventura watched them with a bemused half-smile. "We're nailing Brantley one way or another. You can help, or you can be collateral damage. It's your choice."

20

Getting Samantha Klein's data dump into some semblance of order had been no easy feat, even for Kristina. She had begun by sorting the materials into piles on the conference room table, but had run out of space within the first ten minutes. She'd had to move to the floor. Now she knelt in the center of her system—neat rows of documents, each bristling with colored tabs and Post-It Notes.

"And you made fun of *my* wall of crazy?" Hal said.

Kristina didn't answer. Every time she looked at him, her anger threatened to boil over. Better to focus on the documents.

The Brady rule required the DA's Office to disclose any exculpatory evidence, so Klein had packed eight banker's boxes worth of documents in the classic prosecutor move of burying the good stuff. Reports, photos, lab results, witness statements, anything remotely relevant. Bringing order to this chaos was their only chance of finding that good stuff. *Assuming Klein had provided it at all—Nico wouldn't be the first innocent man she tried to bury.*

"I'm starting to think Samantha might have been joking about that index," Hal quipped.

Kristina's jaw tightened. Lena must have noticed, because she said, "Less talking, Hal." The investigator sat cross-legged, her back braced against the wall, flipping through documents. "More reading."

Kristina could feel Hal's gaze remain on her for a moment longer, but she kept her eyes on her work. After a moment, she heard him sigh and the rustle of him pulling another report from a box.

Three hours later, Kristina's neck ached from hunching over documents, and the office's anemic lighting had spawned a growing headache.

"Klein's good," she said. "Everything *seems* to be here. But good luck finding anything useful."

"There has to be something," Hal said. "She wouldn't have gone overboard like this if there wasn't something she didn't want us to find."

Kristina shuffled through more papers. Bank statements. Phone records. *Wait.* She flipped back to one of the bank statements and pulled it closer.

Hal and Lena stopped working. "Found something?" Hal said.

"Maybe." Kristina reached for one of the other bank statements and placed it next to the first. "It looks like Natalia made a series of cash deposits to a checking account. All of the deposits were made at an ATM. Pretty late at night, too."

"At night?" Hal smirked. "Let me guess—the same nights Nico thought she was at nursing school?"

Kristina's shoulders tensed. "Lena, do you have the schedule Nico gave us?"

Lena rummaged through her notes. "Got it."

"Let's cross-reference the nights she made deposits with her supposed class schedule." She went through the bank statements, reading off the dates.

"Perfect match," Lena said. "Every night when she was supposedly at nursing school."

Despite her lingering anger at Hal, Kristina felt a familiar spark of excitement. This was what they did best together—putting things together, finding patterns. For a moment, the case took precedence over everything else.

She scanned the columns of figures. "The amount of the deposit is different every time. Eight-hundred one night. Two-thousand the next. The largest is a little over four-thousand." She grabbed another statement from her stack. "This has been going on for a few months. Always the same ATM."

"Is there an address?" Lena said.

"Yeah." Kristina read the address out loud, then opened the Maps app on her phone and switched to street view.

Oh.

Hal and Lena stared at her, waiting. She held up her phone so they could see the street-view image. The ATM was next door to a building with blacked-out windows. The establishment's name—*Heartbreakers*—glowed in bright red above a neon outline of a woman twirling around a pole.

"Well," Hal said after a pause. "That explains the cash deposits."

"Hold on," Lena said. "Natalia was a *stripper?*"

"It would explain the deposits," Kristina said. "Most strip clubs operate on a cash basis. The dancers earn money from tips, private dances, the VIP room. The clubs classify the dancers as independent contractors for tax and employment purposes, if they even document them at all. No paycheck, and the amount would be different each night."

"And you know this *how?*" Lena gaped at her, and Kristina could sense her cousin reconsidering how well she knew her. "Don't tell me ... to get through law school ... you—"

"No!" Kristina had to hold back a laugh. "Lena! The Nolan

Law Firm attracts an eclectic clientele." She turned to Hal. "Hand me that pile with the purple sticky note?"

Their eyes met for a fraction of a second before she looked away. Hal walked the documents to her, his hand brushing hers as he handed them over. Police reports. She flipped through them until she found what she was looking for—a notation in an investigative summary.

"Here's a note Detective Coffey made in the file," she said, reading aloud. "*Interviewed club manager and security. Both subjects stated they were familiar with victim.*" She lifted her eyes from the page.

"Sam knows," Hal said.

Kristina nodded. "And now we know."

The real question was whether *Nico* had known. It could explain the neighbors' reports of arguments, of supposedly hearing Nico calling her a slut. And it could explain her murder. Klein's opening statement would practically write itself.

On the other hand, Natalia's side hustle could just as easily benefit the defense. Strip bars weren't known to be the safest places. Obsessive customers, stalkers, even rival strippers—it opened up a lot of possibilities for alternative suspects, if they played this right.

"I'll check out the club," Lena said. "Talk to the other dancers, the bouncers, see what they remember about Natalia."

"No." Hal's voice was firm. "We need you on something else. Something more important."

"More important than finding out what our victim was doing dancing for cash at *Heartbreakers*?" Kristina said. Whatever anger she'd let go of in the moment came rushing back in.

"Yes."

She fastened the bank statements to the investigative summary with a binder clip, wishing she could use it on Hal's mouth instead. Of course he'd make this call without even asking her opinion.

"We need to know more about Natalia's and Nico's marriage," Hal went on. "The Molinas are our best shot at that, but they won't talk to us."

"Can't imagine why," Lena said dryly.

"But maybe they'll talk to you." Hal started to pace—although Kristina noticed he was careful to step around her piled documents. "Remember Gabriel Molina's tattoo? The one I thought was gang-related but turned out to be from that game?"

"*Starborn Cataclysm*," Lena said.

"Turns out there's a game shop near Temple that hosts regular game nights. And guess who shows up every Thursday with his sons to command their little armies?"

Kristina watched her cousin's eyes widen as Lena realized where this was going. "You want to send me undercover? As what? A player?"

"I've lined up an expert to teach you the basics."

"An expert?"

"Well, I mean, he has six-thousand YouTube subscribers...."

"You can't be serious." Lena turned to Kristina. "Please tell me he's not serious."

Kristina didn't need to look at her husband's face to know he was serious. Even worse, she was starting to think it might be a good idea. "It would be helpful to know the truth—if Nico and Natalia were a happy couple or not," she admitted.

"You're actually on board with this?" Lena stared at her with disbelief. "You want me to pretend to be a war gaming enthusiast to spy on a grieving family?"

"We need to understand what was really going on in that apartment," Kristina said. "Did they fight all the time? Or were they happy? After Nico, her father and brothers probably knew her better than anyone."

"And you think they'll just spill their hearts out to some random woman they meet at game night?"

"People bond over shared interests," Hal said. "Especially niche ones like this."

"We had ground rules," Lena said. "No false pretenses. No deceiving innocent bystanders."

Hal's expression was pained. "I mean, is anyone *really* innocent?"

Kristina looked from Hal to Lena. They were running out of options—and time. Samantha Klein's case against Nico was strong. Nico looked guiltier by the day. And jury selection was right around the corner.

"It could be our best shot," Kristina said.

Lena was quiet for a moment. "Fine. I don't like this, but I'll do it I guess. But what about *Heartbreakers*? Someone still needs to check out the club."

Kristina felt Hal's gaze on her. When she looked at him, his lips curved into a devious smile. "What do you say, Kristina? Date night?"

21

———

Dragon's Wing Comics & Games occupied a cramped storefront between a bubble tea café and a sneaker store. Lena paused at the game shop's entrance, then went next door and treated herself to a bubble tea. Memorizing an entire gaming system's worth of rules overnight was hardly standard operating procedure for a PI. Damn right she was expensing this, and with extra boba.

She took a long sip through the fat straw, then headed into the game shop.

Comic books lined one wall, display cases the other. As she scanned the room, her gaze swept over colorful miniatures, gleaming dice sets, and a poster advertising an upcoming *Starborn Cataclysm* tournament. There were tables in the back, decorated with elaborate terrain. A mix of people hunched over the tables, arranging painted miniatures.

She spotted Gabriel Molina immediately—tall and broad-shouldered, salt-and-pepper hair slicked back from his face. He wore jeans and a plain work shirt. A gold crucifix hung from a chain around his neck, catching the light as he leaned forward to carefully place a miniature soldier.

His sons flanked him around the table. From her research, Lena identified the oldest one—built like a linebacker—as Miguel. Emilio, a year younger than Miguel, had his father's high cheekbones. The youngest son was Andrés, barely out of his teens. Andrés held a figure between two fingers while Miguel used tweezers to delicately adjust a tiny flag it was carrying, and Emilio watched. It was hard to imagine these three starting a bar brawl.

"Help you find something?"

A clerk—Kevin, according to his name tag—peered at her with suspicion from behind the counter.

"I heard you guys run *Cataclysm* nights."

Kevin's eyes narrowed. "You play?"

"I'm still a beginner, but I'm looking to get into it. I'm into the Iron Keepers faction."

She saw Gabriel Molina's head turn slightly at the mention of Iron Keepers. The symbol tattooed on his wrist—the one Hal had mistaken for a gang sign—represented the army he commanded on the tabletop.

Kevin seemed to relax a little. "Well, you're in luck. Gabe over there's probably the best IK player in Philly."

"Really? I've been studying the Iron Keepers' resurrection phase mechanics. Still trying to figure out how to time a Faith Chain combo properly...." She walked toward the Molinas' table, but Kevin came out from behind the counter, stopping her.

"Hold on."

Lena froze, reviewing everything she'd just said. She'd spent hours cramming tutorials and talking with Hal's YouTube contact, trying to learn enough game terminology to fake her way through a conversation. Had she messed up some detail?

"You can't bring that in here." Kevin pointed at her bubble tea, then at a trash can by the door.

"Sorry. Of course." With a hint of regret, she dropped the cup into the garbage. Then she headed for the table.

Up close, she could see the incredible detail on Gabriel's miniatures. Each one was hand-painted with impressive precision. The armor looked battle-scarred. Energy weapons glowed. Even the tiny faction symbol of the Iron Keepers was perfectly replicated.

"I hear you're an expert on the Iron Keepers. I'm a new player. Mind if I join you?"

Gabriel looked up, studying her with deep brown eyes. The same eyes Lena had seen in photos of Natalia. "Pull up a chair."

Lena sat, noting how his sons shifted slightly to make room while remaining close to their father. "These miniatures are amazing," she said. "Mine always come out looking globby."

"You'll get there. Takes a lot of practice."

"Dad's been painting minis longer than I've been alive," Andrés said. There was clear affection in his voice, and pride flickered across Gabriel's face.

"My sister tried to teach me some techniques, but...." Lena affected a self-deprecating laugh. "I guess I'm more of a player than an artist."

"Your sister plays?" Emilio asked.

The word *sister* drew all four Molinas' attention. Lena's practiced smile felt brittle. She forced herself to maintain eye contact.

"She used to...." Lena pretended to hesitate, as if the words were difficult. "She's kind of why I got back into gaming. She's going through some rough times with her husband. I thought maybe.... Never mind. I'm sure you don't want to hear about this."

The Molinas exchanged glances. Gabriel's expression softened. "You should encourage her to pick up the game again.

Sometimes returning to old passions can be healing. Is your sister's marriage in trouble?"

The trick to a convincing lie is making it 99% true. Kristina was her cousin, not her sister, but she did seem to be experiencing some marital discord.... "My sister and her husband are business partners. Makes things complicated. They're never apart." Lena looked down, fidgeting with a dice bag. "I don't know why I'm dumping my family drama on you."

"No stranger to family drama here," Emilio muttered.

"What do you mean?" Lena said.

"Our sister was married, too—" Emilio took a breath. Before he could continue, Miguel elbowed him sharply.

"Many churches offer marriage counseling," Gabriel said. "If your sister is a person of faith."

"Thanks. I'll let her know." Lena paused. She held back her desire to pry. That would only break whatever connection she'd built. The Molinas needed to be the ones who decided to share. "It's just hard, you know? Watching someone you care about in a bad situation."

The tension at the table thickened. Lena sensed Emilio's desire to open up, even as Miguel watched him with a warning stare. Andrés stared fixedly at his miniatures.

Gabriel's voice remained steady, but a note of grief that had not been there before now edged his words. "Would you accept the advice of a stranger? If you care about your sister, don't *watch*. Help her. If you don't, a time may come when she is beyond your help."

"Dad...." Miguel started.

Gabriel held up a hand. "*Lo siento.* I am sorry. This subject is emotional for us. I lost a daughter. My sons lost a sister."

"I'm sorry for your loss. I didn't mean to make you feel pain." Even though that was exactly what she'd meant to do, and it made her ill. "Emelio, you said your sister was married. Was she ... happy?"

Ignoring his brother's stare, Emilio erupted half-out of his seat. "Who knows? She stopped speaking to us months before she—" He looked at Lena and his voice lowered. "Before she died."

"What about before that?" Lena said, hoping she didn't sound too nosy.

"I guess they were happy. I never heard Natalia complain."

"Enough!" Miguel slammed a hand against the table, rattling the miniatures. "This is private. And we're here to play. You want to talk feelings, do it at church. Now, are we going to wage war? Or should I go home?"

Gabriel stared at his son until the younger man looked away. Gabriel sighed and turned to Lena. "As I said, this is emotional. But Miguel is right. We are here to play. Let us lose ourselves in the game."

The next hour was surprisingly enjoyable. The Molinas' grief slowly gave way to joy as they rolled dice, checked rules, and bantered about everything from the game's lore to their mother's upcoming birthday to church activities. Lena fumbled her way through her turns as best she could, and the Molinas were patient with her rookie mistakes.

She did not attempt to turn the conversation to Natalia again. Their grief was still too raw, too fresh. She had learned that Natalia had seemingly been happy with Nico. But that had been before Natalia withdrew from her family, months before her death. Around the same time she'd dropped out of nursing school and started stripping.

Finally, Gabriel checked his watch. "Time to pack up." He touched his crucifix, a gesture Lena had noticed him repeat throughout the evening. "It has been very wonderful to meet you, Lena. I hope you will come by the shop again."

"I plan to," Lena said, half-wishing it were true.

Outside, watching the Molinas pile into their car, Lena felt a hollow in her stomach. She'd managed to get some information, but at the cost of reopening the wounds of a grieving family—exploiting their kindness and generosity to secure a tactical advantage in the trial of the man accused of murdering their daughter.

She was glad she'd enjoyed her bubble tea before going inside Dragon's Wing, because now, she felt sick.

22

———

HAL HAD BEEN in strip clubs before. Back in college, when he and his buddies had more hormones than sense and thought throwing money at naked women counted as flirting. But he'd never been to one with his wife.

First time for everything.

Inside Heartbreakers, a main stage jutted into the center of a vast, dark space, with chairs and small tables arranged around it. Men in everything from suits to hoodies filled the seats. Dim track lighting created pools of shadow between the tables, while bright spots lit the stage. Two metal poles gleamed, stretching from floor to ceiling.

He and Kristina sat at the stage. Close enough to smell the heady mix of perfume and baby powder. On stage, a platinum blonde named Valentina wrapped her legs around the pole and spun upside down. Men whistled and waved bills as her sequined thong caught the light.

"And people say we don't have sophisticated interests," Hal said.

He waited for Kristina's reluctant smile, the dimple that

always gave her away. But she sat rigidly beside him, staring straight ahead with her arms crossed, mouth set in a thin line.

"I mean, I know it's not the ballet...."

Still nothing.

He sighed. "You going to tell me what's wrong? Or just never speak to me again?"

Finally she looked at him. "Do you really want to do this here?"

She gestured at their surroundings—the thrumming music, the scantily clad dancers, the men throwing money at the stage. Valentina climbed to the top of the pole, hooked one knee around it, and dropped into a spin with her back arched. Hal had to admit Kristina had a point, but....

"I just want to know what you're so angry about," he said.

Kristina let out a harsh laugh, drawing a few looks from the men around them. "What am I *not* angry about? You embarrassed us at the charity dinner, completely ignored me about the Brantley conflict, got our client beaten in jail, and you're risking our law licenses. Want me to keep going?"

"Not really."

"Then shut up and watch the show like a normal person."

Valentina straddled the pole and leaned back until her long hair brushed the stage, then pulled herself up and turned her hips in a slow roll that had the men around them staring with slack jaws. Hal turned back to Kristina.

"I don't get it. You've always trusted me before."

"Exactly. When are *you* going to trust *me*?"

He opened his mouth, closed it again. "What are you talking about? I trust you."

"No, Hal. You don't. Every time I disagree with you, every time I tell you something's a bad idea, you dismiss it. You think I'm being overcautious, or too hung up on the rules. You never actually believe I might be right."

"That's not fair." Valentina crawled to a group of businessmen and squeezed her breasts together so they could stuff bills into her cleavage. "We're partners."

"Are we? Because when I tell you not to do something, you do it anyway. When was the last time you actually listened to me?"

He started to answer, then shook his head. "I'm trying to save our firm."

"It took *both* of us to build the firm. Why do you think you can save it alone?"

Before he could respond, she stood up and pulled out a hundred-dollar bill. Valentina spun away from the businessmen as if they no longer existed. She lowered herself in front of Kristina, giving her a wicked smile as she parted her thighs.

Hal swallowed. "What are you doing?"

"Speeding this up." She slid the hundred into Valentina's g-string.

The song ended and the DJ's voice boomed through the speakers: "Give it up for the beautiful, the talented, the sexy Valentina!"

Valentina disappeared behind a curtain and the next dancer took her place on the stage.

"Well," Hal muttered, "I can't wait to explain that expense to Brantley."

A moment later, Valentina appeared behind them. She draped an arm over each of their shoulders, her long hair tickling Hal's cheek, and grinned at them. "Generous lady." Hal tried to place her accent—Eastern European, maybe Russian. "You two like private dance, yes?"

Kristina shot Hal a look, then returned the stripper's smile. "We'd love one."

Hal watched Valentina's hips sway as she led them down a hallway lined with small rooms, each screened by a beaded curtain. She parted the curtain of the last room and led them inside. A leather loveseat faced a tiny stage with another pole. Hal hesitated before sitting down, but had to assume from the smell of industrial-grade disinfectant that the leather had been wiped down.

"I love couples dance," Valentina purred. "So much fun." She started moving to the music that pulsed through hidden speakers. "You are married?"

"Almost ten years," Hal said.

"Aww, still newlyweds." She slid onto Kristina's lap. His wife tensed for a moment, then relaxed as Valentina whispered something in her ear that made her laugh.

He wasn't sure if this was the weirdest moment of their marriage or the hottest. *Maybe both.*

Valentina rolled her hips in a slow circle, trailing her fingers through Kristina's hair. She leaned in close, her lips brushing Kristina's ear. "So beautiful," Valentina cooed. Kristina's cheeks flushed, but she didn't pull away. Valentina tossed her hair back and her eyes found Hal's. "You are lucky man."

"Thanks," Hal said thickly.

Valentina slid from Kristina's lap to his. Her coconut perfume washed over him as she twisted his tie around her fingers. "So tense," she said in his ear. "Why no relax?"

Oh, I don't know. Because I just watched you grind figure-eights on my wife's crotch?

"We have work on our mind, actually," Kristina said. She held up her phone, a photo of Natalia Ramirez on the screen.

Valentina's gyrations abruptly stopped. Emotion flashed across her face. "You are cops?"

"No," Kristina said. "Lawyers."

This answer seemed to relax her slightly. "We get a lot of lawyers here."

"I bet," Hal said.

Kristina was still holding out her phone. "Do you know her?"

"Sapphire. She was...." Her voice had lost its seductive hum. She moved back to the pole, but not to dance. To keep her distance. "Management don't like us to talk about other dancers."

"We can make it worth your time." Hal pulled out his wallet.

Valentina's gaze jumped between Hal's face and the bills he was pulling from the wallet.

"Please," Kristina said. "We're representing her husband. We need to know what happened."

"I don't know anything." But her fingers were tight around the pole.

"Did she have any enemies?" Kristina pressed. "Maybe someone here at the club was giving her trouble?"

Valentina hesitated visibly.

"If there's anything you can tell us," Kristina said.

"There was one thing. About one week before ... you know. I hear Sapphire with someone. A man. Here the walls are thin. He yelled at her."

"About what?" Kristina asked.

"I could not hear the words. The music in here is always loud. But after, she is upset. I mean really upset." Valentina's fingers tightened around the pole. "When she leave, she is crying. I never see Sapphire cry before."

Hal shot a glance at Kristina. She returned it, a concerned look in her eyes. They could stop asking questions right now, and probably *should* stop before they learned something they couldn't unlearn.

But neither of them wanted to.

"What did this guy look like?" Hal said.

Valentina shook her head. "I did not see him."

"Did he have an accent?" Hal said, even as Kristina gave him a warning look. "Maybe ... Mexican?"

"Hal," Kristina warned.

Valentina shrugged helplessly. "Maybe he have accent. Hard to hear."

"There was nothing about this in the discovery Klein gave us," Kristina said. "So either she suppressed it, or the police don't know."

"Did you talk to the police?" Hal said.

Valentina looked at him like it was the dumbest thing she'd heard all night—which in this place was saying something. "You think anyone here talk to police?"

"No, I suppose not." He knew from the discovery file that the police had interviewed the club manager and security, but he saw no reason to argue the point. Instead, he shifted to a different question. "You have security cameras, I assume?"

Valentina nodded.

"Think you could introduce us to your security guy?" When she hesitated, he dug into his wallet.

Valentina led them down a darker hallway this time, to a small office near the back of the club. No beaded curtain—this door looked solid enough to be bulletproof. Valentina knocked before opening it. Inside, a thick-necked man in a tight black t-shirt sat watching a bank of monitors. The screens showed the main stage from three angles, each private room, several views of the parking lot.

"Marcus," Valentina said. The man's gaudy gold chain reflected the monitors' glare as he swiveled to face them. "These people want to talk to you."

Marcus's expression didn't change, but his hand moved to rest near what Hal assumed was a weapon. "Val, what the hell? You know the rules."

"They say they are lawyers," she said.

"Even worse. Get them out of here."

Hal stepped forward. "We represent the man accused of Sapphire's murder. We need to see your security footage from the night a man was hassling her. It could be very important, for obvious reasons."

"We don't share footage." Marcus's voice was flat. *For obvious reasons.*"

Hal felt frustration churn in his chest. "I get that your patrons expect privacy, but one of your dancers was killed. Doesn't that matter?" Hal pulled out his wallet again. "Maybe we could—"

Marcus cut him off with a humorless laugh. "You're not hearing me. There was no man. There is no footage. Sapphire was a shit dancer anyway." His voice dropped. "And if you keep asking questions, we're going to have a problem."

"Actually," Hal said, "We already have a problem. One of your dancers is dead, and you seem awfully eager to—"

Marcus pressed a button on his desk. "Dmitri, we got a situation back here."

The door opened behind them. Hal turned to find himself staring at a chest roughly the size of a refrigerator. He looked up —way up—into the impassive face of what had to be Dmitri.

"Show our lawyer friends out," Marcus said. He hesitated for a moment, then added, "And give them a reason not to come back." His chain caught the light one last time as he turned back to his monitors.

Dmitri's massive hands closed around Kristina's upper arms. Hal felt a bolt of panic. "Get your hands off her, now."

"We can walk," Kristina said sharply, trying to break his grip.

"Sure you can." Dmitri's voice was mocking as he leered down at her. "But this way's more fun." He lifted her into the air.

Then they were moving—through the hallway, past the main room where the music thumped and the customers remained fixated on the stage, out a side door into the parking lot. Hal ran to keep up with the giant, his throat tight with rage.

When Dmitri set her down outside, she rubbed her arms, wincing.

"You think you can put your hands on her?" Hal said. "We're gonna sue you into oblivion—"

"Have a nice night." Dmitri slammed the door in his face.

Hal rushed to Kristina's side. "Are you okay?"

She rubbed her arms where Dmitri's fingers had dug in, wincing slightly. After a moment, she forced a smile. "I have to say, I preferred Valentina."

"When we come back, I'll spring for the champagne room."

"*If* we come back, we're bringing a subpoena."

"If?"

"You know there's a chance the man in that video is Nico. If we uncover that, we'll be required to share it with Klein."

"You're assuming he lied to us."

"All clients lie. You said it yourself."

Hal gritted his teeth. That was the dilemma—take Nico at his word and risk everything, or play it safe and stay ignorant.

A woman's voice came from the shadows of the parking lot, breaking his train of thought. "Didn't realize you were such a fun couple." She stepped into the light, followed by a man. Both wore dark suits and definitely did not look like strip club aficionados.

They looked like cops.

Kristina's back straightened. "I think you must have us confused with someone else."

"Otherwise you would *know* we're a fun couple," Hal added.

"No confusion," the woman said. "You're Hal and Kristina Nolan, the defense attorneys representing Nico Ramirez."

Hal instinctively moved closer to Kristina. "And you are?"

The badges came out. Not cops. FBI. "Special Agents Ventura and Glover. We've been watching you."

"Following us, you mean."

"I assume you have warrants?" Kristina said.

"Since when do we need warrants to sit in a parking lot?" Glover, the male agent, tried a smile, but it looked reptilian.

"Let me guess," Hal said. "You're about to tell us our client's only chance is to make a deal with you to deliver Gavin Brantley."

"Finally someone with a brain," Ventura said. Judging by their body language, she was the one in charge—and her smile made Glover's look warm.

"And if Nico's not interested in a deal?"

"Then he should start getting his affairs in order before the lethal injection."

Hal couldn't hold back a derisive laugh. "We'll pass along your offer, but don't expect a yes. We have a strong case. Our client doesn't need a deal."

"I don't think you grasp the reality of your situation," Ventura said. "Even the strongest defense can go wrong at trial. Evidence can go missing. Witnesses can become unavailable." She paused meaningfully. "People can get hurt. Do you understand what I'm saying?"

From the corner of his eye, Hal saw Kristina's back straighten. "It sounds like you're threatening to obstruct justice."

Ventura's smile never wavered. "That's a serious accusation, Ms. Nolan. I'd be very careful about making claims you can't prove. You're not very popular. If something were to happen to you, the investigation might be ... lax."

Kristina went very still, her face pale in the parking lot's harsh lighting.

Hal surged forward. "How dare—" Glover blocked him. Ventura just smirked.

She held out a business card. "Talk to your client. And don't take too long. The offer has an expiration date."

"Nice meeting you," Glover said.

Hal watched the agents walk away, their dark suits melting into the shadows of the parking lot. A minute later, their unmarked sedan peeled out of the lot. Hal's neck prickled as he wondered how long he and Kristina had been under surveillance by those two jackals.

"They just threatened to destroy evidence and intimidate witnesses." Kristina's voice was tight. "And hurt *us* if we don't cooperate."

Hal responded with a nonchalant shrug, even though his hands were shaking. "Not the first dirty cops we've tangled with."

They drove back to the office in silence, both brooding. Finally, Kristina said, "A beating in jail, and now threats from the FBI. How much deeper are we going to dig this hole?"

"All the way down." Hal glanced at her, winced at the hard line of her jaw in the dashboard light. "Do we have a choice?"

"Thanks to you? No."

Hal shook his head, turning toward Old City. They continued through the darkness in silence until their building came into view.

"What the—"

"Did you leave the lights on?" Kristina said.

They hurriedly parked and got out of the car. Hal felt a pit open in his stomach at the sight of their office door, leaning open. Kristina froze in the doorway.

Her meticulous organization of the discovery documents— the neat rows she'd spent hours arranging on the floor, the colored tabs and annotated Post-It Notes—had been ransacked. Sheets of paper carpeted the floor in chaos. Yellow stickies were scattered. Hal could see through the doorway to his inner office, where every drawer in his desk had been yanked open. He assumed Kristina's office would look the same. Someone had destroyed their workspace, searching for ... something.

Kristina put a hand over her mouth, her eyes widening in shock.

Hal's chest tightened. "It's going to be okay." He picked up a legal pad, his eyes fixed on Kristina's neat handwriting. "The place was a dump anyway, right?"

"Hal...." Her voice shook.

"It can't be our new friends," Hal said, then caught himself. "Actually, scratch that. After what Ventura said to you...." He trailed off, remembering her threat about lax investigations.

"You really think they'd risk breaking into a law firm?" Kristina said. "Without a warrant?"

"Brantley seems more likely. Getting nervous, trying to find out what Nico knows."

"He didn't find what he was looking for here. And if he's willing to do this to our office...." Kristina took a deep breath. "What's he going to do next?"

23

———

HAL SAT ALONE at the kitchen table of their darkened apartment, staring at his laptop screen. His document stared back, cursor blinking at the end of a paragraph. He'd loosened his collar and rolled up the sleeves of his white dress shirt. He hated drafting —motions and briefs were Kristina's domain, not his—but he knew he had to do this.

They'd barely spoken since discovering their ransacked office. Kristina had walked through their apartment like a ghost when they'd gotten home, grabbed their keys without a word, and left again. "Meeting with Lena," she'd said, but her tone suggested she just couldn't stand to be in the same room with him.

He sighed and sat back. From his spot at the kitchen table, he could see their entire living space—the couch they'd bought when they first moved in together after law school, the narrow hallway leading to their bedroom, the window looking out over the city they'd been so positive they could conquer.

The apartment felt so quiet without her.

He heard her key in the door. His pulse quickened. "Hey," he said, when she walked in.

"Hey." Her voice was flat, emotionless. "How did it go with Lena?"

"She's going to take a look at our office, see if the intruder left any clues behind."

"Good."

She set down her keys, opened the fridge, and closed it again without taking anything out. She came around to where he was sitting.

"What are you working on?"

"Motion to withdraw as counsel." He kept his eyes on the screen. "We can file it first thing tomorrow morning."

That got her attention. She leaned down to read over his shoulder. "You're transferring the case to *Sawyer*?"

"He's a good criminal defense attorney."

"He's a preening jackass who went to Yale and thinks that makes him better than us." She looked at him with a baffled expression. "You want to just hand him our case?"

"He's got connections we don't. Resources—"

"Stop." She pulled him to his feet, eyes blazing. "What is this, Hal?"

"You were right. I pushed things too far. Got us in too deep. People are getting hurt. *We* could get hurt." He shook his head, misery threatening to overwhelm him. "We're broke, our client got the shit kicked out of him in jail, the Feds and the DA's Office are breathing down our necks, and Brantley's probably going to destroy what little we have left. And that FBI woman threatened—"

"So what? We just give up? Hand all of our cases to Ivy League boys like Ricky Sawyer?" She shook her head. "That's exactly what they expect us to do. It's what they've always expected. We're supposed to know our place. Take the small cases. Stay in our lane."

"Brantley called us bottom-feeders," Hal said quietly. "From a third-rate law school. Said we were suffering from delusions of grandeur."

"*Fuck* Brantley."

Hal let out a strangled laugh. "I'm trying to save what's left."

"I didn't spend all these years building our practice just to hand it over to a trust fund baby. I didn't graduate top our class —third-rate or not—just to stay in my lane. And I sure as hell didn't marry you because you were the type to back down when things get hard."

She leaned down, her fingers finding the keyboard of his laptop. With two keystrokes, she deleted his motion.

"I spent an hour on that!"

"The Nolan Law Firm is ours," she said. "We built it from nothing. And if someone wants to destroy that—Olivia Hazenberg, or Gavin Brantley, or a couple of dirty FBI agents—let them try."

Something tightened in his chest as he watched her—the color rising in her cheeks, a loose strand of hair falling across her face, her eyes fired up, fierce. He couldn't look away.

"But you said it yourself—we've dug ourselves into a hole. *I've* dug it."

"That's why I sent Lena to the office. She's there right now. If someone was stupid enough to search our office, she'll find proof. And then we'll have something to make them back off."

"And then?"

"And then we convince twelve citizens of Philadelphia that Nico Ramirez is innocent."

"Or we lose everything."

"Well, you know ... been there, done that, right?" She moved closer, knocked her shoulder against his with a smile that was almost shy.

"I miss this," he said. "Miss us being a team."

"We're always a team." Her hand came up to cup his face. "Even when I want to strangle you."

He leaned into her touch, laughing. "Which seems like most of the time lately."

She pressed her mouth to his—their first kiss in days, maybe weeks. His hands tightened around her.

"I'm sorry," he said. "For a while there, I guess I forgot who you were."

"Do you remember now?" She caught his lower lip between her teeth.

And that was all it took.

He pushed her suit jacket roughly off her shoulders and backed her against the wall. She gasped as his mouth found her neck, his hands gripping her hips. He savored her scent, the heat of her skin.

"Hal," she breathed. She kicked her heels off.

His shirt joined her jacket on the floor. He hiked up her skirt, his fingers digging into her thighs. Her head fell back as she fought with his belt. Then she held his shoulders as he lifted her.

He considered the couch, but it was three steps away. He couldn't wait that long.

They ended up on the floor. Her skin was hot under his hands. Their breath mingled, bodies pressed together, moving together like they'd never been apart, in the rhythm they both knew so well.

When it was over, when both of them were sweaty and spent, Kristina propped herself on an elbow and smiled at him. Her face was flushed, her hair a wild curtain.

"So," she said, "about Nico."

Hal burst out laughing. Of course she was already back to the case. It was one of the things about Kristina he loved most— her relentless mind.

"The strip bar has to be the key, right?" he said. "Valentina said someone made Natalia cry. We find that man, and we find our defense strategy."

"Unless it was Nico who made her cry."

"Yeah. That would suck."

"Eloquent as always."

Naked and still breathing hard, they lay there in silence, both thinking about the risks. Somewhere in that strip club was the truth about Natalia Ramirez's last moments alive. That truth would either save or bury Nico—and The Nolan Law Firm along with him.

"It's time to talk to our client," Hal said.

24

———

THE NEXT MORNING, Riverside Correctional seemed almost cheery. *Amazing what a night of makeup sex can do to your perspective.* Gray walls, metal table, heavy, clunking, industrial-strength locks—today they all had a certain *je ne sais quoi.* Hal pulled in a deep breath of fragrant prison air, stealing a glance at Kristina.

Correctional officer Juan Gomez gave them a once-over even more suspicious than his usual. "What happened? Someone die and leave you money?"

"Just having a nice morning," Kristina said. She leaned into Hal's side, one arm looping around his waist.

Gomez continued to stare. "Oh, I get it." His face relaxed into a grin. "Perk of working with *tu amor,* right, Nolan?"

"Are you going to bring our client or what?" Hal said.

Gomez snorted. "Try to control yourselves while I'm gone. Can't vouch for the cleanliness of that table." He closed the door behind him with a heavy clang.

Kristina sat at the table. "Are we that obvious?"

"No one ever accused us of subtlety."

Kristina laughed, shaking her head. The way she was

looking at him made him want to throw her onto the table, Gomez's warning be damned.

Hal forced his mind back to Nico's case as he sat down in the metal chair beside her. They had maybe fifteen minutes before Gomez would return with their client. Time to plot their approach.

"I say we hit him with Heartbreakers the moment he sits down," Hal said. "See how he reacts."

"Seriously? He's been through a lot. You want to start his day by telling him his wife was a stripper?"

"I want to know if he already knew."

She started to reply, but her phone buzzed. She checked the screen. "It's Lena."

"Put her on speaker."

Kristina tapped the screen. "You're on speaker. We're at Riverside, about to meet with Nico."

"Got something for us?" Hal said.

"I tracked down one of Natalia's classmates from nursing school." Hal could hear the sympathy in Lena's voice even through the phone's speaker. "Andrea Soto. She said Natalia was struggling. Like, really struggling—barely scraping by in Pathophysiology, failing Pharmacology. Andrea tried to help, but Natalia would have mini-breakdowns during their study sessions. She was overwhelmed and unhappy."

"No wonder she dropped out," Kristina said.

"There's more. Natalia told Andrea she wasn't even sure she wanted to be a nurse. Said it was her husband's idea."

Hal and Kristina exchanged a look. *So he worked overtime to pay for a degree she didn't want, while she stripped behind his back. Not exactly the stuff of romance novels.*

"Did Andrea know about what Natalia was doing after she dropped out?" Hal said.

"Nope. They weren't close friends. Once Natalia quit school, they lost touch."

"Anything else?" Kristina asked.

"Not yet, but I have a few more people at the school I plan to talk to."

"Okay," Kristina said. "Let us know what you learn." The door opened and Gomez appeared in the doorway with Nico. "Gotta go."

Kristina ended the call and slipped her phone off the table as Gomez guided Nico to the chair across from them.

Hal observed their client as Gomez secured him. Nico's hair was a ratty mess, his jumpsuit wrinkled, dark circles under his eyes.

"Back in forty-five minutes," Gomez said.

Nico managed a wan smile as he looked across the table at them. "Morning." There was a roughness in his voice, as if he hadn't spoken in hours. *Administrative segregation—basically solitary confinement with less sadistic guards.* After the attack, Judge Harding had placed Nico into "protective custody," as if locking a man in a cell for twenty-three hours a day was doing him a favor.

"How are you doing?" Kristina said.

"I'm alone all day in a cell the size of my supply closet back at Brantley Capital. What happened to innocent until proven guilty?"

Hal's jaw clenched. Nico should have been released on bail, but that was a battle they'd already lost twice. Jury selection was only days away. They needed to focus on the trial.

"At least no one's bothering you now," Kristina said.

"No. I'm safe." Nico's eyes dropped. "So what have you got? Good news, I hope."

Hal was about to throw Heartbreakers into Nico's face and

see how the man reacted, but Kristina's warning look stopped him. *Fine, we'll play it your way.*

"We confirmed that Natalia dropped out of nursing school," he said. "The prosecution could try to spin that as your motive for killing her."

"What?" Nico stared at him. "How is that a motive?"

"You were the one who wanted her to be a nurse, right?" Kristina said gently.

"Who told you that?" Nico's hands fidgeted, the chain rattling on the metal table. "None of this makes sense. Why would Nat have me drop her off at school every night? Why would she tell me about her classes, her teachers.... Why would she lie?"

"Could she have been afraid of disappointing you?" Kristina said. "You were working so hard to support her education. Maybe she couldn't bear to tell you."

Nico's shoulders slumped and his hands stilled. A muscle along his jaw spasmed as he worked through some emotion. Hal studied him, trying to determine if that emotion was sadness or something worse—like rage.

The perfect time to push him. "That's not all we learned," Hal said.

Nico looked up, wary.

"We found evidence of late-night ATM deposits in Natalia's bank account. Cash deposits, every few days. All made at an ATM next to a club called Heartbreakers."

Something flickered across Nico's face. Recognition? Bewilderment? Hal couldn't tell.

"Heartbreakers is a strip club," he said, watching Nico's reaction carefully. "Natalia was working there. She called herself Sapphire."

The color drained from Nico's face. "No."

"Kristina and I went there ourselves. There's no question—"

"No," Nico repeated. His voice sounded dull, shellshocked. "She wouldn't go back to that."

Wait—what? He exchanged a quick glance with Kristina, catching the widening of her eyes. He leaned forward. "What do you mean, *back to that?*"

Nico shifted in his chair. When he spoke, his voice was barely audible. "I told you we've been together since high school, but there was a break. Right after we graduated."

"A break?"

"I got drunk at a graduation party." Nico's face twisted with the memory. "Natalia found me in the basement with another girl from our class." He stared down at his cuffed hands. "We were just ... kissing, but that was enough. Natalia dumped me."

"But you worked things out?" Hal said.

Nico paused, collecting himself. "Eventually we did. But first we spent eight months apart." Nico's eyes went distant. "Nat met another guy. Nice car, fancy clothes. He told her she could make easy money. He started her dancing." Nico's hands clenched into fists.

"I know this is hard." Kristina reached across the table and folded her hand over his. Slowly, Nico's fist relaxed. "We need to hear the whole story."

Nico managed a shaky nod. "One night, she called me. Crying. Said she missed me." A ghost of a smile touched his lips, then vanished just as quickly. "I swore I would never hurt her again. And a few months later, I proposed."

"Why didn't you tell us this before?" Hal's tone was harsher than he'd intended, and Nico's gaze snapped up to meet his.

"Because I love her! Because she hated that part of her past. Because she deserved better than to have everyone remember her as a dead stripper!"

His words echoed in the small room. Somewhere in the distance, a pipe clanked.

"I wanted to protect her memory." Nico's voice cracked.

"That's gallant," Hal said, "but our job is to protect *you*, and when you hide the truth from us, you make that job harder."

"I didn't hide the—"

"You knew, didn't you? You knew she went back to stripping."

"No." Nico's gaze met Hal's with sudden intensity. "I swear. I thought she was still in school."

"This is very important, Nico." Kristina's voice was warmer than Hal's, but just as intense. "Have you ever been to Heartbreakers? Even once?"

"No."

"Did you have an argument with Natalia there?" Hal said.

"No."

"The club has cameras," Kristina said. "It's possible the police and the DA's Office could obtain security footage, assuming they haven't already."

"I told you, no!" Nico shook his head emphatically. "I've never been there!"

Hal leaned back in his chair, sensing Kristina relax beside him. They'd served too many expert liars to ever completely believe a client again, but Nico's raw pain seemed genuine. For the moment at least, they believed him.

"I know what you're thinking," Nico said. "That maybe I found out she was stripping again and lost it. But I wouldn't...." He drew a shaky breath. "You have to understand, I would have forgiven anything. After that eight month separation, I could never lose her again."

His shoulders began to shake. "All those nights I dropped her off.... She must have been so ashamed. Hiding it from me. She didn't have to."

"She knew you loved her." Hal touched Nico's shoulder, but he shrugged him off.

"No. I pushed her too hard about nursing school. Working

all the time, never home.... I didn't even notice what she was going through—*what I was putting her through*. This is my fault."

"No," Kristina said firmly. "It's her killer's fault. And we need to find him."

Hal leaned forward. "Tell us more about the boyfriend with the fancy clothes."

Nico's face twisted with disgust. "Marcus Medrano."

Hal felt a jolt. The security guy at Heartbreakers had been named Marcus. *Could it be that simple?*

He kept his voice carefully neutral. "Can you describe him?"

"Never met him in person, but Natalia had some photos. He looked tall—like maybe over six feet. Dark hair slicked back with lots of product. Gold chain." Nico's voice hardened. "Had a smug look, even in the photos, like he knew something you didn't."

Before Hal could press for more details, the door opened and Gomez stepped into the room. "Stop saying anything attorney-client confidential, because time's up."

"We need five more minutes," Kristina said.

"Then make another appointment, because time's up."

Kristina looked like she might argue, then sighed. "Okay." To Nico, she said, "We'll be back tomorrow."

Outside, they walked to the car. "You think it's the same Marcus?" Kristina said.

"I certainly hope so. And Nico's description...."

"Is hardly conclusive," she finished. "We need more."

"I'll call Lena." But before he had a chance, Lena called them. Hal answered his phone with a laugh. "Your timing is impeccable—"

"I found something in your office," Lena cut him off, and there was no smile in her voice. "How quickly can you get here?"

25

"So?" Hal said when they were back in their Old City office. "What did you find?"

Lena didn't answer immediately. She stood in the middle of their ransacked office, studying their faces with a scrutiny that reminded Hal why she was a good investigator. "Something happened at Riverside. You two have that look."

"What look?" Hal said, but his denial only drew a smirk.

"Come on, Hal." She tilted her head. "What did Nico tell you?"

"We'll get to that," Kristina said. "First tell us what you found here."

Lena nodded, clearly reluctant to let it go. It was then that Hal realized the office looked even worse than when they'd discovered the break-in. Lena's investigation had scattered the papers further, leaving no trace of Kristina's careful organization. She'd pulled desk drawers completely out of their housings, shoved furniture aside. Even the drop ceiling panels had been shifted.

"You searched the ceiling?" Hal said.

"Checking for cameras and listening devices. I didn't find any."

"What did you find?" Kristina said.

"The person who was here conducted a targeted search, focused on the Ramirez discovery materials. Other drawers were opened, but the contents were undisturbed. They knew what they were looking for."

"Makes sense," Hal said. "Brantley would only care about Nico. If he sent someone—"

"It wasn't a professional," Lena said. She held up a small Ziploc bag. Her mouth tightened at the corners. "And I don't think it was Brantley."

Hal took the bag, lifted it up to the light. Inside was a single, colorful piece of cereal.

"A Froot Loop?" Hal turned the bag in his fingers, watching the cereal piece tumble. Something nagged at his memory.

"I found it in your office," Lena said. "And I've never known you to eat Froot Loops."

"I'm more of a blueberry muffin kind of guy." Then the memory hit him. The hearing in Judge Harding's chambers, arguing for a reconsideration of bail after Nico's beating. Samantha Klein had arrived late, and when she'd walked past his chair, he'd smelled Froot Loops.

"Sam Klein," Hal said. "But why would she break in to rifle through the discovery *she* gave us?"

Kristina's expression hardened. "We need to tell Judge Harding. Klein should be fired. Disbarred. Breaking and entering, violation of attorney-client privilege, interference with right to counsel—Harding will have to declare a mistrial and refer her to the Ethics Committee." She was already reaching for her phone.

"Hold on." Hal caught her wrist before she could dial. "Let's talk to her first."

"What?" Kristina yanked her arm free. "Why?"

"Because she's desperate, and desperate people make mistakes." Hal's voice lowered. "Think about it—an assistant DA breaking into a defense attorney's office? She's risking everything. Just like we risked everything when we took Brantley's money."

Kristina let out a sharp laugh. "She is nothing like us. She's everything we fight against. A prosecutor who hides evidence, who'd rather win than see justice done—"

"She's scrappy," Hal said. "An underdog. And whatever drove her to break in here wasn't about winning—it was about survival. Remember how it felt when we couldn't pay for lunch at Bistro Cannata?" He glanced at the scattered papers. "Klein's terrified of something. I think we should find out what it is before we destroy her."

"Oh, please. She works for the DA's Office. She has a steady paycheck, benefits, job security—"

"Does she?" Hal raised an eyebrow. "How much job security do you think she has after that *Orozco* screwup?"

"*Orozco* wasn't a screwup, Hal. It was prosecutorial misconduct."

Lena cleared her throat. "I did some digging into Klein. She's a single mom. She has a daughter, Emily, seven years old."

"That's irrelevant," Kristina said, but her crossed arms loosened. She moved to the window. A group of college students strolled past the building looking happy and carefree.

"We should hear her out," Hal said. "Give her one chance to explain herself."

"We're officers of the court, Hal. We have an affirmative duty to report this."

"Our duty to report doesn't have a time limit. Sam broke in here looking for something. Wouldn't you rather know what that is before we blow everything up?"

He watched Kristina's face as she wrestled with an internal battle.

"Fine, one chance." She returned to his side, threading the narrow path between scattered files. "But if I don't like what I hear—"

"Then we go straight to Harding," Hal said.

Lena began gathering her things. "Are you going to tell me what you learned from Nico, or just leave me hanging?"

Kristina filled her in about the security guy at Heartbreakers who just happened to share a name and a physical description with Natalia's sleazy rebound boyfriend who'd introduced her to the world of pole-dancing.

"I'm starting to think you manufacture these surprises just to keep me employed."

"It's hard enough to keep ourselves employed," Hal said.

"We need to know everything you can find out about Marcus Medrano," Kristina said. "He could be Natalia's killer."

"And even if he isn't," Hal added, "if we can make the jury think he is, that's reasonable doubt, and the whole ball game."

26

───────

THE NEXT MORNING, the sun warmed the worn brick of Samantha Klein's walkup. It was the kind of building where blue-collar parents—and white-collar ones on government salaries—did their best with what they had. The facade attempted dignity with its classic bricks and neat rows of windows, but the effect was undermined by the ghost of graffiti someone had tried to scrub away. The concrete steps leading to the door were ravaged by cracks.

"Are you sure her home is the right place for this confrontation, Hal?"

"Poetic justice. She violated our office, so now we violate her personal space."

"First thing in the morning?"

"We need to catch her before she leaves for the office."

"Is that really your reason?" Kristina paused on the step and arched an eyebrow. "Or are you hoping a peek at her home life will make me see her as a struggling single mom and not the snake who broke into our office?"

He winced. She knew him too well.

"Some conversations need to happen off the record," he said.

Inside, Hal knocked on apartment 3A. On the other side of the door, feet thundered across a hardwood floor and a child's voice yelled something indistinct. The door opened. Samantha Klein was still facing behind her as she said, "Emily, the bus will be here in—" She froze when she turned and saw them.

"We would have brought coffee, but someone knocked over our coffee maker last night."

Sam's face hardened. "What are you doing here? I'm getting my daughter ready for school."

"We'll wait."

Sam's jaw worked as her gaze moved from Hal to Kristina and back again. She made a useless attempt to fix her hair, still damp from a shower, then stepped back. "Fine."

The apartment was small, the kitchenette inches from the entryway. Sam hurriedly gathered legal documents from the counter, shoving them out of sight.

Emily sat at a small table in what passed for a dining area, fisting dry cereal into her mouth. She looked up at them with curious eyes.

"Who are *they*?"

"Nobody. Finish your breakfast." Sam opened a colorful backpack on one of the chairs and rifled through it. "Did you pack your music folder?"

"Yes."

"Show me."

Emily rolled her eyes but dutifully clambered to her mother's side.

Hal exchanged a glance with Kristina, then casually studied the apartment. A wall calendar was crammed with overlapping commitments—Emily's activities and playdates, Sam's court appearances, a parent-teacher conference. A basket of unfolded laundry dominated the couch, and next to the toaster, a stack of envelopes stamped with red and orange warnings. Past-due notices. As Kristina had said the night before, *Been there, done that.*

"You want to tell me what you're doing here?" Samantha zipped up the backpack, glaring at him. "It's highly inappropriate."

Kristina shook her head and leveled an incredulous look at the woman. "As inappropriate as breaking into someone's office?"

"Tie your shoes, honey." Sam knelt to help her daughter with the laces. "I have no idea what you're talking about."

"Someone went through our files last night," Hal said. "Specifically, the Ramirez discovery files."

"Sounds like you need to invest in better security." Shoes tied, Sam rose to her feet. "What does that have to do with me?"

Hal pulled the Ziploc bag from his pocket and held it next to the Froot Loops box by Emily's bowl. "Why don't you tell us?"

Samantha stiffened. "Just let me get her on the bus, okay?"

They waited in tense silence while Sam walked Emily downstairs. When she returned five minutes later, her prosecutor's mask was firmly in place. "A Froot Loop doesn't prove anything."

"You might be surprised how persuasive we can be," Kristina said.

Sam's laugh was bitter. "So this is a threat?"

"This is mercy," Kristina said. "And you can thank Hal. I wanted to go straight to Judge Harding."

"Of course you did. Little Miss Law Nerd."

"At least I never needed to break the law to do my job."

Hal got between them. "Hey, why don't we all take a deep breath?"

"I told you this would be a waste of time," Kristina said. She pulled out her phone. "Let Judge Harding deal with her. Or Burke."

Hal saw a tremor run through Sam at the mention of Aldo Burke, but she regained control of herself quickly. "Please." Her voice oozed sarcasm. "I have two FBI agents threatening to re-open custody of my daughter. They may have already gotten the restraining order against my ex lifted. Colten is a monster, so if you think I'm worried about a couple defense attorneys tattle-tailing to the judge, you're wrong."

FBI agents? Hal exchanged a quick glance with Kristina. "The same agents working the Brantley investigation?" he said, keeping his voice casual.

"Like I would discuss an ongoing federal investigation with the two of you."

"Ventura and Glover," Hal said. Sam's jaw worked, but she said nothing. "Yeah, we've met them. They made quite an impression."

"Then you know what I'm dealing with."

"Did they tell you to break into our office?" The logic didn't work, but Hal was trying to understand the connection. He settled onto her couch, moving the laundry basket to make room. "*Hypothetically.* Why would a prosecutor break into a defense attorney's office to look through the same discovery materials that same prosecutor had herself provided?"

Sam looked at him. "She wouldn't."

"The Froot Loop indicates otherwise. So help me under-stand. Hypothetically. Otherwise...." He let his gaze swing to Kristina, who still held her phone.

Sam's jaw flexed. Hal saw the flash of calculation in her eyes and reminded himself to tread carefully. "Maybe the pros-ecutor disclosed something, and then had second thoughts about whether it really fell within the obligation of the Brady rule."

Kristina let out a derisive laugh. "You really didn't learn anything from *Orozco*, did you?"

"Hypothetically," Sam continued as if Kristina hadn't spoken, "maybe given the pressure exerted by these FBI agents, the prosecutor didn't want to take any chances with her daughter at risk. So she corrected the oversight."

"Understandable," Hal said. "Now, maybe if that evidence were returned, the defense attorneys would forget the break-in ever happened."

Kristina shot him a sharp look, but did not contradict him. They could both see that Sam was wavering, that they were close to retrieving whatever she had taken.

"I wouldn't know anything about that," Sam said. But she walked to her attache case, removed a manila folder, and set it on the coffee table with a defeated look.

"Neither would we." Hal picked up the folder.

Back in their car, Kristina flipped through the pages while Hal drove. "I still don't think we should just let her get away with this."

"Because she called you Little Miss Law Nerd? That was a low-blow." He flashed her a smile, but she did not return it.

"Because she's dangerous."

"What's in the file?"

Kristina flipped through more pages. "Looks like lab results. And Detective Coffey's notes from a conversation with the ME...." She fell silent as she studied the documents. Hal navigated the Camry toward their office.

"Seriously?" he said after a long moment. "How long are you going to keep me in suspense?"

"Klein and Coffey sent the USB cable to the police lab, along with a tissue sample from Natalia, hoping to find DNA evidence proving it was the murder weapon."

"And they didn't?" Hal said. "That's great."

"The lab found metal particles embedded in the tissue sample."

"What does that mean?"

Kristina shook her head. "It wasn't pursued any further—probably because Klein shut Coffey down." She flipped pages. "The ME told Coffey that the abrasion patterns were unusual for a rubber cable."

"So maybe the USB cable was planted after the fact," Hal said. "It wasn't the real murder weapon."

"Metal particles," Kristina mused. "Sounds more like a chain."

"We know someone who wears a chain," Hal said, thinking of Marcus Medrano's thick neck. The strip club's head of security had been awfully quick to throw them out ... and awfully reluctant to let them learn who Natalia had argued with. He'd also conveniently neglected to mention he had a history with her—assuming he was the same Marcus that Nico had told them about.

An assumption Hal was more than willing to make.

"Ventura and Glover were at that club," Kristina said. "We assumed they followed us. But what if they were already there?"

"Investigating the real killer?" Hal shook his head. "That doesn't make sense."

"Not investigating," Kristina said. "*Protecting*."

"What?" Hal took his eyes off the road and met Kristina's gaze.

"Ventura and Glover want Brantley. Enough to threaten us. Enough to blackmail Klein, by meddling with her restraining order and threatening her custody of her daughter. They think Nico can give them the evidence they need if they exert enough pressure. And what better way to keep the pressure on him than to make sure he's facing an airtight murder charge?"

"So they hide the real killer." Hal was quiet for a moment, processing. Then he laughed. "You realize what this means?"

"That Ventura and Glover are even more vile than we thought?"

Hal's laughter died. "I was going to say it means we can prove Nico's innocence."

"If they let us live that long."

27

Kristina tried to remain calm in spite of the sensory overload that was Philadelphia's Reading Terminal Market—competing food smells, hundreds of conversations, the constant crush of anonymous bodies. She and Hal had managed to claim a small table near some trash cans—and even for this real estate, they'd had to fight a family of four.

"Want coffee or anything?" Hal said. She could barely hear him over the sounds of commerce—a man ordering a cheesesteak, a woman haggling over kale. "We passed a baked goods place on our way in."

Kristina gestured past Hal. "He's coming."

FBI Special Agent Charles Cooley navigated toward them. Kristina had always found his look slightly unnerving—navy blue suit, shirt starched and blindingly white, tie knotted with the precision of a cyborg—but today, the sight provoked even more unease as she realized how similar he looked to Ventura and Glover.

Cooley might seem like an ally. He was leading the investigation of the cyberattacks on their firm, after all, and had done them a favor in the past. But at the end of the day, he was law enforcement, and Kristina had learned the hard way that law enforcement's priorities rarely aligned with theirs. The same Bureau that was supposedly helping them recover from Olivia Hazenberg's attacks was also home to agents like Ventura and Glover. How much loyalty did agents really have to each other versus the truth?

She realized too late that this meeting might be a huge mistake. But Hal was already rising from his chair and waving to Cooley like they were old friends meeting for brunch.

"Charles," Hal said, extending his hand. "Thanks for meeting us."

Cooley's handshake was brief, his gaze assessing.

"I was about to go grab coffee and maybe some muffins," Hal said. "Let me guess—you take your coffee black?"

Cooley settled into the third chair. "I don't need anything. Thanks."

"I'm good, too," Kristina said.

She saw Hal suppress a pout as he sat down. "Okay. No muffins then."

"How's the Ramirez case progressing?" Cooley's voice was neutral. "I understand jury selection starts tomorrow."

"Which is actually why we need to speak with you now," Hal said. "We need your help."

Cooley's posture shifted. "Go on."

Hal looked at her—he had agreed to let her do the talking—but now she hesitated. She studied Cooley's maddeningly neutral expression. "We had a run-in with two of your colleagues," she said. "FBI agents."

"About the Ramirez case?" Cooley looked puzzled, which would be the appropriate reaction—the FBI had no jurisdiction over Natalia Ramirez's murder. But that didn't mean his reaction was genuine.

"It wasn't a pleasant conversation," Kristina said. "They ambushed us outside a strip bar."

"A strip club?" Cooley's eyebrows rose.

She waved a hand. "That's not important. The point is, they threatened us."

"They're also pressuring the prosecutor," Hal said.

Cooley's gaze remained steady. "That's a serious accusation."

"We're not making it lightly," Hal said.

Cooley's voice dropped lower. "Maybe you could be more specific about who you're talking about."

Kristina took a breath. They'd already told Cooley too much to stop now. She only hoped they could trust him. "Lilliana Ventura and Austin Glover."

As she spoke the names, she caught a slight tightening around his eyes and an almost imperceptible tensing of his shoulders.

"Do you know them?" Hal said.

"Why would they interfere in your murder trial?" Cooley asked, ignoring Hal's question.

"Because they're building a case against Gavin Brantley," Kristina said. "Nico Ramirez worked at Brantley Capital. Ventura and Glover want to use the murder charge to leverage Nico to provide evidence against Brantley."

Cooley rubbed his face and gazed at the crowd.

"Agent Cooley," Kristina said, "Charles. We're not here to cause problems for you or the Bureau. But these two FBI agents are actively interfering with our ability to defend our client at trial."

Cooley let out a sigh. "And what exactly are you hoping I'll do about this?"

"Well," Hal leaned forward. "We thought that maybe being on the inside, you could help rein them in."

"You're asking me to work against members of my own agency based on allegations I have no way to verify."

"You don't trust us?" Hal said.

"Is that a serious question, Hal?"

Kristina let out a frustrated sound. "We're not talking about overzealous investigators. This goes way beyond that. The prosecutor—Samantha Klein—has a restraining order against her daughter's abusive father. Ventura and Glover are working to vacate it, and threatening to reopen custody as well. They're threatening a child's safety in order to coerce her to follow their agenda. They're breaking the law."

Cooley scanned the busy market around them again, and she wondered if he was avoiding their eyes—or watching for someone else. Finally, he said, "Ventura and Glover are ... not my favorite people." The admission—such as it was—was barely audible over the din.

"So you know them," Kristina pressed.

"Our paths have crossed."

"And?" Hal said.

"They have a reputation for getting results."

"At any cost?" Kristina asked.

Cooley's jaw tightened. His silence was its own answer.

"Look," Hal said, leaning forward, "it's no secret that Kristina and I bend the rules on occasion. The same could be said for Sam Klein. But Ventura and Glover? What they're doing is a whole other level of bad."

"Is it possible," Cooley said carefully, "that a plea deal could be in your client's best interest?"

"No." Kristina stopped herself from saying more. There was a limit to what they could confide to Cooley, and telling him that there was no deal to make—because Nico didn't actually know anything about Brantley's business practices—was beyond that limit. Telling him would violate attorney-client confidentiality, not to mention jeopardizing the funding of his defense.

"You sound very certain of that."

"We are," Kristina said.

"We can't tell you more than that," Hal added. She felt his knee touch hers under the table, a subtle gesture to let her know they were on the same page.

Cooley seemed to study them for a long moment. "Ventura and Glover have done this type of thing before."

"And the Bureau allows it?" Kristina said.

"As I said, they get results."

"At the expense of innocent people."

"Usually those people aren't particularly innocent."

Kristina felt a flare of anger. "That's not right. They can't just—"

A group of tourists with oversized shopping bags bumped into their table, jostling it.

"I need to go," Cooley said, checking his watch.

"Wait," Kristina said. "You're not going to help?"

Cooley stood, straightening his suit. "I'd advise you to watch your backs. Ventura and Glover are not the type of enemies you can afford to make right now, especially in your precarious position."

Precarious position. The phrase stung because it was accurate. Their firm was hanging by a thread, financed by Brantley based on a lie, and their only client was facing death row. Now they were making enemies of FBI agents with a track record of playing dirty.

"Think about what I said," Cooley said. "If there's any chance that a plea deal could work in your client's favor—"

"We're picking our jury tomorrow," Kristina said, rising from her chair to remain level with him. "And we intend to win at trial."

Cooley nodded. "Good luck." She thought she saw a hint of respect in his gaze, but maybe it was just pity.

He turned and disappeared into the market, leaving Kristina and Hal alone at the table. She waited until he was completely out of sight before speaking. "Well?"

"Not exactly the resounding pledge of support we were hoping for." Hal flashed her a sardonic smile, but she could hear the tightness in his voice.

"Looks like we're on our own," she said. "As usual."

28

IN HER OFFICE, Samantha Klein's hands shook. The words of the court order swam before her eyes as she read them for the fourth time—as if they might miraculously rearrange themselves into something less devastating.

...AND THEREFORE, it is the decision of this Court that the restraining order against Colten Roth regarding Samantha Klein and minor child Emily Klein is hereby VACATED, effective immediately...

Not an empty bluff by the Feds. Not a hollow threat. Reality, printed on official court letterhead and signed by some asshole judge who'd been bribed or compromised by Ventura and Glover, probably both.

The man who'd put her in the hospital three times now had the legal right to approach her. And Emily. To show up at their doorstep in the middle of the night.

No hearing. No opportunity to present evidence. Just ... vacated.

And this was only the beginning, a mere show of force. Ventura had made clear that if Sam failed to deliver Nico Ramirez's testimony against Gavin Brantley on a silver platter, the next court order would address child custody.

Colten could obtain a legal right to be alone with Emily.

Sam's stomach twisted so hard that for a moment, she couldn't breathe.

Years of stressful legal battles to protect Emily, gone in one swift judicial stroke.

A rap on her door made her jump.

She shoved the papers into a drawer just as the door swung open and Aldo Burke entered.

She realized that a stack of jury questionnaires remained in plain view on her desk. She grabbed for them, knowing even as her hands touched the papers that she was already too late.

One bushy eyebrow arched as Burke watched her. "Guilty conscience, Klein?"

He advanced into her tiny office, reached down, and jerked the top sheet from her fingers. Her heart sank as his eyes scanned the document.

"*Voir dire* scheduled for...." His gaze flicked up to meet hers. "Tomorrow morning."

Sam straightened in her chair. "I've been meaning to update you." Hoping he didn't hear the crack in her voice, she forced a confident smile past her held-back tears. "Everything's ready to go. Detective Coffey and I have prepared a solid case."

Burke's eyebrows knitted together. "A solid case you neglected to mention to me."

"That's ... that's not true, Aldo. You assigned it to me. At the time, Ramirez had a public defender. I just.... I got busy and I didn't get around to updating you when the Nolans took over his representation—"

"The Nolans." His eyes darkened and his large frame suddenly felt menacing in the tight confines of her office. Her heart rate sped.

"I ... I was going to schedule some time to update you—"

"And it's going to trial tomorrow?" Burke flung the jury questionnaire at her. The paper hit her chest before drifting to her desktop. "The last I heard, this was going to be a quick plea deal. The public defender, Jerry Newman—"

"When the Nolans took over for Jerry, Ramirez rejected the plea offer. I meant to update the case file." She gestured vaguely toward her computer. "But—"

Burke loomed over her desk, and she had to fight the instinct to retreat—not that there was anywhere to go. "Do you actually believe that I am this easy to deceive, Klein? I know you hid this from me intentionally, and I know why. A big murder trial against infamous defense attorneys? You thought that was your ticket to the big time."

She swallowed. What was the use in denying it?

"There is no ticket to the big time," Burke continued. "Not for you. I'm reassigning the case to Wyatt Donovan."

His words hit her like a bucket of ice water. Her mouth opened, but panic strangled her voice. She couldn't let him take this case from her. Not now. It wasn't just pride anymore, not just her career at stake. Emily's safety hung in the balance.

As Burke turned to leave, she popped out of her chair. "That didn't work out so well last time."

Burke stopped in the doorway. Turned. Glared at her. She flinched from that glare, legs threatening to give way beneath her. But then something Dan Coffey once told her played in her mind. *When all else fails,* the detective had said, *sometimes you have to take a baseball bat to a hornet's nest.*

"Donovan lost to the Nolans," she heard herself say, "just like you."

Burke's jowls quivered. His face reddened.

"So let's discuss this like professionals," she said. "Close the door."

To her own astonishment, Burke did as she said.

"And *you* think you can beat them?" His voice dripped with contempt.

"I know I can."

"You don't know anything. You're a failure of a lawyer. You're a liability and an embarrassment to this office."

Sam felt heat rise to her face, and the sting of oncoming tears in her eyes. She held all of that back. She'd had years of practice managing her emotions. A lifetime, really.

And he wasn't done. "You should have been disbarred after *Orozco*."

"But I wasn't."

"No, because instead of admitting fault and taking responsibility, you slithered out of it like a sleaze. You're the kind of prosecutor who gives all prosecutors a bad name."

"People say similar things about Hal and Kristina." The steadiness in her voice surprised her. "Did it ever occur to you to fight fire with fire?"

Burke sneered. "More like trying to clean mud off a floor with a dirty mop."

That's really how he sees me—as dirt, mud.

The realization shouldn't have hurt after all this time, but it did. All these years grinding away in this office, handling cases no one else wanted, trying to work her way back into his good graces—and her goal had never actually been achievable. Because Burke would never see her as anything more than the prosecutor who violated the *Brady* rule.

So own it.

"You've tried everything else. What's the worst that could happen? I lose—like everyone else has against the Nolans? Or I get a plea deal and put Nico Ramirez in prison?"

Burke shook his head and let out a weary sigh. "I don't have time to reassign this. It wouldn't be fair to dump your mess on another prosecutor with one day to prepare."

She felt a weight lift from her shoulders. "Thank you, Aldo. You won't regret—"

"But Klein—a plea deal is not enough. I want a courtroom victory. A first-degree murder guilty verdict. I want the Nolans to lose, publicly and completely. That's your job. Do that, or you're done—for good this time."

The silence stretched between them, so quiet Sam could hear the hum of her computer. A drop of sweat slid down her back.

Ventura and Glover demanded a plea deal, and if she failed to deliver it, they would put Colten back in Emily's life. If she made this deal with Burke, she would have to break it to save her daughter.

"Deal," she said.

Burke turned and left her office, closing the door with a controlled but forceful click. Not quite a slam, but close enough.

29

___

HAL SAT at the defense table and pretended to review the jury questionnaires Kristina arranged in front of them—while really side-eying the pool of potential jurors as they filed into the gallery. Ordinary Philadelphians annoyed at this disruption of their schedule, who'd been forced to fight the morning commute into the city for a duty they didn't ask for, who would rather be anywhere but here. It would be up to Hal and Kristina to find twelve people from the crowd open-minded enough to give their client a fair shot.

A moment later, the deputies escorted Nico into the courtroom. Hal had provided him with a charcoal gray Brooks Brothers suit from his own closet. It hung loose on Nico's frame, but still looked good on him—and a hell of a lot better than a prison jumpsuit. Nico's face was drawn, but there was a gleam of optimism in his eyes as he shook Hal's hand.

"So this is when you pick the people who will judge me?" Nico said quietly.

"Don't think of it that way. Think of it as building your defense team. Twelve people who will see through the DA's case and get you out of jail."

Nico nodded, his gaze darting around the gallery. "They all look so ... uninterested."

"We're good at making people interested," Kristina said.

The three of them sat down. Across the aisle, Samantha Klein arranged her own files. She seemed even more tightly wound than usual, her movements jerky, her smile brittle. And she wasn't alone. A middle-aged man, tall and reed-thin, sat beside her with a laptop open in front of him.

Hal leaned close to Kristina. "Sam has backup. Junior prosecutor maybe?"

"That's Elliott Snow," Kristina whispered. "Jury consultant to the stars. We considered him once. His rates start at five grand a day."

Hal whistled. "We're in the wrong line of business."

"No way Klein can afford him on a DA's Office trial budget. And judging by her apartment, she's not in a position to pay him out of her own pocket. So...."

"Ventura and Glover," Hal said.

"That's what I'm thinking."

It made a kind of twisted sense. The FBI agents would want to ensure Sam had every advantage, because the worse this trial went for Nico, the more leverage they would have to coerce him to make a deal against Brantley.

If he'd known they'd be outgunned at jury selection, Hal would have pushed Brantley to fund their own fancy consultant. But he hadn't expected this. Sam had blindsided him.

"It doesn't matter," he said, as much to himself as Kristina. "Jurors are people. We don't need a high-priced nerd to tell us which of them will take our side."

Kristina didn't argue, but her tightened posture told him she had her doubts. She slid a few jury questionnaire forms toward him, each marked with her notations in the margins. "Get these three in the box if you can. Working class backgrounds, skeptical of authority figures—good defense jurors."

Hal glanced at the forms. A mechanic, a daycare worker, and a postal employee. "And what about what we talked about?"

Kristina's posture stiffened. "Hal...."

"We need every advantage we can get. Especially now, with Snow over there running algorithms in realtime."

"Victim-shaming is not a strategy," she said tightly. "It's a shady tactic used by desperate lawyers."

"In case you didn't notice, we *are* desperate lawyers."

Kristina's jaw clenched. She slid a questionnaire in front of him. "Frank Matthews."

Hal skimmed the document. Fifty-seven. Accountant. History of conservative comments on social media, many about the country's loss of traditional values.

"Thanks."

Hal's strategy was threefold. First and foremost, he wanted jurors who were skeptical of authority figures—the bread-and-butter of a defense-friendly jury, people likely to question the police and DA narratives. Second, he wanted working-class male jurors, Latino if possible, guys who were likely to see themselves in Nico the janitor, and sympathize with him. And third, even though it sickened him as much as it did Kristina, he wanted haters.

People who, the moment they learned Natalia Ramirez had been dancing naked at a strip bar, would decide she was a worthless slut who got exactly what she deserved.

People like Frank Matthews.

The bailiff cut off his thoughts. "All rise. Court is now in session, the Honorable Judge Callum Harding presiding."

Harding emerged from his chambers. The rookie judge did a good job projecting the confidence of an old hand, but Hal had his doubts. Jury selection could be a minefield for a judge, especially with a professional snake like Elliot Snow using every trick to help the prosecution exploit the process.

"Be seated," Harding said after settling into his chair. "*Commonwealth versus Ramirez*, scheduled today for jury selection. Are both sides prepared to proceed?"

"Yes, Your Honor," Sam said.

"Defense is ready as well, Your Honor," Hal said.

Harding turned his attention to the gallery. "Ladies and gentlemen, thank you for appearing here this morning. My name is Judge Callum Harding. As you know, you've been called here today as potential jurors in a criminal case."

Hal watched the jurors' faces as Harding launched into an explanation of the *voir dire* process, courtroom procedures, and the responsibilities of a juror under the criminal justice system. It all sounded dry and burdensome, and that was reflected in the faces of the potential jurors, which ranged from bored to annoyed.

When it was Hal's turn to talk, he would need to shake things up.

"We will now begin *voir dire*," Harding said. "Both the prosecution and the defense will ask you questions. This is necessary in order to ensure we seat a fair and impartial jury. Mr. Nolan, you may now proceed with general questioning."

Hal rose and faced the throng. "My name is Hal Nolan, and if you are selected for jury duty, we'll be getting to know each other." He offered his most charming smile. "I represent the defendant in this case, Nico Ramirez. But before we start talking about Mr. Ramirez, I'd like to share a quick story from when I was a kid."

He paused, ensuring he had their attention. From the prosecution table, he heard Sam mutter under her breath.

"When I was about ten," he continued, "my mom and dad took a vacation for their anniversary. They left me with a sitter

—an older woman from the neighborhood named Mrs. Baxter."

He waited as several of the jurors' postures relaxed, a natural response to the shift from legalese to personal anecdote.

"Mrs. Baxter wasn't too bad, overall. She kept me fed, made sure I went to school and did my homework. But one afternoon, Mrs. Baxter suddenly accused me of hiding her purse. She was furious—shaking her fist in the air, face red, the whole bit. I swore I was innocent, but nothing I said made a difference. I realized she'd already made up her mind. She wasn't listening to me. In fact, she was already telling me all the punishments I could look forward to." Hal shook his head ruefully. "But just when all seemed lost, she suddenly said, 'Oh—you put it on the bannister by my coat.'"

A ripple of laughter spread through the jury pool. Hal let it settle before continuing, his expression growing more serious.

"I tell you this story because it taught me something about human nature. Once we *think* we know what happened, it can be incredibly hard to see any other possibility." He leaned forward, making eye contact with several potential jurors. "The key to being a good juror—to carrying out your duty if you are chosen—is to keep an open mind."

Hal proceeded to ask the standard questions about impartiality, reasonable doubt, and the presumption of innocence. He paid careful attention to each response, trying to suss out the open-minded jurors, not just by their words, but by their body language and glances toward Nico. When he finished, he returned to his seat.

"How'd I do?"

"I never knew about Mrs. Baxter," Kristina whispered. "That must have been terrible for you."

Hal shrugged. "It would have been, if it had actually happened."

Kristina tried to give him a stern look, but he saw the twinkle of begrudging amusement.

Sam rose for her turn at general questioning. She took an hour, but the time was well-spent. She established herself as passionate but professional, and skillfully planted the seeds of the prosecution's theory—that Natalia had been murdered by her controlling husband because she'd failed to follow the course he'd decided for her. Kristina placed a hand on Nico's and whispered something in his ear—probably reminding him to maintain a neutral expression. Throughout Sam's performance, Elliot Snow watched the jury pool like a hawk, his gaze moving from the jurors to his laptop. Hal caught himself grinding his teeth.

After a brief recess, individual questioning began. Judge Harding called the first batch of potential jurors to the box. Hal and Sam took turns, each working to expose biases harmful to their own side while attempting to slide prejudices favorable to their case past the other's scrutiny.

Some jurors were dismissed "for cause" when their answers revealed biases Judge Harding had to concede would prevent fair judgment, while others needed to be knocked out via peremptory challenges—those precious few strikes each side could use to remove jurors without specific justification. Each side had only seven peremptory challenges, making them a limited commodity neither Hal nor Sam could afford to waste.

Hal focused on Etta Farrell, a retired nurse in her sixties. "Ms. Farrell, according to your questionnaire, your daughter was a victim of domestic violence?"

The woman's voice quavered. "That's correct."

"If you were to hear allegations during this trial—for example, that neighbors often heard my client and his wife having loud arguments—do you believe you could maintain an objective perspective given your daughter's experience?"

The woman's jaw set. "I can be fair, if that's what you're asking."

"Are you sure?"

"Asked and answered, Your Honor," Sam said to the judge.

Before Harding could rule, Farrell said, "I understand the difference between my daughter's situation and this case."

Like hell you do. Hal had not failed to notice how the woman's hands squeezed into fists whenever she looked at Nico.

"Your Honor," Hal said, "the defense moves to strike Ms. Farrell for cause. Ms. Farrell's personal connection to domestic violence creates an inherent bias that would prevent her from fairly evaluating the evidence."

"Seriously?" Sam shook her head. "Your Honor, Ms. Farrell just stated, clearly and on the record, that she can be impartial."

Judge Harding seemed to consider for a moment, studying Ms. Farrell. Hal could see the indecision in the young judge's features. "Ms. Farrell, can you assure this Court that you will set aside any personal experiences and judge this case solely on the evidence presented?"

"Absolutely, Your Honor." Her voice was firm, but her eyes flicked toward Nico with disdain.

"Motion to strike for cause is denied," Harding ruled. "Ms. Farrell may remain in the pool."

Hal shot a quick look to Kristina and was not surprised when she gave him a decisive nod. Farrell was too dangerous.

"The defense will exercise a peremptory challenge to dismiss, Ms. Farrell, Your Honor."

"That makes five strikes," Sam said under her breath as she traded places with him in front of the jury box. She tucked a strand of red hair behind her ear, allowing a smirk to show for the split-second her hand hid her face. "Running low, Hal."

"More than enough to handle whatever your overpaid consultant is feeding you."

"Maybe math isn't your strong suit."

Judge Harding cleared his throat. "Is this a private conference, or something you'd like to share on the record, counselors?"

"Sorry, Your Honor," Hal said. "I was just offering Ms. Klein some advice on trial strategy."

Sam, glaring at him, had no chance to respond before Judge Harding said, "I strongly suggest you move along. We're on a tight schedule."

"Of course, Your Honor."

Their next battleground came in the form of Truett Booker, a young bartender with sleeve tattoos and a perpetual sneer. During Sam's questioning, he admitted to distrusting cops. "I've seen too many of them lie. So yeah, I'd question what they say."

Blunt, but exactly the kind of juror Hal wanted.

He approached the jury box with a casualness he didn't feel. "Mr. Booker, just to clarify—you're not saying you would *automatically* disbelieve testimony from a law enforcement officer, right? Just that you would look for evidence to support or contradict their claims, like any reasonable person."

Sam turned to the judge. "Your Honor, Mr. Nolan is putting words in the potential juror's mouth."

"I'd like to hear Mr. Booker's answer," Harding said. "But Mr. Nolan, going forward, please be more careful about leading questions."

Hal maintained eye-contact with Booker. "Go ahead."

Booker shifted in his seat. "I wouldn't *automatically* disbelieve a cop, no."

"But you would apply a different standard to police testimony than to other witnesses, wouldn't you?" Sam said.

Booker frowned. "I don't think so...." Not exactly the most convincing response.

"You wouldn't be more skeptical?" Sam pressed.

"I mean, not on purpose," Booker faltered. "I mean, it's kind of an instinct at this point to ... you know...."

Stop talking, Hal silently urged the man.

Sam nodded to the man with make-believe sympathy, then swung toward the bench. "Your Honor, the Commonwealth moves to strike Mr. Booker for cause."

Hal spread his hands. "Your Honor, Mr. Booker merely expressed a healthy skepticism, not an inability to be fair."

Judge Harding grimaced. "I agree with the Commonwealth on this one. Motion to strike for cause is granted. Mr. Booker, you are excused."

Hal struggled to keep his poker face as the bartender made his way out of the jury box.

By mid-afternoon, Hal had a dull headache, the courtroom had grown stuffy—even Judge Harding had loosened his collar —and both sides' stores of peremptory challenges were dwindling. But the worst part was Hal's growing certainty that he was losing, badly.

And then they came to Frank Matthews.

The middle-aged accountant survived Sam's initial questioning, answering in a voice that sounded reasonable and measured. Hal had feared that the man might reveal subtle tells, but if he held narrow views about women, he hid those prejudices well.

"Does the defense have any questions for this juror, Mr. Nolan?" Judge Harding said.

"No, Your Honor. Mr. Matthews appears to be a perfectly acceptable juror."

"In that case, let's move on to—"

"Hold on, Your Honor," Sam said. As she spoke, Hal caught movement at the prosecution table. Snow was gesturing urgently to her, his fingers flying across his keyboard. Sam strode quickly over. Snow spoke into her ear, angling his laptop screen toward her. Sam's eyes widened, then narrowed with predatory focus.

Uh-oh.

Sam returned to the jury box. "Mr. Matthews, how would you react if trial evidence were to show that the victim engaged in behavior some might consider morally questionable?"

Hal held his breath.

"Well, my job as a juror would be to evaluate evidence, not pass moral judgment," Matthews replied without hesitation.

"And if the victim worked in what some consider a controversial profession? For example, if she was a stripper?"

Matthews blinked—just once, quickly—and shifted slightly in his seat. "I would focus on the facts of the case."

"Do you think stripping is morally wrong, Mr. Matthews?"

"Your Honor." Hal managed to keep his voice level despite the tension building in his chest. "Mr. Matthews's personal opinion of exotic dancing is irrelevant. He's already stated that he would be impartial."

"The Commonwealth has the right to test that statement, Your Honor."

Judge Harding seemed to study Sam for a moment, then gestured for her to continue.

"Mr. Matthews, I'm curious about something else. What would you say if I told you that in addition to being a prosecutor, I'm also a single mother?" She crossed her arms.

"I wouldn't care."

"Really?" Sam tilted her head. "Because according to your social media posts from last year, you stated that, and I quote, 'Children raised by single mothers are statistically more likely to become criminals, which is why traditional family values matter.'"

Matthews's face flushed. "Well, that's taken out of context."

"Is it though?"

Matthews shifted uncomfortably. "That was about statistics, not individuals."

"Statistically, would a stripper evince 'traditional family values?'"

"Your Honor, may we approach?" Hal said.

Harding nodded, and Hal and Sam met at the judge's bench.

"Your Honor, Ms. Klein's line of questioning is completely inappropriate. I mean, telling a potential juror about her personal life? Reading his own social media posts on the record in a courtroom?"

"The only thing inappropriate here is Mr. Nolan's defense of a misogynist bigot because he thinks the man will applaud his client's vicious murder."

"Right. As opposed to the small business owner you wanted on the panel who believes jobs are being stolen by 'those Mexicans.'"

"He was dismissed."

"Over your objection."

"And Mr. Matthews should be dismissed over yours."

Harding frowned. "Mr. Matthews has stated emphatically that he can and will be an impartial juror."

"Exactly," Hal said.

"He's lying." Sam took a deep breath. "My consultant has discovered that Mr. Matthews served on a jury in a sexual assault case three years ago. During deliberations, he reportedly told other jurors that 'women who dress provocatively are asking for trouble.' The defendant in that case was acquitted despite substantial evidence."

How the hell did Snow dig that up?

Hal forced an incredulous laugh. "Your Honor, we have no way to verify what Mr. Matthews may or may not have said during confidential jury deliberations in another case."

"I can ask him right now," Sam countered. "Although I suspect he would just lie again."

"To what end?" Hal said. "Your Honor, this is jury manipulation, plain and simple."

Sam glared at him. "No, Hal, it's *voir dire*."

"I guess the rumors are true. You can't win a trial unless you cheat—"

"Enough." Harding's voice was a harsh whisper. "I don't know what's going on between you two, but my courtroom isn't the place to settle it. Pull yourselves together or I'll finish jury selection without either of you."

Hal fell silent, as did Sam beside him, but he could feel her seething.

Harding continued, "Mr. Nolan, while Ms. Klein's concerns are valid, I agree that there's insufficient evidence of bias. The motion to strike for cause is denied. Ms. Klein—"

"Then I'll use a peremptory."

"That's your right."

And just like that, Hal watched their secret weapon walk out of the jury box.

At least his conscience would be clear—victim-blaming was off the table.

The rest of *voir dire* continued with similar intensity. By the end of the day, the final jury was set—four women (all young and seemingly liberal), five middle-aged men (four married, one divorced, all white-collar professionals with a healthy respect for authority), two retired teachers (one male, one female, both from affluent neighborhoods), and an older female paralegal who once worked as a cocktail waitress.

Not a single working-class male. Not a single Latino. Not a single authority skeptic. A stacked jury, and not the good kind.

Judge Harding thanked the seated jurors and provided instructions for their return the following morning. As court adjourned, Hal and Kristina quietly packed up their files. "How'd we do?" Nico said.

Hal forced a smile. "All good. Couldn't ask for a better panel." But Nico did not look reassured—their client wasn't stupid. "We'll make it work," Hal said.

Deputies appeared at Nico's side. Hal waited until they'd escorted him from the courtroom before he let his smile drop.

"Klein outmaneuvered us," Kristina said softly.

Hal watched the jurors file out of the courtroom. "We can still win them over."

"We're going to need to."

30

HAL PACED the length of their Old City office's common room, holding an egg roll in one hand and a draft of his opening statement in the other.

"You're nervous." Kristina looked up from the conference table. "That's not like you."

"Well, we just impaneled a jury that would give any prosecutor a wet dream. So yeah—I'm nervous."

Kristina pushed a strand of hair behind her ear. "Pacing won't fix it."

"Moving helps me think."

He glanced at his watch. 9:42 PM. Tomorrow morning, he would be standing in Judge Harding's courtroom, making an opening statement to the jury. If it wasn't a good one, Nico would be relocating to a new cell on death row.

"Focus on our defense theory," Kristina said. Her voice was maddeningly calm. "The police arrested the obvious suspect— the husband—without conducting a diligent investigation. We will show that not only is there reasonable doubt as to Nico's guilt, but there is actually compelling evidence pointing to a different killer—a dangerous man from Natalia's past who'd recently returned to her life."

"That would be great if we actually had any compelling evidence."

The knock at their office door made both of them pause. It was a little late for a visitor—even the bill collectors usually kept to business hours.

Hal put down his food and moved to the door. Lena Randall stood outside, carrying a portfolio under her arm and looking far more energized than anyone had a right to be at this hour. Behind her, the sounds of Old City nightlife drifted in—laughter from a group of friends passing the building, music spilling from an open doorway down the street—the carefree sounds of people who didn't need to worry about their client receiving a lethal injection.

Hal stepped back to let Lena in. "Let me guess," he said. "Marcus has an airtight alibi and spends his weekends rescuing kittens."

"That kind of day, huh?" Lena strode inside, her gaze sweeping the room, taking in the leftover Chinese takeout and their disheveled workspace. "I guess jury selection didn't go as planned?"

"It could have gone better," Kristina said.

Lena set her portfolio on the conference table. "Maybe this will help."

She unzipped the portfolio and began spreading out documents across the desk. "I confirmed that the security guy at Heartbreakers is Marcus Medrano."

Hal and Kristina exchanged a glance. That was one detail nailed down—Marcus the Heartbreakers goon was the same Marcus who'd been Natalia's boyfriend years ago, who'd gotten her into stripping.

"Good job," Hal said. "How'd you confirm it?"

"Called in a favor with a buddy who works at the PA Department of Labor." Lena looked pleased with herself. "He had access to Heartbreakers' employee records based on an audit from a few years ago. I also got a visual match."

Lena produced two photographs and placed them side by side—one was a reproduction of Marcus Medrano's driver's license, the other a surveillance photo taken outside the strip club.

"It's him alright." Studying the images, Hal felt a spark of hope. They would still be relying on innuendo and circumstantial evidence to suggest that Marcus was the killer, but the fact was he looked dangerous in these photos—surly, nasty—and appearances could go a long way with a jury.

"Hold on," Lena said, spreading out more documents. "I haven't gotten to the good stuff."

Hal looked at Kristina, who arched an eyebrow. "Criminal record?" Kristina said.

"Bingo."

Hal picked up the printouts. "Multiple assaults." He felt a smile spread across his face. "Including one against a former girlfriend. Lena, this is amazing."

She acknowledged the praise with a curt nod. "Most of the charges were either reduced or dismissed, but they show a pattern of violence, especially toward women."

Kristina came around the table to look at the documents. "He's wearing a gold chain in both photos."

Hal picked up the surveillance photo and examined it closely. The chain around Marcus's neck was thick, made of metal links that gleamed in the headlights of a passing vehicle.

The discovery materials Klein had tried to conceal from them had indicated that Detective Coffey had not been convinced the USB cable was the real murder weapon, because of the pattern and the metal particles in Natalia's wounds.

"We need a better look," he said, squinting.

"I can enhance these," Lena said, "maybe get a clearer image. Would that help?"

Kristina found the ME's report and placed it on the table, flipping immediately to a page she'd marked with a color-coded sticky note—an autopsy photo of Natalia's throat. "We'll need a forensic pathologist to analyze the two patterns. I can reach out to some experts—assuming we have the budget."

Hal winced at the thought of going to Brantley with another request for funds. But he knew Brantley would cover it—too afraid of what Nico might tell the FBI if a guilty verdict became imminent. "I'll take care of Brantley, but.... I don't think a zoomed-in photo is going to be enough. We need the actual chain."

Kristina nodded. "I'll draft a subpoena request. Judge Harding—"

"No," Hal cut her off. "That's the worst possible approach."

"Excuse me?"

"A subpoena would alert Sam Klein—and Ventura and Glover—that we're onto Marcus. They could warn him in time for him to destroy the real necklace and give us a decoy."

"That's against the law," Kristina said.

Hal gave her a look until she exhaled with a curse. "Okay, then what's your idea, Hal? Break into the guy's home and steal it?"

"That might not be admissible as evidence."

"I know," Kristina said. "I was being sarcastic."

Hal started to pace again, thinking. "What if we could get him to hand it over voluntarily?"

Kristina's eyes narrowed. "Why do I feel like your next sentence is going to make me want to update our malpractice insurance?"

Hal turned to Lena. "How do you feel about going undercover again?"

Lena's expression was guarded. "Manipulating the grieving members of Natalia's family was not my finest moment, Hal."

"Maybe not as a human being, but as a private investigator, it was up there. You have a talent for it."

Lena's posture loosened, but only slightly. "What do you have in mind?"

"You pose as a jewelry appraiser. Pretend to run into Marcus and notice his chain. Tell him it might be valuable, a collector's item or something."

Lena nodded slowly and he could see the muscles in her face shift as she considered. "I can offer to examine it for him. But I'll say I need to take it for a few days to make a proper appraisal."

"Exactly," Hal said. "And during that *appraisal*, our forensic experts run it through their labs."

"A guy like Marcus won't be easy to fool. I'll need a credible cover identity—business cards, a website, maybe even a fake storefront."

"I'll arrange all of that," Hal said, thinking of Brantley's wallet again.

"Hold on," Kristina said. "Even if we put aside the obvious downsides to this plan—like putting Lena's life in danger—it doesn't legally hold up. Obtaining evidence through deception isn't voluntary consent for search and seizure."

"The Fourth Amendment applies to government actors, not private citizens," Hal said. "We're not cops."

Kristina shook her head. "We're still officers of the court. Even if the Fourth Amendment doesn't directly apply, we have ethical obligations. Rule 8.4 of the Pennsylvania Rules of Professional Conduct specifically prohibits dishonesty, fraud, deceit, or misrepresentation. Harding could exclude the evidence—"

"He could," Hal said. "But only if he finds Klein's arguments more compelling than yours. And you're the best legal researcher in that courtroom."

"Even if that were true—"

"Kristina," Lena put in, "you just recited the rules of professional conduct from memory."

Kristina stopped short. A flush crept up her neck and into her cheeks as she tried to shake off the compliments.

"We're not committing fraud," Hal pressed. "We're investigating. There's a difference, and if anyone can make Judge Harding understand that, it's you."

"What about chain of custody issues?"

Hal felt his jaw tighten. They would need to document exactly what happened with the necklace at all times. Otherwise, Sam could argue that *they* switched the chain with a decoy.

"We'll need to record everything," Hal said. "Video, photographs ... from the moment Marcus gives Lena the chain until we bring the chain into the courtroom."

"I can wear some kind of recorder," Lena said.

"Which puts you in even more danger." Kristina crossed her arms. "Are you forgetting this man has a violent history, particularly toward women?"

"I handled worse than him in Afghanistan," Lena said. But she looked at the floor as she said it, and Hal sensed some doubt behind the woman's bravado. Lena was confident, but not naive. She knew the risk was real.

"Look." Hal softened his voice. "It's not a perfect plan—"

"Far from it," Kristina said.

"But it's the best one I've got. We're facing opening statements tomorrow with a hostile jury and a prosecutor with no problem bending the rules. We need a game-changer."

Lena took a moment. A tense silence fell over the office. Her chin lifted and she met Hal's gaze. "I'll do it."

Relief flooded through Hal. They had a plan. A risky, probably unethical plan, but a plan. "Let's get to work."

31

LENA WATCHED MARCUS MEDRANO. Although she'd surveilled him from a distance, this was the first time she'd been this close to him, a mere ten feet away in a small Wine & Good Spirits liquor store in Center City. Up close, his face was hard and unpleasant, the angles too sharp. Even in the simple act of browsing a display of small-batch bourbons, his gaze seemed angry, menacing, as if he were barely containing a coiled violence beneath the surface. He stood about six feet, with a thick neck and broad shoulders. He obviously spent serious time at the gym.

But he'd built a physique designed to intimidate rather than for health or athleticism.

Lena had known men like Medrano in the Corp—men who didn't simply handle trouble, but enjoyed it.

Her gaze shifted to his chain—ridiculously thick and gaudy now that she could see it in person—gleaming under the store's rack lighting. She reminded herself of her purpose here.

She shifted uncomfortably in her pencil skirt and silk blouse —not her usual attire. The outfit was from Kristina's closet, meant to project the image of a professional with refined tastes.

It was riding up in all the wrong places, which she supposed might be helpful with a man like Medrano.

He pulled a bottle of Four Roses off the shelf. *Now or never.*

Lena adjusted the lapel pin affixed to her blouse, making sure it was positioned correctly. Inside the accessory was a miniature camera and wireless antenna—not exactly the latest in covert surveillance tech, but good enough for the task at hand. She touched it lightly, activating the recording function with a subtle press of her fingertip.

One of her high heels twisted under her as she crossed the polished floor, making her cringe inwardly. Medrano hadn't noticed her yet, thankfully. Lena came up beside him, positioning herself at an angle that would give the lapel camera a clear shot, and pretended to check out the bourbon selection.

Marcus reached past her for a bottle on a higher shelf. As his arm extended near her, she made a show of noticing his chain.

"That's a beautiful piece," she said, gesturing toward the hideous gold links straining around his bull neck. "Franco style. Late seventies, if I'm not mistaken."

Marcus froze momentarily, his hand still on the bottle. He turned, seeming to notice her for the first time. His gaze swept her from head to toe.

"Sorry," she said. "I didn't mean to disturb you. Professional curiosity. Comes with the job."

"You're some kind of jewelry expert?"

She extended her hand. "Alexandra Lloyd. I'm an appraiser. I specialize in vintage jewelry and precious metals."

"Marcus," he replied, taking her hand, not offering a last name. He released her hand but continued to study her with skepticism.

"Well, Marcus, you have excellent taste," Lena said, nodding toward his chain. "That's a superior example of gold chain craftsmanship. The alternating link pattern is characteristic of a specific Italian workshop from the late seventies. Not many of those around anymore."

The information was straight from the artificial intelligence app that she, Hal, and Kristina had fed a digital image of the necklace the night before. Lena hoped the app knew what it was talking about.

Marcus's posture shifted slightly. "It was my grandfather's. I never take it off. Been through a lot with me, this chain."

I bet it has.

"Your grandfather was very generous," Lena said. "He must have really loved you, to give you such a valuable gift."

He was good at hiding his reaction, but she saw his eyes widen slightly. "It's that valuable?"

"Well, I couldn't say for certain, without doing an appraisal, but ... pieces like that can be quite valuable, especially with provenance." She let the implication hang in the air that he'd been obliviously wearing an invaluable treasure all these years.

He seemed to reassess her, his eyes lingering a bit longer than necessary. "You don't look like a jewelry appraiser."

A chill gripped her, but she forced a note of flirtation into her voice. "What's a jewelry appraiser supposed to look like?"

The flirtation seemed to work. He smiled, showing teeth, and even let out a quiet laugh. "I don't know. Older."

"How about you, Marcus? What do you do?"

"I run security at a club." He straightened his shoulders, standing a bit taller.

"That must be exciting."

"Sometimes." Marcus leaned in closer. Lena resisted the impulse to step back and establish distance. She reminded herself that he was not a threat. Not yet, anyway.

"You know, I could take a look at it for you. The necklace, I mean. The market for vintage pieces has been surging lately."

"And how much would that cost me?"

"First consultation is complimentary."

Marcus seemed to consider the offer. He put the bottles back on the shelf, his arm brushing against her and causing the lapel pin to shift. She could feel it pulling downward, threatening to detach from her blouse.

"Cold in here, isn't it?" She adjusted her blouse, using the motion to secure the pin more firmly, trying to ignore the hammering of her heart.

"So you'd need to take it with you? For how long?"

"Three to seven business days," Lena replied, relieved that the crisis had been averted. "We document everything, of course. Provide a detailed receipt. We're very careful with our clients' pieces. And the item would be fully insured while in our possession."

She reached into her purse and extracted a business card with a logo, contact information, and the name "Lloyd Appraisal Services."

Marcus took the card but shook his head. "I don't know. Like I said, I never take it off." He touched the chain again, his fingers tracing the links.

Lena nodded. *Don't push too hard.* "I understand completely. Sentimental value is always more important than monetary worth." She picked up a bottle of Knob Creek Single Barrel. "Well, it was very nice meeting you, Marcus. If you change your mind, my number's on the card."

Three steps to the register and she heard his voice. "Hey, wait."

Gotcha.

Lena turned. "Yes?"

Marcus stood there for a moment, conflict evident on his face. Then he reached up and unclasped the chain from around his neck.

"Three to seven days, right?" He held the chain in his fist, not yet extending it toward her.

"For a preliminary appraisal? Might even be quicker."

She reached into her purse again and removed a small velvet pouch.

Marcus hesitated, then extended his hand and dropped the chain into the pouch. It was heavier than Lena had expected, and she almost dropped it.

The murder weapon.

She kept her expression professional as she carefully drew the strings closed. "Let me write you out a receipt. And I'll need you to write down the best way to reach you."

"Yeah. Good. Thanks for doing this."

"Of course," Lena said. "Thank you for trusting me with this piece, Marcus." She paused, then couldn't resist adding, "I think you'll be surprised by what we find."

She paid for the overpriced bourbon—an expense she would absolutely be billing to Hal and Kristina—and exited the store with measured steps, fighting the urge to run. Only when she was safely in her car did she allow herself to exhale.

Lena turned to ensure her lapel pin had a clear view as she removed an evidence bag from her glove compartment. With gloved hands, she transferred the chain from the velvet pouch to the plastic bag, carefully sealing and labelling it.

Her phone rang as she pulled into traffic.

"Please tell me you got it," Hal said.

"Hello to you too. And yes, I got it. No complications."

"Never doubted you," he said, but the relief in his voice was audible. "How soon can you get it to us?"

"On my way now."

32

HAL SHIFTED UNCOMFORTABLY at the defense table in Judge Callum Harding's courtroom, trying not to look at the empty jury box. He knew the jurors were waiting in the deliberation room, probably growing more hostile by the minute. He glanced at his watch. 9:47 AM. With each passing minute, the empty chair beside him and Kristina seemed to be lit by a spotlight.

Where the hell was Nico?

Of course something would have to go wrong now, right after they'd finally caught a break. Right after his plan, against all odds, had actually worked, and Lena had obtained Marcus's necklace voluntarily—sort of.

Something always went wrong. He should really be used to it by now.

Hal stole a glance at Harding. The judge—not as experienced as Hal in the art of courtroom catastrophe—clenched his jaw rhythmically as he struggled to control his emotions and did a poor job of it. Mild annoyance had progressed to growing irritation to what now could only be described as simmering rage. No one would call him a rookie judge after this trial. *Maybe a Nolan defense should be part of the orientation program.*

Across the aisle, Samantha Klein had stopped even pretending to review her notes. She now sat with arms crossed, occasionally making a show of checking her watch and sighing loudly enough for the judge to hear. *Subtle as ever, weaponizing our misfortune and enjoying every second of it.*

He suppressed a smirk. He really did like the woman.

Beside him, Kristina somehow caught the micro-expression. "You think this is funny?" she whispered.

"I think it's a disaster, but I try to find the humor in professional humiliation—"

"Mr. Nolan." Judge Harding's voice cut through the uncomfortable silence like a machete. "Ms. Nolan. I believe we've been patient enough, not to mention the twelve citizens who have taken time away from their jobs and families to sit in an empty room and twiddle their thumbs. Would you care to explain to this Court exactly what is going on?"

Hal and Kristina rose from their seats together. "Your Honor," Hal said, "we sincerely apologize for the delay. I'm assuming there must be some confusion with the transport from Riverside Correctional—"

"Your Honor," Sam cut in, "if the defense feels their client's presence at his own trial is unnecessary, perhaps we should proceed to opening statements without him."

"Mr. Ramirez has the right to be present at his trial." Kristina shot Sam a venomous look.

"We'll get him here," Hal interjected. "Give me ten minutes to make some calls. I promise I'll resolve this."

Harding's expression suggested serious doubt, but he let out a sigh. "We'll take a fifteen-minute recess. Bailiff, please inform the jurors back in the jury room."

Hal was pulling out his phone as he and Kristina walked into the hallway. The courtroom door closed behind them, mercifully cutting off the whispered commentary from the gallery.

"You *promise*?" Kristina said. "We have no idea what's going on, Hal."

They found a quiet corner and Hal leaned against the wall. "Relax. Harding's not going to hold me to it." He scrolled through his contacts, looking for the main number for Riverside.

Kristina watched him, incredulous, one eyebrow arched. "Harding's going to hold us in contempt."

"That would make us special—they always remember their first time."

A voice came on the line. Before Hal could speak, he realized it was recorded. A droning voice recited a list of menu options. He stabbed 0, hoping to reach a human.

"Riverside Correctional." The voice sounded bored, but human—barely.

"My name is Hal Nolan. I'm legal counsel for one of your inmates, Nico Ramirez. He was supposed to be transported to the Criminal Justice Center this morning for trial. Judge Harding's courtroom. He's not here."

"One moment."

Hal was put on hold. Tinny R&B played in his ear.

Kristina was watching him, arms crossed. "I'm on hold," he said.

The muzak cut off and a new voice said, "Inmate Transport."

"This is Hal Nolan, attorney for Nico Ramirez. He was supposed to be transported to the Criminal Justice Center—"

"Not on the list."

"What?"

"No transport order for Ramirez today."

"He was scheduled for court." Hal struggled to keep his voice steady.

"Hold on. Looks like he was on the list, but his transport got cancelled."

"What? Who cancelled—"

"Let me transfer you."

"No, wait—" The music returned. He was on hold again. He looked at Kristina, whose expression had shifted from worry to anger.

"Processing," another voice said, this one female.

Hal took a breath. "This is Hal Nolan, attorney for Nico Ramirez. We're in court right now, and my client hasn't been transported. Apparently his transfer order was cancelled? I need to know—"

"Can you spell it?"

"Spell it?"

"Your client's name."

"Ramirez.... R-A-M-I-R-E-Z."

He heard her typing. "Nico Ramirez. Yes. He's listed as unavailable for transport today."

"Unavailable? What does that mean? He's in jail. He doesn't exactly have a busy schedule." Hal couldn't keep the edge from his voice.

"Just says 'unavailable'. Hold on, I'll transfer you—"

"No, wait!" Hal realized he was yelling. Lowered his voice. "Listen, can you connect me with Juan Gomez? He's a correctional officer there."

"I can transfer you."

After a moment, a familiar voice said, "This is Gomez." Hal never thought he'd be so grateful to hear the guard's gruff voice.

"Juan, it's Hal Nolan. We can't find Nico."

"What are you talking about, Nolan? He's in Inmate Health Services."

"Is he hurt again?"

Gomez let out a harsh laugh. "What, are you pretending you don't know about the psych eval?"

"I don't know anything about a psych eval." Hal exchanged a look with Kristina, whose eyes widened. He felt his blood pressure spike. "Who's performing it?"

"Some shrink named Pugh." Hal heard a rustle of paper. "Dr. Westley Pugh. Came in early this morning. Are you claiming there's a problem?"

"Yeah. A big one. Stop the eval. We're coming right now."

Hal ended the call and turned to Kristina. "We need to go."

He started to move. She grabbed his arm, stopping him. "Judge Harding only gave us fifteen minutes."

Hal glanced at his watch. They had less than three minutes left. "Screw Harding. We need to get over there now."

A psych eval? What the hell was going on?

"*Hal.*" Kristina's grip tightened on his arm. "We can't just run out of here. We need to go back in the courtroom, get a continuance—"

"We don't have time."

"Think about it. If Harding holds us in contempt, we can't help Nico at all."

He took a deep breath. Knew she was right. "Fine."

"I'll do the talking." She straightened her jacket. "Let's go."

Back in the courtroom, Kristina went straight to the bench. "Your Honor, we have an emergency situation. Our client is being subjected to a psychological evaluation at Riverside. We were given no notice. No opportunity to object. We need to postpone today's proceedings and get over there immediately."

Harding's face darkened. "Ms. Nolan, this Court's schedule is not subject to the whims of counsel. You had months to arrange any psychological evaluations."

"Your Honor, we didn't arrange this evaluation."

Sam was on her feet now. "This sounds like another delay tactic."

"It's not a tactic." Kristina's voice cut through the courtroom. "Please, Your Honor."

Harding studied them for a long moment, then sighed deeply. "Ms. Klein, do you have any objection to postponing opening statements until tomorrow morning?"

Sam hesitated, and Hal could practically see the calculations behind her eyes. Apparently she decided fighting the delay wasn't worth it. "No, Your Honor, but I want it on record that the defense requested this postponement."

"So noted," Harding said. He turned back to Hal and Kristina. "You have until 9 AM tomorrow to sort this out. If your client isn't here and ready at that time, I'm going to consider sanctions."

Kristina nodded. "Thank you, Your Honor."

They turned for the door, but Sam stepped into their path. Lowering her voice, she said, "What's really going on?"

"Exactly what we told the judge," Hal said, not breaking stride. "Someone's messing with our client."

Sam narrowed her eyes. "If I find out this is a stunt—"

"It's not *our* stunt," Kristina said. "And for your sake, it better not be yours."

JUAN GOMEZ MET them outside the interview room, shoulders hunched and jaw tight. "Whatever you're scheming this time, don't bother," he said before they could speak. "I reviewed his paperwork three times. It's in order. I followed procedure."

"Nobody's questioning your sterling performance," Hal said. "Is he still in there with Nico?"

"Yes."

"How long have they been at it?"

"About two hours now."

Hal felt sick. Two hours of unmonitored questioning. Heaven only knew what this shrink asked Nico, or what Nico told him.

"Is the session being recorded?" Kristina said, stepping closer to Gomez.

"Yes, the doctor specifically requested we record."

Of course he did. "Turn it off," Hal said. Gomez's eyebrows shot up, but before he could protest, Hal added, "Let's go in."

Gomez hesitated. "Dr. Pugh said not to interrupt."

"Officer Gomez," Kristina cut in before Hal could speak, "you know that blocking counsels' access to their client is grounds for a formal complaint."

Gomez frowned, but stepped aside.

Hal opened the door without knocking. Inside, Nico sat at a small table. A lean man with calculating eyes perched across from him, his pin-striped suit far too expensive for a prison interview room. There was an unpleasant sharpness to his features as he looked up with annoyance at the interruption. "Excuse me, we're in the middle of an evaluation."

"No, actually, you're done," Hal said.

Nico's face was pale, his hands trembling on the table as he looked at Hal. "About time you got here," he said, his voice unsteady. "I've been telling him I have court today." He gestured toward Pugh. "He won't listen. Insists everything was cleared. He's been at this for hours, asking about my childhood...." He swallowed hard. "About Natalia. About whether I have anger issues."

"Is that so?" Hal got in the psychiatrist's face. "And what makes you think you have any right to evaluate our client without our knowledge or presence?"

"I was hired to do this," Pugh said. His posture stiffened.

"By who?"

Kristina circled behind Pugh and slipped the legal pad from beneath his loosened grip.

"Hey. You can't—"

"Who hired you?" Hal said, his anger rising.

"Those are my notes." Pugh gestured at Kristina, whose expression was hardening as she scanned the pages.

"'Patient exhibits persecutory delusions,'" she read aloud. "'Possible diminished capacity at the time of the offense.' 'Demonstrates emotional instability when discussing wife.'"

"This is the last time I'm going to ask nicely." He planted both palms on the table, leaning into Pugh's space. "Who hired you?"

"The Nolan Law Firm." Pugh swallowed hard. "Isn't ... isn't that you?"

Hal caught Kristina's eye, recognizing the same realization dawning in her expression that was forming in his own mind— that this was even more of a train wreck than they'd imagined.

"You need to leave. Now." Hal injected every ounce of authority he could muster into his voice.

Pugh rose from his chair, his composed demeanor crumbling. "But my evaluation—"

"There is no evaluation." Kristina clutched the legal pad to her chest as she stepped back from the table.

Pugh's eyes darted to his notes in Kristina's hands, then back to Hal. The utter disintegration of his condescending attitude gave Hal some satisfaction, but not nearly enough to outweigh the panic threatening to overwhelm him.

"We're keeping those notes." Hal moved to stand between Pugh and Kristina. "The recording of this session, too. And by the way, every minute you spent in here with our client was a violation of our client's constitutional rights."

Hal strode to the door and yanked it open, pointing to the hallway where Gomez waited. Pugh scurried out, nearly colliding with the correctional officer. Hal slammed the door after him.

He leaned against it for a moment, taking a deep breath to calm himself. Then he turned to Nico.

"What did you tell him?"

Nico shook his head. "He just kept asking the same questions different ways. He wouldn't stop."

"Nico." Hal forced himself to soften his voice. "It's okay. Whatever you said, we'll fix it. But to do that, we need to know what you told him."

"He wanted to know if I had any memory gaps or if I ever blacked out. I said no." Nico rubbed his temples. "He asked if I ever lost my temper with Natalia. If I ever found myself doing things I couldn't remember doing. I told him that was crazy. That I'd never hurt Natalia. That I remembered every minute of that night—coming home, finding her...." His voice broke.

Kristina was still reviewing Pugh's notes. "It looks like he was building a case for diminished capacity."

Nico gave Hal a questioning look.

"Insanity defense," Hal said.

"I'm not crazy!" Nico's voice rose in panic. "You can't let them say that. I didn't kill Natalia. I didn't black out. I didn't forget anything. Someone else did this to her!"

"We know that." Hal placed a steadying hand on Nico's shoulder. "We know."

The man nodded, and Hal felt the tension drain from Nico's shoulder. "Thanks for coming—for stopping that guy."

"It's our job."

"Just hold tight," Kristina said. "We'll see you in court tomorrow."

"Okay. Thanks."

They left Nico in Officer Gomez's custody with strict instructions that no one—absolutely no one—was to speak with him without both attorneys present.

Back in the car, Hal rubbed his temples. "Had to be Brantley, right? Thinking he knows our job better than we do?" He shook his head in disgust. "I'll deal with him."

"No," Kristina said firmly. Her eyes met his. "This is going to take both of us."

33

———

BRANTLEY'S SMUG smile made Kristina's skin crawl. He lounged behind his desk, tossing a stress ball from one hand to the other. He smiled broadly, as if greeting old friends.

"How's jury selection going? Oh wait, that was yesterday, wasn't it? Heard it didn't go so well." His eyes sparkled with undisguised amusement.

"Cut the games, Gavin," Hal said. "What the hell were you thinking with Dr. Pugh and the unauthorized psychiatric evaluation?"

Brantley's eyebrows shot up in feigned surprise. "Unauthorized? I thought I was paying for the defense. That makes me the client."

"No," Hal shot back, taking another step forward. "*Nico* is the client. Your money doesn't buy you control of his defense strategy."

"Doesn't it, though?" Brantley set the stress ball on his desk and leaned back in his chair. "I'm footing the bill. Without me, your innocent janitor would be stuck with a public defender and a one-way ticket to death row."

Kristina took her place beside Hal in front of Brantley's desk.

"What were you trying to accomplish?" She kept her voice level, professional—though inside she was seething. "We already have a strategy—"

"A lame one." Brantley spread his hands in a gesture of reasonable explanation. "Mine is better. The learned Dr. Pugh will diagnose our friend Nico with paranoid schizophrenia, a condition that directly affects perception of reality. Perfect for our needs."

"*Our* needs?" Hal's voice had a heated edge. "Or *your* needs, Gavin?"

"Both," Brantley replied easily. "This gives us a fallback defense if your 'someone else did it' theory falls apart. Which, let's be honest, is a real possibility given that jury you're stuck with."

"Bullshit," Hal said. "Insanity's not a fallback plan. It's a completely different strategy that undermines everything we've been building."

Brantley shrugged. "Well, it's your strategy now."

"The hell it is," Hal snapped.

Brantley's relaxed demeanor shifted, his voice hardening. "You don't get it, do you? The FBI, the SEC—they're closing in on me. And if they break Nico, I'm finished."

"We've built a solid defense for Nico," Kristina said. "We have evidence pointing to someone else as the real killer."

"Yes, I saw Hal's request for additional funds. You want to engage a ... what was it, a metallurgist?" He scoffed. "To analyze some necklace? You seriously think a jury is going to be convinced by that?"

Kristina's eyes narrowed. "With all due respect, we're the ones with law degrees—"

"From a fourth-tier law school." Brantley's smile was dismissive. "An insanity defense is the safer play. If we demonstrate that Nico suffered a psychotic break—say the poor bastard doesn't even remember killing his wife, or whatever sob story Pugh cooks up—then whatever testimony he might later give about *my* business dealings becomes worthless."

And there it was. The only thing that really mattered to him. As long as he believed Nico could hurt him, his only goal would be to silence the man, at whatever cost necessary.

Kristina exchanged a look with Hal. As if reading her mind, his eyes pleaded with her. *Don't say it.* He shook his head minutely, mouthing *No.*

The air between them seemed to still. Hal's expression was raw with desperation. She knew if there were time to speak, he would say to stall, negotiate, find some clever scheme that would maintain the flow of Brantley's cash while they clung to whatever limited control of the defense they could grasp.

But looking at Brantley—at his smug, self-satisfied smirk, his absolute certainty that they would fall in line, that they were *his* —she knew Hal was wrong.

And there was only one way to stop this runaway train—to derail it completely.

She mouthed back, *Sorry.*

"Gavin," she said, her voice calm and measured, "Nico has nothing to give the Feds."

The hedge fund manager froze, brow furrowed. "What?"

"There is no incriminating information. No damaging evidence. There never was."

Hal made a strangled sound beside her, like air escaping a punctured tire. His shoulders tensed and she could feel him fighting the urge to jump in, to try and salvage this. But he remained silent, grinding his teeth.

Brantley's face remained eerily still for several seconds before a deep crimson flush began creeping up from his collar. His hands, which had been casually resting on his desk, slowly curled into fists. When he spoke, his voice was ominously soft.

"You're lying."

"Nico never overheard anything in your offices," she said. "Never saw any incriminating documents. He made it up because he knew you'd pay for his defense if you thought it was the only way to save your own ass. Clearly he was right."

The silence that followed was so complete that Kristina could hear the soft hum of the building's ventilation system. "So this whole time...."

"Nico was never a danger to you," Kristina finished for him. "The threat was hollow."

"You played me." It wasn't a question.

"We represented our client's interests."

Brantley shot to his feet. His chair flew backward and slammed into the window behind him. Kristina's pulse jumped and she took an involuntary step back as Hal moved closer to her.

"You're finished! Done! You'll have to get law licenses in fucking Somalia when I'm through with you!"

Kristina braced herself against his rage. In some ways, she knew, they deserved it. They had lied to him, played on his fears, taken thousands of dollars from him. Who wouldn't be furious?

"The money stops now."

"We had a deal!" Hal said.

"Deal's off." Brantley's voice seethed as he regained his composure. "You want to play heroes for your innocent janitor? Do it on your own dime. Oh wait, you don't have a dime, do you?" His lips curled in a cruel smile. "Congratulations. You're officially bottom-feeding losers again. Back in the gutter where you belong."

"Gavin, please." Hal's voice was stripped of its usual bluster. "We're so close."

Kristina had seen Hal's vulnerability before, but never in a professional setting, never in front of a client, certainly never in front of someone like Brantley. The man who approached every negotiation as if he held all the cards—even with a losing hand—was gone. She watched him, too stunned to speak, and felt her throat tighten.

He was begging, but not for himself.

"We just need you a little longer—just long enough to hire the experts to analyze the chain. If you pull out now, Nico will go to prison for life—or worse." Desperation choked his voice. "For a crime he didn't commit."

"Oh, I see." Brantley smirked. "You're appealing to the kindness of my heart." He leaned forward, hands splayed on his desk. "Get the fuck out of my office."

Hal sighed, defeat visible in his eyes, and nodded. He turned to leave. Kristina kept her gaze on Brantley.

"You're not seeing the upside," she said.

Brantley raised an eyebrow. "Aside from scraping two parasites off my bank account?"

"The FBI agents investigating you—their names are Ventura and Glover—have been breaking the law to build their case."

Brantley's expression shifted from dismissive to interested. "Explain."

"They told us that if Nico doesn't make a deal, evidence will disappear and witnesses will become unavailable. They also ... threatened us personally. And they've used similar tactics to pressure the prosecutor."

"I guess the joke's on them." Brantley shook his head. "They got played, too."

"Exactly. And we can use that to set a trap," she said. "If we can prove Ventura and Glover are corrupt—that they're trying to railroad an innocent man just to get to you—it taints their entire investigation."

Brantley's eyes narrowed, but she could see she had the selfish prick's attention now.

"Keep talking."

"If we expose them, you walk away a free man."

Interest sparked in Brantley's eyes, though his skepticism was still evident. "From the criminal charges, maybe. What about the SEC investigation into my fund?"

"The Feds' misconduct could torpedo both cases," Kristina said. "It's called the 'fruit of the poisonous tree' doctrine. When federal agents engage in misconduct, everything that flows from that misconduct becomes tainted evidence—inadmissible in court. Assuming you're represented by good lawyers."

A slow smile spread across his face. "You're still gunning for the job." His voice was tinged with something that sounded almost like admiration. "After all this. You still want to be my lawyers."

"We're good at what we do," Kristina said. She exchanged a quick look with Hal, and saw the smile in his eyes. "Fourth-tier law school notwithstanding."

Brantley tapped his fingers on the desk. "Fine. Focus on trapping Ventura and Glover, and I'll continue funding Nico's defense."

"And our experts." Kristina barely managed to maintain her professional demeanor.

Brantley waved a dismissive hand. "Yes. Them, too."

Kristina nodded. She and Hal turned to leave.

"One more thing," Brantley said—because there was always one more thing with guys like him. "If we have to have this conversation again, even your silver tongues won't save you. Do you understand me?"

Kristina looked at him. "Oh, I understand you perfectly."

As they left Brantley's office and rode the elevator down to the lobby, neither of them spoke. It wasn't until they reached the parking garage that Hal finally broke the silence.

"That was...." He shook his head.

She felt a warmth spread through her chest and grinned. "I love when you're at a loss for words. It's so rare." She gave his shoulder a playful nudge.

"You're incredible. You just saved our client and our firm in one meeting."

"I bought us time."

A ghost of Hal's usual confidence returned to his smile. "Then let's not waste it."

34

—————

HAL WATCHED the jurors file into the courtroom and take their seats in the jury box. He tried to catch their eyes, searching for a friendly face. He found none. All twelve of them—fourteen counting the alternates—looked ready to crucify his client. Hand-picked to convict.

He glanced over at the prosecution table, where Samantha Klein sat in a charcoal suit, her red hair pulled back. Her gaze caught his and she smirked.

"Don't let her get in your head," Kristina whispered. They sat side-by-side at the defense table, joined this time by Nico. He wore a suit they'd provided, and his hands were folded in front of him—expression appropriately somber, but not guilty, exactly as they'd coached him. But it was going to take more than good courtroom comportment to win this.

In the gallery behind the prosecution sat Gabriel Molina and his three sons. The grieving family of the victim. Natalia's brothers wore suits that didn't quite fit. Gabriel wore a dark suit with a white shirt buttoned to the collar, no tie, his Iron Keepers tattoo hidden beneath his sleeve.

And in the back row, FBI Agents Ventura and Glover. They

weren't even attempting to hide their presence. They *wanted* it known that they were watching.

Quite the audience for today's performance.

"We'll begin with opening statements," Judge Harding said once everyone was settled. "Ms. Klein?"

Sam Klein rose from her seat, gave a respectful nod to the judge, and approached the jury box. Her movements were deliberate, unhurried. She managed to look warm without smiling—a trick Hal would need to learn—as she took a few seconds to make eye contact with each juror.

"The Commonwealth does not bring first-degree murder charges lightly. We bring them when the evidence is overwhelming. When the brutality is unmistakable. When a human life has been deliberately, viciously extinguished."

Hal felt his throat tighten and he resisted the urge to exchange a glance with Kristina. *Talk about coming out of the gate swinging.*

"And that is precisely what happened to Natalia Ramirez. At this trial, you will hear about a sacred vow that was broken. A marriage that ended not in divorce papers, but in violence. A woman whose voice was permanently silenced by the one person who promised before God and family to cherish and protect her. This trial isn't merely about murder. It's about betrayal in its most raw and personal form."

Sam paused, allowing the words to hang in the air. Hal scanned the jury box. Juror number four was already nodding along. Two others were leaning forward. Not a skeptical face among them, and Sam hadn't even mentioned a scrap of evidence yet.

Nico's knuckles had gone white where his hands were clasped together. Hal willed him to maintain his composure, knowing no amount of coaching could prepare a man for this.

"On the evening in question, Natalia Ramirez returned

home. She unlocked her apartment door, stepped inside, and closed the door behind her. And she never left that apartment alive."

Simple, direct, effective. Aldo Burke had been a fool to bury someone with her talent.

"What happened to Natalia Ramirez in that apartment?" Sam continued, her voice gaining intensity. "The defendant—her husband, Nico Ramirez—strangled her with a computer cable. Natalia suffered tremendously in her final moments. The cable dug deep into her flesh as she struggled for breath. Her hyoid bone fractured from the force applied to her throat. She would have been conscious through much of this ordeal, feeling her life being squeezed out of her by the man who had promised to love and protect her."

Hal watched several jurors wince at the details. Juror number six even touched her own throat. *Great.*

Sam moved away from the jury box, her gaze now directed toward Nico. "Why would he do this? Because Natalia didn't conform to his expectations—she didn't do what she was supposed to do. She didn't follow his plan for her life."

Nico was shaking his head, a slight movement at first but becoming more pronounced. From the corner of his eye, Hal saw Kristina touch their client's arm, trying to steady him. *Keep it together.*

"Mr. Ramirez had invested everything in his wife becoming a nurse," Sam continued, her voice rich with accusation. "He worked long hours as a janitor to support her while she attended nursing school. Or at least, that's what he thought. In reality, Natalia had dropped out of school months earlier because she hated it. She didn't want to be a nurse. Wasn't suited for it. But she tried to conceal that from her husband."

Sam lowered her voice, compelling the jurors to lean in. "Why attempt to keep that a secret? You'd think she'd want to tell her husband, wouldn't you? Her life partner, there to comfort and support her? But the evidence will show that Natalia had good reason to fear her husband's reaction. Their neighbors heard frequent arguments. One witness will testify that the defendant called his wife terrible names—including the word 'slut.' Another saw her crying outside their apartment the day before her murder."

In other words, not just a murderer but an abusive control freak, too.

Sam's voice softened, taking on a confidential tone. "Now, I hesitate to tell you this, because I don't want you to judge Natalia." She paused, drawing the jurors in. "After dropping out of nursing school, Natalia began working at a gentlemen's club. A strip bar."

Murmurs rippled through the jury box and the gallery. Hal glanced at Gabriel Molina and his sons, whose faces had hardened into masks of shock and grief. In the back row, Ventura and Glover smiled tightly. Nico had gone completely still.

"Imagine," Sam continued, "the sense of betrayal the defendant must have felt when he discovered all of these deceptions. Working those long hours, exhausting himself, all to put his wife through school—while she was secretly taking off her clothes for strangers."

Sam paused, then leaned slightly toward the jury box. "But understand this—Natalia's choices don't diminish her humanity. Her right to live. Whatever your personal feelings about her decisions, she did not deserve what happened to her. No one does."

Her gaze swept across the jury. Several jurors looked away, unable to meet the intensity of her stare.

"The evidence will show that the defendant, Nico Ramirez, deliberately and with premeditation, strangled and killed Natalia. This was not a crime of passion—it was a calculated decision by a controlling husband who had finally decided his wife's disobedience warranted the ultimate punishment. We will prove this beyond any reasonable doubt, and at the conclusion of this trial, we will ask you to return the only verdict supported by the evidence. Guilty of murder in the first degree."

With that, Sam returned to her seat. The courtroom felt unnaturally quiet in the wake of her opening statement. Hal had to admit, it had been prosecutorial rhetoric at its most lethal—a virtuoso performance in character assassination, practically a nuclear strike. Now he had to perform the legal equivalent of battlefield surgery.

Judge Harding was watching the defense table, growing impatient.

Hal took a deep breath and started to rise from his chair. Kristina's hand on his wrist stopped him.

"Don't hold back," she whispered.

He felt a smile quirk the edge of his mouth. "Do I ever?"

"I'm serious." There was no smile on her face. "You need to take it to eleven this time."

He nodded. Coming from Kristina, that was something. She was usually the one applying the brakes, not hitting the gas. They must be in even worse shape than he thought. "Eleven. Got it."

He straightened his tie as he crossed the well of the courtroom. But instead of standing in front of the jury box, he perched on the corner of the prosecution table, inches from Sam Klein's carefully arranged notes. She stiffened, scowled at him, but didn't object, and a few of the jurors' eyes widened— exactly the reaction he'd hoped for.

Because nothing says you're not afraid of the prosecution's case like invading their personal space with your ass.

"Raise your hand if you've ever been lied to by someone you love," he said.

The jurors stared at him, visibly confused.

"Not a rhetorical question."

A few hands tentatively went up. Others followed. Hal made eye contact with the hesitant ones. He waited, swinging his leg against Sam's table. He had all day.

Within moments, every juror had a raised hand.

"Keep your hand up if you murdered them for it."

Every hand went down. An uncomfortable ripple moved through the jury box.

"Exactly," Hal said, finally hopping down from the prosecution table to close the distance with them. "Yet that's the prosecution's entire theory of this case. That my client was so enraged by his wife's deception that he transformed from a loving husband into a killer in the span of a single evening."

He had their full attention now. Level eleven achieved.

"And I haven't even told you the most important part—Mr. Ramirez *didn't even know* he was being lied to. He didn't know his wife had dropped out of nursing school. He didn't know she was dancing at Heartbreakers. Every night, he dropped her off at what he thought was her nursing program. He waited in the car while she walked into the building. He picked her up when she texted him after 'class.' They even had a favorite Thai restaurant near campus where they'd sometimes eat. Her deception was so good, so complete, that he didn't even believe the truth when my law partner and I explained it to him in his jail cell." Hal paused, letting that sink in. "So ... there goes the prosecution's motive."

Hal glanced back at Nico, who was staring down at the table now, his shoulders slightly hunched. When Hal returned his gaze to the jury box, he no longer found a uniform wall of hostility. Some jurors looked angry. Some looked confused. Several looked introspective. Like a synchronized swimming team suddenly forgetting their routine. Hal suppressed a smile.

"Now let's talk about evidence. After all, that's what the prosecution is required to provide." He took another step forward, his voice gaining intensity. "Let me tell you what the evidence will show. On the night Natalia died, Mr. Ramirez was at work, witnessed by multiple coworkers, at a time that overlaps the window in which the medical examiner estimates his wife was killed. There is no evidence that Mr. Ramirez confronted his wife that night. The arguments overheard by neighbors occurred on different occasions. And that's assuming the man they heard was even my client."

Hal paused, letting his points about the timeline sink in. The jury was listening now—even the most law-and-order jerk-offs among them. He glanced at Sam, who glared back at him like she wanted to rip his throat out. *Always a positive sign.*

In the gallery, Ventura and Glover weren't smiling anymore.

Hal stepped back, as if to wrap up, then abruptly turned and approached the jury again. He could never resist a good courtroom head-fake.

"But all of this—the lack of motive, the timeline problems— it's just the appetizer. Because the most glaring hole in the prosecution's case is actually the murder weapon. Or what the prosecution *claims* is the murder weapon."

Hal stepped away from the jury box, gesturing toward the prosecution table.

"When police arrived at the scene, they found a USB cable wrapped around Natalia Ramirez's neck, with my client's fingerprints on it. The prosecution wants you to reach the same conclusion the police did—that this cable was the murder weapon."

He paused, letting his eyes meet each juror in turn. "However, the medical examiner—the prosecution's own witness— discovered metal fragments embedded in the wounds on Natalia's neck. Metal fragments, not rubber residue. Furthermore, she documented that the pattern of bruising didn't match the dimensions or structure of the USB cable."

Several jurors straightened in their seats as Hal walked backward, toward the center of the courtroom. "Someone strangled Natalia Ramirez. But not with that USB cable." He turned abruptly. "And not my client."

Hal paused, scanning the jurors' faces. Time to go for broke.

"There was another man in Natalia's life." He gestured toward the gallery without looking back. *Not that Marcus Medrano was actually in the courtroom—but you don't win trials without taking some creative license.* "A man with whom Natalia had a complicated past. A man who knew her secrets."

Hal lowered his voice, drawing the jury in. "A man who wears a thick metal chain around his neck."

"Objection!" Sam Klein stood, her composure finally cracking. "Counsel is making unsupported claims about evidence not in the record."

Not in the record *yet*.

"Sustained," Judge Harding said. "Mr. Nolan, confine your opening to what evidence will be presented."

Hal spread his hands wide, the picture of reasonable cooperation. "That's exactly what I'm doing, Your Honor." He turned back to the jury. "Unlike the prosecution, we will provide all of the evidence needed to back up our claims."

Assuming Kristina gets Marcus's chain into evidence, and assuming our experts deliver....

Time to wrap things up. He approached the jury box for the grand finale. "Ladies and gentlemen, I want to tell you something else." His voice dropped, intimate and confessional. "I've defended guilty people. Knowingly. Not my favorite part of the job, but hey. Someone's gotta do it."

The jury shifted uncomfortably. Sam's head snapped up, instantly suspicious.

"Nico Ramirez is not guilty." Hal pointed at his client, who sat perfectly still. "Nico's that rare thing in my line of work. An innocent man. A man who loved his wife so much he scrubbed toilets so *she* could chase what he thought were *her* dreams. Even as she lied to him, manipulated him, danced behind his back, grinded in men's laps to make money she deposited in a secret bank account."

"Objection, Your Honor!" Sam was on her feet. *Too late, sweetheart.*

Judge Harding glowered at him. "Mr. Nolan, do I need to remind you that the victim is not on trial here?"

Hal held the judge's gaze for a moment before returning his attention to the jury.

"You know what keeps me up at night the most about this case? The knowledge that while we're sitting in this courtroom, the real killer is watching. Laughing at us. But he won't be laughing for long. Because before this trial is over, we will have dragged him into the light."

The statement was completely inappropriate, but Judge Harding—still a rookie—failed to stop him. Instead, the judge moved uncomfortably in his seat.

"Thank you." As Hal returned to the defense table, Kristina met his eyes. Her lips barely moved, but he caught the whispered *Eleven* as he passed. Beside her, Nico sat straighter, shoulders back, as if someone had removed a fifty-pound weight from his spine.

Hal felt a strange mix of satisfaction and anxiety. He'd delivered an eleven—hell, maybe even a twelve—but this was no time to celebrate. He'd be lucky if one juror remembered his opening statement a week from now. Speeches didn't win trials. Trials were fought in the trenches of witness testimony, evidence, and cross-examination.

This wasn't over. Far from it.

35

"DETECTIVE COFFEY, how long have you been with the Philadelphia Police Department?"

"Thirty-two years. Twenty-four of those in Homicide."

Standing by the witness stand, Sam was really working that charcoal gray suit—it was the perfect balance of professional and form-fitting, and Hal's brain couldn't decide whether to focus on her words or her ass. Coffey looked his part, too. Veteran homicide detective, complete with thinning hair and world-weary scowl.

The way he was looking at Sam was different, though. Almost with a paternal concern.

Interesting.

Hal filed the observation away for later.

"Can you please walk us through your involvement in the investigation of Natalia Ramirez's murder?"

Coffey nodded, shifting in his chair. "I was called to the scene at approximately 11:43 PM. When I arrived, officers had already secured the apartment. Inside, I found the victim, Natalia Ramirez, deceased on the living room floor."

"And what did you observe about the scene?"

"The victim was lying face-up. She had ligature marks on her neck consistent with strangulation. There was a USB cable on the floor next to her body."

As Coffey described the crime scene, Hal pretended to take notes while scanning the jury box from the corner of his eye. Several of the jurors were nodding along with Coffey's every word like he was dispensing gospel. *Great.*

"Did you recover the USB cable as evidence?"

"Yes. It was photographed in situ, then collected according to standard evidence protocols."

Standard evidence protocols. Police-speak for sticking it in a plastic bag.

Sam strode to the prosecution table and returned, holding that very bag now. "Is this the USB cable you collected from the scene?"

Coffey examined it. "Yes, that's the cable."

"Your Honor, I'd like to enter this exhibit into evidence."

Judge Harding nodded. "So entered."

Sam continued walking Coffey through the investigation—the identification of the victim, the preliminary determination of the cause of death, the notifications made to next of kin. Building a foundation, brick by brick, for Nico's death sentence.

"Detective Coffey, who was the primary suspect in this case?"

"The victim's husband, Nico Ramirez."

"And why was Mr. Ramirez considered a suspect?"

"Initially, we focused on Mr. Ramirez because of his access to the apartment and the weakness of his alibi. Crime scene techs then identified his fingerprints on the USB cable. And once we started digging, we found evidence of ongoing marital problems."

Several jurors exchanged glances. Sam's opening statement

had promised them juicy marital discord. Now they leaned forward for the payoff.

"What evidence did you find of marital problems?" she said.

"We interviewed several neighbors in the building. Multiple witnesses reported hearing arguments between Mr. and Mrs. Ramirez in the weeks leading up to her death. One of the neighbors heard Mr. Ramirez call his wife a slut."

From her seat beside Hal, Kristina rose to her feet. "Objection, Your Honor. Hearsay."

Sam turned to Kristina with an expression of mild annoyance. "Your Honor, Detective Coffey is merely explaining the course of his investigation and what led him to focus on the defendant. He's not offering the neighbors' statements for the truth of the matter asserted."

"Of course he is," Kristina said. "That's the entire point of Ms. Klein asking the question."

Judge Harding looked uncertain, his gaze jumping from Sam to Kristina. After a moment, he said, "Overruled. I'm going to allow Detective Coffey to continue, but the jury should understand that the detective's testimony about what neighbors reported is being admitted not for its truth, but to explain the detective's subsequent actions. The neighbors themselves will need to testify if the prosecution wishes to establish that these arguments actually occurred."

Kristina sat down.

"Rookie ruling," Hal whispered.

Kristina's gaze was on Judge Harding, and it was not kind. "We can't afford too many of those."

Sam waited until the room quieted, then turned to Coffey again. "What else did your investigation reveal about the Ramirez marriage?"

"We learned that Mrs. Ramirez had dropped out of nursing

school several months before her death, but she pretended to continue to attend classes each evening, even having her husband drive her to the school."

"And where was she going instead?"

"To a gentlemen's club called Heartbreakers." Coffey paused dramatically, and turned to face the jury. "Where she worked as a dancer under the name Sapphire."

Kristina's butt lifted from her chair. This time, Hal stopped her.

She gave him a look, whispered, "Relevance."

"Yeah, but look," he whispered back. A few of the jurors had visibly stiffened at the phrase *gentleman's club*, and one of them, an elderly woman in the front row, had actually made the sign of the cross.

"Sam's introducing this for motive," Kristina said.

"And it hurts her more than it helps her."

She met his gaze, questioning. But he held firm. Yes, it was true that Natalia's work as a stripper added to his alleged motive. But these jurors had been cherry-picked by Sam and her consultant because they were upper-class, law-abiding folk. Traditionally, not the biggest fans of women who gyrate on poles to get dollar bills stuffed in their g-strings.

Kristina must have read his thoughts. She frowned, but she settled back into her seat.

Meanwhile, Sam had already moved on. She continued her examination for another twenty minutes, extracting a detailed account of the investigation from Coffey. The detective did a good job making his work sound thorough, even though he'd never even considered an alternate suspect. By the time Sam finished her direct examination with a satisfied "No further questions, Your Honor," Hal was raring to punch holes in the man's testimony.

Judge Harding turned to the defense table. "Cross-examination?"

"Thought you'd never ask." Hal stood, stepping into the well of the courtroom like a prizefighter entering the ring. "Detective Coffey."

Coffey watched him warily. "Mr. Nolan."

"Let's start by clarifying something. You said Mr. Ramirez's fingerprints were found on the USB cable, right?"

"Yes."

"That surprised you? You didn't expect to find Mr. Ramirez's fingerprints on his own belongings in his own home?"

Coffey's eyes narrowed slightly. "I made no assumptions about whose fingerprints would be found on the murder weapon."

Hal held back a wince. Coffey was good at this. But Hal was good at this, too.

"Were any other fingerprints found on the cable, Detective?"

"No, just the defendant's."

"Just my client's? Not even the victim's fingerprints?"

Coffey froze, realizing what he'd stepped into. He looked pissed off now. Off-balance. Just the way Hal liked his law enforcement witnesses.

"You'd think Natalia Ramirez, struggling for her life, clutching desperately at that cable around her throat, would have been as likely if not more likely than the killer to leave prints behind. Strange."

"Objection." Sam glared at him. "None of these facts are in evidence. Mr. Nolan isn't even asking a question!"

"Mr. Nolan," Judge Harding said, "please phrase your comments as questions."

"Of course, Your Honor. Detective Coffey, wouldn't you expect to find the victim's fingerprints on the cable if she had been struggling against it during strangulation?"

"Objection. Calls for speculation."

"Well, that shouldn't be a problem for Detective Coffey," Hal said, looking to the jury instead of the judge. "As far as I can tell, his whole investigation was speculation."

"Your Honor!"

Judge Harding's face flushed red. "Mr. Nolan, do not test this Court's patience."

Hal raised his hands, palms out in mock surrender. "I'll move on. Death by USB cable ... was that the official cause of death?"

"The cause of death was strangulation," Coffey bit out each word, no doubt fully aware of where Hal was going.

"As determined by the Medical Examiner's Office, correct? Assistant Medical Examiner Julia Reyes?"

"Yes."

"Did Dr. Reyes's report note any unusual findings related to the strangulation?"

"Objection." Sam's voice was starting to sound hoarse from so many objections. *Hope you brought cough drops.* "Dr. Reyes will be testifying later today. Mr. Nolan can ask her his questions directly."

"This question was for Detective Coffey," Hal said.

Judge Harding gritted his teeth. "Please answer, Detective."

Coffey shifted slightly in his seat. "There were some metal particles found in the wound."

"Metal particles? That's weird, huh?"

"Objection—"

"Did the ME's finding of metal particles strike you as inconsistent with the theory that the murder weapon was a plastic USB cable, Detective?"

Coffey's expression tightened. "Yes, but there could be any number of explanations—"

"Speculating again. I'm told that's frowned upon here." Hal

paused, hoping the detective would take the opportunity to call him an obnoxious douchebag, or otherwise lose his cool in front of the jury. He didn't. "Notwithstanding this finding by the ME, your investigation focused exclusively on the USB cable and Mr. Ramirez, didn't it?"

"We pursued multiple avenues of investigation."

"Did you pursue the avenue of investigation that the murder weapon might have been made out of metal? For example, a chain?"

"No, not specifically."

"No. Did you interview any other suspects?"

"There was no need. The evidence—"

"No patrons of the strip bar where Mrs. Ramirez was dancing? No coworkers? No ex-boyfriends?"

Coffey sighed. "We interviewed the club manager and its security head, but not extensively. Our investigation focused primarily on the home environment and the husband."

"Did you conduct any follow-up investigation regarding the source of the metal particles found in Mrs. Ramirez's wounds?"

Coffey's gaze ticked past Hal to Sam, and he knew what it meant. She'd told him to stop digging, afraid of what he might find.

"Yes or no, Detective."

"No."

"Detective Coffey, did your investigation uncover any evidence that Mr. Ramirez knew about his wife's withdrawal from nursing school, or her employment at Heartbreakers, prior to her death?"

"It would have been very hard for her to hide that. It seems much more likely that he discovered what she was really—"

"Speculating again...." Hal warned.

"Objection!"

"Sustained."

"Detective, did your investigation uncover any history of violence or abuse in the Ramirez marriage?"

"Neighbors reported hearing arguments—"

"I'm not asking what you learned from nosy neighbors. I'm asking about violence. Abuse."

"No, we did not find evidence of prior domestic incidents."

"No calls to the police? No hospital visits for suspicious injuries?"

"No."

"In fact, Mr. Ramirez has no history of violence whatsoever, does he?"

"Not that we discovered, no."

"One final question, Detective. You mentioned Mr. Ramirez has—in your words—a weak alibi. But it is possible, based on his wife's estimated time of death and the time Mr. Ramirez left work, that he was not home at the time of the murder. Isn't that correct?"

"It's possible. Time of death isn't an exact science. But it's also possible—"

"*Possible.* Not the strongest word to use when you're telling a jury that a man killed his wife. No further questions, Your Honor."

Hal returned to his seat, catching Kristina's gaze. His confident swagger masked a gnawing uncertainty in his gut. The cross had gone well enough—he'd landed several solid points—but whether any of it mattered to this jury remained an open question.

"How'd I do?"

"You're not going to win any awards from the Fraternal Order of Police."

He grinned. "I'll take that as a compliment."

Sam stalked to the witness stand for redirect. "Detective Coffey, during your investigation, did you find any evidence of anyone other than the defendant having a motive to harm Natalia Ramirez?"

"No, we did not."

"Thank you, Detective." Coffey had barely stepped down before she was calling her next witness. "The Commonwealth calls Dr. Julia Reyes to the stand."

36

—————

HAL SAT FORWARD in his seat. Dr. Julia Reyes was hands-down his favorite Philadelphia medical examiner—though the feeling was not exactly mutual. It wasn't just her brains he appreciated. Brains were overrated in his field. It was her perfectionism, so pathological it made Kristina's organizational skills look haphazard by comparison.

In all his years crossing swords with her, he'd never once seen her shade the truth to help either side. She was meticulous to the point of obsession—borderline OCD—and always answered honestly.

Julia Reyes never fudged the science. They couldn't have asked for a better ME for Nico's trial.

There was just one problem. In their last courtroom face-off, Hal had weaponized her obsessive-compulsive tendencies against her to fluster her on the stand. Not his most virtuous moment. Reyes hadn't spoken a civil word to him since. Which was why he and Kristina had agreed that Kristina would handle this particular cross-examination.

He watched Reyes enter the courtroom now, and hoped she wouldn't hold his sins against Kristina.

After being sworn in—and shooting Hal a withering look—Reyes began arranging three black pens in parallel alignment about four inches from the edge of the witness box.

Sam waited patiently while Reyes completed her ritual, then began the standard credentials recitation—medical degree from Johns Hopkins, residency at the University of Pennsylvania Hospital, board certification in forensic pathology, and eight years with the Philadelphia Department of Public Health. The whole shebang was designed to impress the jury—and Hal couldn't deny that Reyes's CV was intimidating.

"Dr. Reyes, did you perform the autopsy on Natalia Ramirez?"

"I did," Reyes replied in her usual clipped tone. She glanced down at the pens, as if reluctant to stop adjusting them.

"What did you determine to be the cause of death?"

"Asphyxiation due to strangulation."

Sam strode to the prosecution table, where she slid a set of glossy prints from a folder. "Your Honor, I'd like to enter these photographs as prosecution exhibits."

Judge Harding examined them, then nodded. "So entered."

Sam placed the first photo on the witness stand in front of Reyes. She also handed a copy to the jury and another to Hal. He forced himself not to grimace. A classic dead-body candid, showing the ligature marks on Natalia's neck, livid against her pale skin. Several jurors flinched.

Hal leaned close to Kristina's ear. "Nothing like a little death porn before lunch."

She didn't respond, but her jaw flexed.

Nico's head dipped into view on her other side as he leaned forward to see the photo. Instantly, his face drained of color. Part of Hal wanted to turn the photo over, spare him from the brutal reality of what someone had done to the woman he loved—but he knew the sight of him looking physically ill would play well for the jury.

"Dr. Reyes, can you describe what we're seeing here?"

"These are ligature marks consistent with strangulation by a cord or cable-like object. The pattern of bruising indicates that significant force was applied for at least two to three minutes."

"Is that how long it would take to cause death?"

"Typically, yes. Unconsciousness usually occurs within thirty seconds to a minute, but death requires sustained pressure for several minutes."

"So this wasn't a momentary loss of control? The killer had to maintain the strangulation for a prolonged period? He intended to kill her?"

"Objection," Kristina rose to her feet beside him. "Calls for speculation about the killer's state of mind. Ms. Klein is also attempting to elicit a legal conclusion."

"Sustained," Judge Harding ruled.

Only slightly flustered, Sam worked methodically, having Reyes explain the evidence of strangulation in clinical detail—the broken blood vessels in Natalia's eyes, the fracture of the hyoid bone, the bruising pattern on her neck. The testimony was precise and clear, as it always was when Reyes was on the stand. Hal watched Kristina making careful notes, underlining key points for her cross.

"Dr. Reyes, the defense has raised a question about certain metal particles found in the wound. During your examination, did you find any such substances?"

Reyes straightened her already perfect posture. "Yes. I detected small metal fragments embedded in the victim's tissue, specifically in the subdermal layer of the anterior neck region."

"Were you able to determine the source of these metal fragments?"

"No. My laboratory analysis identified them as a nickel-chromium alloy, but not their specific origin."

"Based on your expertise, does the presence of metal fragments alone mean that Mrs. Ramirez was not killed with a plastic USB cable found at the scene?"

Reyes hesitated slightly. *Here we go*, Hal thought. *Science versus the prosecution's narrative.* "No. The metal particles alone do not rule out the USB cable as the murder weapon."

"In fact, based on your experience, these metal fragments could have come from another source, correct?"

"Objection," Kristina said. "Leading the witness."

"I'll rephrase. Are there explanations for the presence of these metal fragments unrelated to the murder weapon?"

"Yes. For example, the metal particles could have been transferred from jewelry worn by the victim during the struggle."

"Could the USB cable still have been the primary murder weapon, despite these fragments?"

"Yes."

Appearing satisfied, Sam switched gears. "Dr. Reyes, did you determine a time of death?"

"Based on body temperature, rigor mortis, and lividity, I estimated death occurred between 11:00 PM and 1:00 AM on the night in question."

"Thank you, Dr. Reyes. No further questions."

Judge Harding looked at the defense table. "Cross-examination?"

Kristina stood. "Yes, Your Honor."

As Kristina approached the witness stand, she projected professional precision—mirroring Reyes to put the witness at ease. Hal wasn't the only one who employed courtroom techniques.

"Dr. Reyes, good morning. I'd like to start with the metal

fragments you found. Metal fragments would be a different composition than a plastic USB cable, correct?"

"That's correct."

"In fact, you testified that your lab identified the metal fragments as an alloy of nickel and chromium?"

"Yes."

"Is that consistent with jewelry? Perhaps a chain?"

"It could be, yes."

"Regarding the bruising pattern on the victim's neck, you testified that it was consistent with the USB cable, but could it also be consistent with other cord-like objects?"

Hal braced himself for Sam's objection, but the prosecutor held her tongue for now.

"Potentially, yes."

"Could it be consistent with a metal chain that had been wrapped around the victim's neck?"

Reyes considered this. "It's possible."

Hal watched the jury, trying to gauge if they were following the technical testimony. Most seemed engaged, though a couple in the back row appeared to be losing focus. It had been a long day.

"Dr. Reyes, in your report, you noted what you called 'unusual abrasion patterns' on the victim's neck. Could you explain what was unusual about them?"

Hal held his breath. This was where some medical examiners would hedge, trying to serve the prosecution's case. He could see that thought flicker behind Reyes's eyes, but only for a moment.

"The abrasions had a granular quality that suggested something with a rough texture had been in contact with the skin. The USB cable had a smooth exterior."

Thank you, doctor.

A tight smile flashed briefly on Kristina's face. "Given the inconsistent bruising pattern and the unexplained presence of metal particles, isn't it possible that the victim's wounds were actually inflicted with a chain, rather than the USB cable?"

"Objection," Sam said. "Calls for speculation."

"I'm asking for her professional opinion based on the forensic evidence," Kristina countered.

"I'll allow it," Judge Harding said. "The witness may answer."

Reyes straightened. "Based solely on the physical evidence, I cannot rule out that possibility."

Several jurors exchanged glances, and Hal noticed a few of them nodding.

"Thank you, Dr. Reyes."

As Kristina returned to the defense table, Hal gave her a subtle thumbs-up.

"Not bad for a girl who got Cs in science class," he whispered.

"They were A-minuses." She cut him a glare, but there was a hint of a smile on her lips. "And that's still a sore point."

"Noted."

Sam declined to redirect, and Judge Harding checked his watch. "It's approaching noon. We'll break for lunch and resume at 1:30 with the Commonwealth's final witness."

____

37

After lunch, Sam called her last witness.

"The Commonwealth calls Gabriel Molina."

A hush fell over the courtroom as Natalia's father entered. *Classic prosecution move,* Hal thought. *Nothing like a grieving parent to seal the deal as the final witness.* Molina wore a dark suit that hung loosely on his frame, evidence of recent weight loss. His salt-and-pepper hair was slicked back from his face, revealing the same high cheekbones he'd passed on to his daughter—a subtle reminder of what was lost. His dignified bearing commanded attention, and several jurors sat up straighter as he took the stand.

Even in grief, Gabriel Molina carried himself with a quiet authority that filled the room. As he passed the defense table, Hal caught a glimpse of the blue-black tattoo on his wrist—the Iron Keepers emblem Hal had mistaken for a gang tat. *One more reminder that appearances lie.*

After establishing that Molina was Natalia's father, Sam guided him through gentle questions about his daughter—her childhood, her dreams, her marriage to Nico. Molina's answers were measured, his grief evident but controlled.

"Mr. Molina, when was the last time you saw your daughter alive?"

"Two months before she died. She came to Sunday dinner at our house."

"How did she seem to you?"

"Distant. Not herself."

"Had you noticed this change in her before?"

"Yes, for several months. She used to call me every few days. Then the calls became less frequent. She stopped coming to family gatherings as often."

"Did you ask her about these changes?"

"Yes. She said she was busy with nursing school, that she and Nico were doing fine. But I could tell something was wrong."

"Did she ever mention any problems in her marriage?"

"Objection," Hal said. "Calls for hearsay."

"Your Honor, this falls under the state of mind exception," Sam argued.

"I'll allow it," Judge Harding said. "The witness may answer."

State of mind? Hal leaned toward Kristina's ear. "Did she seriously just make that up?" He drummed his fingers against his legal pad, leaving small indentations in the yellow paper. "You gotta be kidding me."

"Rule 803(3)," Kristina said under her breath. She touched his hand, stilling his fingers. "State of mind, emotional condition —it's a legitimate exception."

"Since when?"

"1892?" Kristina said dryly. "Admissible to show her emotional state leading up to the murder? Seriously, none of this rings a bell?"

Sam glanced over her shoulder at their whispered exchange, a small, satisfied smile playing at the corner of her mouth.

Hal gritted his teeth. "I'll let you handle the objections."

"You can answer," Sam urged her witness.

Molina shook his head. "Natalia never said anything specific about marriage problems. But a father knows."

This time, Kristina was on her feet. "Objection, Your Honor. The question calls for an improper lay opinion, speculation, conclusory statement, in addition to foundation issues—"

"Sustained," the judge said. "The jury will please disregard Mr. Molina's last statement."

Kristina flashed Hal a superior smirk.

He rolled his eyes. "What? No *Father Knows Best* exception from 1783?"

"Nope."

Sam continued, drawing out testimony about how Molina learned of his daughter's death, his identification of her body, and the devastating impact it had on his family. Even Hal recognized a few opportunities for objecting, but Kristina mostly held her tongue. They both knew objecting too frequently during the testimony of a grieving relative could backfire with an emotionally invested jury.

And this jury was fully invested. By the time Sam finished, several jurors were blinking back tears.

"Thank you, Mr. Molina. No further questions."

Judge Harding turned to Hal. "Cross-examination?"

As Hal stood, he felt Kristina's hand on his wrist. Her fingers gave a quick, meaningful squeeze. When he glanced down, her expression said to go easy.

Hal gave a stiff nod, then approached the stand.

"Mr. Molina, I'm very sorry for your loss."

Molina nodded slightly, his expression guarded.

"I just have a few questions. You testified that Natalia seemed distant in the months before her death, is that correct?"

"Yes."

"And you attributed this to possible problems in her

marriage? Based on, let's see"—he made a show of checking his notes—"fatherly intuition."

He felt rather than saw Kristina flash him a look from the defense table.

"I didn't know what to attribute it to," Molina said. "I just knew something was wrong."

"Were you aware that Natalia had dropped out of nursing school during this period?"

"No. I didn't know that until after her death."

"Were you aware that she was working at a gentleman's club called Heartbreakers?"

Molina's face darkened. A flash of something beyond grief—shame for his daughter, or anger at Hal, or maybe both—twisted his features before he regained his composure. He gripped the edge of the witness stand.

"No." The single word carried a chilling weight. Hal remembered the man was active in his church, a youth group mentor to neighborhood kids. He felt a moment of guilt dragging his daughter's dirty secret out in court.

But it was a brief moment.

"You didn't know she was stripping? Giving lap dances in the VIP room, wearing nothing but a G-string and body glitter? Calling herself Sapphire?"

"I told you I didn't know!"

"Objection!" Sam lurched forward. "Asked and answered! Mr. Nolan is harassing a grieving father!"

Kristina was going to tear into him later, but his instincts told him to push. Molina was not an open-minded dad, and if Hal could transfer even a tiny bit of Molina's disapproval to the jurors, he might make them less eager to punish Nico.

Hal raised his hands in a gesture of surrender he had no intention of honoring. "That wasn't my intent, Your Honor. Mr. Molina, I sincerely apologize if my questions are upsetting. I'm only trying to establish the truth—that Natalia was keeping secrets not just from her husband, but from you as well."

"Objection! Argumentative!"

"Sustained. Mr. Nolan, find a new line of questioning."

From the corner of his eye, he saw Kristina give him a tight shake of her head.

"Did you know that Natalia had previously worked as a dancer years ago, before she married Nico?"

Molina's eyes widened slightly. "No. I didn't know that."

"Are you familiar with a man named Marcus Medrano?"

"Objection! Beyond the scope of discovery! The Commonwealth has received no prior notice about this Marcus Medrano, and this appears to be an attempt to introduce an alternative suspect theory without proper disclosure."

Hal remained calm. "Your Honor, Marcus Medrano is hardly beyond the scope of discovery. He was interviewed by the police during their investigation. Detective Coffey testified that they spoke to the management and security at Heartbreakers. Mr. Medrano is the head of security at that establishment. His name appears in the discovery file provided by the Commonwealth."

Judge Harding looked at Sam. "Ms. Klein?"

Sam's jaw tightened, but she lowered herself back into her chair.

"Please answer the question, Mr. Molina," the judge said.

"I don't know anyone by that name."

Hal nodded. "Mr. Molina, based on everything we've just heard, would it be fair to say that there were aspects of Natalia's life that she kept private, even from you?"

Molina stared down at his hands. Something in his face seemed to collapse inward. When he finally looked up, his eyes held a distant look and his voice was barely audible. "I suppose that's fair to say."

"No further questions."

As Hal returned to his seat, he could feel Kristina's barely suppressed anger. "What the hell was that?"

"I rattled him."

"You rattled the jury. Look how uncomfortable they look. The sympathy on their faces."

Hal peeked at the jury box. His jaw clenched. "Maybe I got carried away."

Judge Harding leaned forward. "Redirect, Ms. Klein?"

"No thank you, Your Honor." She turned to the jury with a grave expression. "At this time, the Commonwealth rests its case."

As the witness stepped down, Judge Harding checked the time.

"It's nearly five o'clock. We'll adjourn for the day and resume tomorrow morning at nine. The defense will present its case."

As the jury filed out, Hal tried to focus on his thoughts and not on Kristina's glare. Sam had presented a strong case, but they'd managed to plant a few seeds of doubt with each witness.

Tomorrow would bring new challenges.

He leaned close to Kristina. "Don't worry. Once that chain hits the evidence table, the jury won't make it past their first coffee break in deliberations."

"Assuming Judge Harding *allows* it into evidence. You heard Klein—she's already setting up for a discovery violation motion."

"When has a little thing like the rules of evidence stood between us and a win? Relax—I have a plan."

38

HAL'S PLAN WAS PUBLICITY. In the small prep room adjacent to one of the event spaces of the Philadelphia Marriott Downtown, he examined himself in a wall-sized mirror and adjusted his tie. Behind him, Kristina was pacing. The sound of her heels on the polished floor matched his heartbeat—fast and anxious.

"Will you stop?" he said, without turning around. "I know what I'm doing."

"Do you?" Kristina stopped pacing. "Because what you're doing is undermining the judicial process."

"It's a press conference, Kristina."

"It's trying the case in the media."

"Which is not, technically speaking, illegal." Hal turned to face her. "Look, I have total faith in your legal abilities. I know you can beat any argument Sam makes for excluding the chain from evidence. Your brain is a deadly weapon."

"Uh-huh." Her eyes narrowed skeptically. "But?"

"But we obtained Medrano's chain through deception, without a warrant, with questionable chain of custody, and with zero notice to the DA's Office."

Kristina cringed. "There's precedent supporting—"

"I'm sure there is." Hal straightened his spine. "Just think of this press conference as insurance ... in case there isn't. Judge Harding is new to the bench. A rookie judge. And rookie judges are particularly sensitive to outside pressure. A little media attention on our side creates a ... friendly environment for your arguments in support of admissibility."

Kristina moved closer, lowering her voice even though they were still alone in the room. "You're being smug."

"I'm being smart."

"If this backfires, we're looking at contempt charges."

"If it backfires, the least of our problems will be contempt charges. Without the chain proving Medrano killed Natalia, Nico is going to death row." Hal held her gaze. "You know I'm right."

Kristina sighed. She glanced anxiously at the door to the event room. "Just ... don't go to eleven this time."

"You seemed pretty happy when I took my opening statement to eleven."

"That was in court. This is a press conference. Keep it to an eight, okay?"

"Eight and a half?" He grinned, hoping to coax a smile from her.

Kristina's expression darkened. "Hal, the last time you ignored my advice, which was"—she checked her watch—"a few hours ago, you emotionally devastated a grieving father and turned our entire jury against us."

"Eight it is."

"And the second I give you the signal, you wrap it up."

"What's the signal?"

She seemed to mull it over. "Given how annoyed I am at you right now? I think kicking you in the shin will work."

"Joke's on you. I like it rough."

Kristina just shook her head, frowning.

Hal felt his own smile fade. "Are we sure we'll have the forensics by morning?"

"Lena just checked. The lab tech is finishing up the comparison between the metal fragments from Natalia's neck and the chain. Everything's on schedule."

"Good. Then let's start the show."

The door opened and a hotel staff member stuck his head in. "Mr. and Mrs. Nolan? The reporters are all set up. Whenever you're ready."

Hal nodded. "Two minutes."

When the door closed, Kristina stepped closer to him. She smoothed his collar, tugged his lapels—gestures that might have seemed affectionate if she didn't add, "Try not to sound like a used car salesman."

"I would have been an excellent used car salesman."

"First thing you've said today that I agree with." But he finally won a smile, and that was something.

They walked into the adjoining event room together, presenting a united front they didn't quite feel as camera flashes erupted around them. Even with Brantley's money, the room was smaller than Hal would have liked, but still respectable, easily fitting a dozen reporters from local outlets, plus a few bigger fish from national publications. Lena lurked at the back of the room, arms crossed, scanning the crowd of reporters like she'd rather be anywhere else.

Hal and Kristina took positions at the podium facing the reporters.

"Thank you all for coming on such short notice," Hal began, leaning slightly toward the microphones. "I'm Hal Nolan. This is my partner, Kristina Nolan. We represent Nico Ramirez, who has been wrongfully accused of murdering his wife, Natalia."

As if any of these vampires needed a recap.

A reporter from the local ABC affiliate raised her hand. "Mr.

Nolan, given that the trial is ongoing, why are you holding this press conference now? Has something changed?"

Perfect setup.

"Excellent question." Hal smiled, channeling his confidence. "Yes. New evidence has come to light. We're here tonight because tomorrow morning, we intend to introduce that evidence."

The room stirred. He had their attention.

"The prosecution would have you believe that Nico Ramirez killed his wife with a USB cable in a jealous rage. That narrative has a fatal flaw—the USB cable is not the murder weapon."

"What makes you so sure?" a voice called out from the crowd.

Hal locked eyes with the reporter. "Because we have just obtained physical evidence that identifies the actual murder weapon—and it is not the USB cable that the prosecution has built their case around. The medical examiner herself testified that metal fragments were found in the wounds on Natalia's neck, fragments that do not match the USB cable. Our evidence explains her finding."

The room erupted in questions. Hal held up his hands.

"This isn't just about proving *what* didn't kill Natalia. The actual murder weapon leads directly to someone who isn't our client—someone the police never bothered to investigate because they were fixated on Nico from the beginning. From day one, this investigation suffered from tunnel vision."

From the corner of his eye, Hal saw Kristina watching him carefully. Remembering her warning, he dialed it back a notch.

"I'm sure the police did their best, but the fact is, they over-looked other suspects, other motives, and most crucially, forensic evidence that didn't fit their theory."

"Are you saying you can identify the real killer?" another reporter called out, this time from the *Inquirer*.

Hal smiled. "You'll have to be in court tomorrow morning to find out. But I can tell you this—the real murder weapon belongs to someone with a documented history of violence against women and a personal connection to Natalia that the prosecution never explored. When you see this evidence, you'll understand why we're confident Nico Ramirez is an innocent man wrongfully accused of a crime he did not commit."

A man called out from the back of the room. "Mr. Nolan, don't you think it's unethical to try your case in the media like this?"

Hal paused, licked his lips. He didn't recognize the man from any of the networks or local newspapers.

"I'm not trying my case in the media. I'm simply alerting the public to a significant development that will be presented in court tomorrow."

Then he spotted them—Agents Ventura and Glover, standing near the exit, arms crossed and chins raised in identical poses of challenge. The interrogator was a plant. Hal winced inwardly but managed to keep his expression neutral.

"But isn't there a risk that this press conference could influence the jury?"

"The jurors have been instructed to avoid press coverage of the trial." Hal swallowed. The man's objective was to disrupt the press conference. Hal needed to get things back on track. "The citizens of Philadelphia have a right to know when the police and DA's Office are conspiring to frame an innocent janitor rather than investigating a real killer walking among us."

Kristina's heel connected sharply with his shin behind the podium.

"What I mean," Hal quickly amended, "is that all elements of law enforcement should be focused on finding the truth, not just securing convictions."

"Is it true you're being paid by hedge fund billionaire Gavin

Brantley?" This from a thin man with wire-rimmed glasses, another plant judging by the grin on Ventura's face.

Kristina leaned forward, nudging him away from the microphone. "Our fee arrangements with our clients are confidential. What I can tell you is that Nico Ramirez deserves the best defense possible, regardless of his financial situation. Thank you all for coming. We won't be taking any more questions tonight. Everything will be made clear when trial resumes tomorrow morning."

As the reporters continued shouting questions, Hal and Kristina made their way toward the side exit. Lena fell in behind them, creating a buffer between them and the press. Hal didn't let his smile drop until they were safely back in the prep room.

"Did you see Ventura and Glover skulking by the exit?" Hal loosened his tie with an angry tug. "Those reporters asking the hostile questions—FBI plants."

"They're interfering with your interference of the trial." Lena smirked. "Must be frustrating."

"It is!"

"We need to deal with Ventura and Glover before they can do more damage," Kristina said.

"Oh, we will." Hal felt his expression harden. "By the time we're done, Ventura and Glover are going to wish they'd never crossed paths with us." He checked his watch. "But first things first—we need to get that chain into evidence tomorrow morning. No matter what."

39

No professor in law school had prepared Kristina for how much of her career would be spent waiting. If she ever got the chance to create her own curriculum—a remote possibility given her firm's controversial reputation, but a girl could dream —she'd make this crucial skill a required course for all future litigators.

She paced the hallway outside Judge Harding's courtroom. Every few seconds, she checked her phone, willing it to ring. The lab results should have come in hours ago.

She glanced at the courtroom door and winced, imagining what must be going on inside. Hal was no doubt buying them time with his special combination of charm, bullshit, and courtroom tap-dancing, but even his considerable repertoire of delaying tactics wouldn't hold Judge Harding at bay forever. After forty minutes, she knew even Hal must be reaching his limit.

The door opened and a court officer emerged, his face pinched with annoyance.

"Ms. Nolan? Judge Harding is asking if you'll be rejoining the proceedings or if your husband plans to keep telling old war stories until lunch."

She forced a polite smile. "Tell His Honor I'll be right in. I'm just waiting for an urgent call from a witness."

The officer gave her a skeptical look before retreating back into the courtroom.

Crap. Crap. Crap.

She checked her phone again. Nothing.

Her heart hammered in her chest. This was their last gambit—their only real shot at creating reasonable doubt. Without the lab results connecting Medrano's chain to Natalia's murder, they had nothing but circumstantial evidence and wild theories.

A young attorney walking past gave her a curious look. Kristina realized she must appear slightly unhinged, muttering to herself. She forced herself to settle down. Smoothed her suit and tried to project an air of calm confidence she absolutely did not feel.

Her phone vibrated in her hand, and she nearly dropped it in her haste to answer.

"Lena? Please tell me you have something."

"Results just came in from the lab."

"Thank goodness," Kristina breathed, allowing herself a momentary sigh of relief.

"*Not* good, actually." She heard the reluctance in Lena's tone—the voice of someone delivering bad news. "The necklace isn't a match, Kristina. The lab found none of Natalia's DNA or fingerprints. Not a single cell or tissue fragment."

The hallway seemed to tilt slightly. Kristina leaned against the wall, suddenly needing its support. "Medrano could have cleaned the necklace. What about the metal particles in her neck tissue—"

"Not a match to the chain, according to your metallurgy expert."

"The abrasion patterns—"

"Inconclusive. The patterns aren't inconsistent with a chain like Medrano's, but they're also not inconsistent with dozens of other objects—including a USB cable used with enough force."

"Oh God." Kristina's stomach dropped as if she'd missed a step on a staircase. "Please tell me they didn't put that in writing."

"Of course not."

She glanced at the courtroom door again, imagining Hal inside, burning through his last delaying tactics thinking the cavalry was on its way.

But there was no cavalry, and they were out of options.

"Kristina? You still there?"

"Klein will rip us apart if we try to introduce the chain now. She'll paint us as desperate defense attorneys grasping at straws to save a guilty man." She closed her eyes, trying to think through the fog of disappointment. She still believed Marcus Medrano was the killer. But what evidence did they have? Their past relationship? An overheard argument at the club? Not enough.

"We need the security footage," she realized suddenly, opening her eyes. "From Heartbreakers. The night Natalia had that argument. If we can show it was with Medrano, that might be enough for reasonable doubt...."

"But Medrano threw Hal and you out when you asked to see it."

"Yes, but...." Kristina hesitated, an idea forming. "*You've* established a rapport with him."

A long pause on the line.

"Kristina. No."

"He liked you, Lena."

"He liked 'Alexandra.'"

"Exactly! If you wore something sexy, visited him at the strip club—"

"Are you serious right now?" Lena's voice was sharp over the phone line. "You want me to *seduce* the security footage from a potential murderer? Am I Mata Hari now?"

"You're being dramatic, Lena. Just, you know … flirt a little."

"Have you *seen* me flirt? This guy works with strippers. They're like expert-level flirts. I'm … not."

"He already showed an interest in you. Keep doing what you did at the liquor store. You don't need to marry the guy. Just get access to his office and locate the video files."

Another long pause.

"You're sounding more like Hal every day," Lena finally said.

The accusation stung, partly because Kristina had been thinking the same thing. "I'm trying to save an innocent man's life, and you're criticizing me?" she snapped.

"I'm not criticizing you," Lena's voice softened. "I'm worried about you. I get that you're under enormous pressure, but I don't want you to lose yourself. Who you are."

Kristina swallowed hard. "I haven't lost myself. I'm just … adapting to the situation. Sometimes doing the right thing means bending the rules a little."

Exactly what Hal would say.

"Kristina—"

The courtroom door swung open. The court officer reappeared, his expression even more annoyed than before.

"Mrs. Nolan, Judge Harding is insisting you return immediately or he's holding both you and Mr. Nolan in contempt."

"Tell Judge Harding I'll be right there," Kristina said, trying to keep the desperation from her voice.

As the officer disappeared back into the courtroom, Kristina returned her attention to the phone.

"Lena, I have to go. Please, will you do this for me?"

"Okay," Lena said reluctantly. "But you owe me big."

"I'm good for it."

Kristina ended the call just as the courtroom door opened again. This time it was Hal who emerged, his face grim.

"I convinced Harding to give us fifteen minutes, but he's already pissed off about the press conference and he's itching to throw us in a jail cell if we don't deliver. Where are the lab results?"

"Forget the lab results."

Hal blinked, but didn't need to ask any questions to understand what she meant. "Shit."

"Yeah."

He ran a hand through his hair. "So we've got nothing?"

"Lena's on it, but we need another day."

"Another day?"

"I asked Lena to go back to Heartbreakers tonight as Alexandra to try and get that security footage."

Hal's eyebrows rose.

"Don't look so shocked."

"I'm not shocked. I'm impressed. It's a good idea. But Harding isn't going to just hand us another day because we ask nicely."

"I'll handle it."

She headed into the courtroom, Hal right behind her. As she walked to the defense table, she caught Sam Klein watching her from across the courtroom. The prosecutor's lips were curved in the faintest hint of a smile. Klein might not know exactly what had gone wrong, but she obviously sensed something had. Like a shark scenting blood in the water.

Kristina broke eye-contact. She didn't have time for Klein right now, with Judge Harding glaring down at her like he wanted to take away her law license.

"So glad you could rejoin us, Ms. Nolan. Are we finally ready to proceed?"

Kristina took a deep breath and straightened her shoulders. "Your Honor, I need to request a brief continuance until tomorrow morning."

Judge Harding's face twisted. "Ms. Nolan, I've already indulged your team's delays far beyond what court protocol dictates. What possible reason could justify further postponement?"

Kristina felt the courtroom's attention focus on her. From the corner of her eye, she could see Klein already out of her chair, ready to object. Hal, standing at her side, looked like he wanted to disappear.

Kristina grabbed her stomach and bent over, letting out a groan. "Your Honor, I apologize profusely for the inconvenience, but ... I'm battling what I believe is food poisoning. I was hoping I could push through, but...." She groaned again and gritted her teeth.

Klein threw her hands in the air. "Your Honor, this is beyond absurd! The Commonwealth strongly objects—"

"Are you suggesting my partner would risk her professional reputation by fabricating an illness?" Hal glared across the room at Klein.

Judge Harding's gaze shifted between the three of them, clearly flustered. "Uh ... Ms. Klein, your objection is noted, but.... Ms. Nolan, you look kind of pale...."

"Your Honor," Kristina said, clutching her stomach more dramatically, "I hate to be graphic, but if I don't get to a restroom in the next thirty seconds..." She grimaced and shifted from foot to foot. "...there's going to be a mess."

The court reporter rolled her chair a few inches backward.

"Go!" Judge Harding said. "Court will adjourn until 9:00 AM tomorrow!"

"Thank you, Your Honor."

Klein shook her head in barely contained fury as Kristina and Hal headed toward the door.

"But," Judge Harding added, "I expect you to be prepared to proceed tomorrow morning without further delays." He fixed her and Hal with a stern look. "No more last-minute maneuvering—and no more talking to the press. Am I clear?"

"Perfectly clear, Your Honor. Thank you."

In the car, Hal burst out laughing. "Food poisoning? That was the best you could come up with?"

"It worked, didn't it?"

Hal was still laughing as he started the car, and Kristina found herself laughing with him. Hardly her most impressive courtroom moment, but she'd gotten the job done. They had one more day. One last chance to save Nico. She just hoped Lena could deliver.

40

───────

Sam Klein sat in a folding chair against the wall of Dance Foundations, arms crossed, still wearing her court attire. The other mothers were in yoga pants and athleisure wear, chatting and planning playdates, showing off photos from their recent family vacations. No one glanced Sam's way. She was used to it, used to being the weird prosecutor woman always rushing in at the last second to pick up her daughter. Not mommy clique material.

Emily's face scrunched in concentration as she executed a wobbly but determined spin that ended with a little bow. Her red hair—the same shade as Sam's—slipping from its ponytail. Every few seconds, her eyes went to Sam, as if confirming her mother was really there.

Sam mentally chastised herself. *You're just projecting your guilty feelings.*

But it was nice being able to watch Emily's whole dance lesson for once, instead of catching the last thirty seconds. It almost made her less angry about Kristina Nolan's theatrical "food poisoning" episode. Almost.

Not that she wasn't on her phone anyway.

The device buzzed with yet another incoming text from Dan Coffey: *They don't actually have anything. If they did, they would have introduced it today.*

Sam shook her head, responded: *Even the Nolans wouldn't make promises in a press conference if they didn't think they could deliver. Something changed overnight.*

Coffey: *So they thought they found the real murder weapon, then learned they were wrong. Last-minute lab results?*

Sam: *What I'm thinking.*

Coffey: *So who's their scapegoat?*

Sam thought about that as a dozen seven-year-olds pirouetted across the hardwood floor with varying degrees of success. The Nolans had clearly been building up to the reveal of an alternative suspect as a means of creating reasonable doubt, but had been hiding the fall guy's identity as long as possible to prevent her from preparing a counteroffensive.

She tapped out: *Hal asked Molina about Marcus Medrano yesterday on cross.*

Coffey: *Strip club security guy.*

Sam: *Are you sure that's his only connection to Natalia?*

Coffey: *I'll see what I can dig up.*

Sam: *Do it fast.*

The truth was, the evidence about the metal particles nagged at her like a loose tooth. After watching the press conference, she'd spent last night combing through the case file, looking for a hint of what the Nolans had claimed to discover. Medrano was the best answer she could come up with. And then the unexpected delay this morning plunged her straight back into uncertainty.

The dance studio door swung open, admitting the sound of traffic and the smell of exhaust. Sam's eyes flicked toward the intrusion with annoyance, then locked on the figure in the doorway.

Colten.

His eyes swept across the mirrored walls, the polished hard-wood floor, the cubbies filled with tiny sneakers. He seemed momentarily disoriented by the pastel colors and tinny classical music.

Sam's stomach twisted at the sight of him—tall, with the same rugged good looks that had once fooled her into thinking he was someone she wanted to build a life with.

The same good looks that had helped him talk his way out of trouble with cops the first two times he'd put his hands on her.

Sam's heart stuttered in her chest, then began to pound. The physical reaction was as immediate as it was infuriating. Six years free of him, with a restraining order that had kept her safe, and her body still remembered the danger.

Colten's eyes met hers, and he smiled. It wasn't a confrontational smile. It was ... *pleasant*, which made it so much worse.

He strolled toward her, hands in the pockets of his jeans. Sam kept her expression neutral, even as her mind raced. Emily hadn't noticed him yet. She and the other girls were focused on Miss Katie, who was demonstrating a new step.

"Hello, Sam." His voice was the same too, smooth and deceptively gentle. "Long time."

"What are you doing here, Colten?" She didn't flinch, didn't raise her voice. A few other moms were watching them now, their eyes curious.

He turned to watch Emily and a grin broke across his face. "Wow, she looks just like me."

Narcissistic bastard.

Sam's hand moved to her phone, sliding it into her lap. "You don't belong here."

His smile widened. "Haven't you heard? That ridiculous restraining order was vacated. I'm free to see my daughter whenever I want."

"This isn't the place or the time. You're going to upset her."

He shrugged. "That's your opinion."

"Stay away from us." The words came out as a hiss.

Colten took the empty seat next to her, sliding it as close as possible. "That's not how it works anymore." His voice dropped to a threatening murmur in her ear. "And you better get used to it, because my lawyer is working on getting me visitation rights next. And I intend to exercise them."

Sam felt her throat tighten. Emily was still oblivious to his presence, thank God. But she needed to do something. Keeping her hand casual, she unlocked her phone without looking down. Her text chain with Coffey appeared, the last app she'd had open. Hiding her movements with her thigh, she tapped out a single word.

Help.

"Why are you doing this?"

Not that she needed to ask. Even if she hadn't had years of firsthand experience living under his thumb, she'd been a prosecutor long enough to understand that for men like Colten Roth, it was always about control.

He stretched his legs out, getting comfortable. "Maybe I just want to spend time with my little girl."

"You don't care about Emily. You haven't paid a dime in child support. You don't even know her."

"And whose fault is that? You're the one who told the court I was dangerous, that I needed to be kept away." His voice had that familiar unhinged tone now, the one that always preceded the worst moments. "All because of a few little disagreements."

What he calls throwing me down a flight of stairs when I was four months pregnant.

Sam kept her voice steady despite the fear coiling in her gut. "If you actually gave a damn about Emily, you would leave now and never come back."

"I've changed, Sam. Got my act together."

"Right." She risked another glance at her daughter, who was now looking over, her face showing confusion. Colten followed her gaze and gave Emily a little wave. Emily ducked her head and turned away.

"She looks like she's afraid of me," Colten said, his voice hardening. "That's on you."

Sam turned to face him fully. "Get the fuck out of here, Colten. Last warning."

He smirked. "Or what?"

The door to the studio opened again. Sam felt a surge of relief at the sight of Dan Coffey's weathered face. The detective's eyes scanned the room until they locked on her and Colten. He moved toward them with a determined stride.

"Everything okay here, Sam?" Coffey asked, positioning himself directly in front of Colten.

Sam watched Colten's face darken. "Who's this old guy, Sam? Your boyfriend?"

Coffey flashed his badge. "Detective Dan Coffey, Philadelphia PD."

"Yeah, well, we're having a private conversation, *Detective*." Colten's voice took on the edge Sam remembered all too well.

"Not anymore." Coffey's tone was firm, his gaze hard in a way that made the knot in Sam's stomach loosen slightly.

"This is bullshit," Colten said, rising to his feet. His hands curled into fists. For a moment, Sam thought he might actually take a swing at Coffey in the middle of the dance studio. But then he took a step away from the detective. Colten's bravado had always been directly proportional to his opponent's vulnerability.

"This isn't over," he said to Sam. Then, to Coffey: "And you should mind your own business, Detective."

With that, he stormed out, slamming the door behind him.

"Thanks." Sam let out a ragged breath and sank back into her chair as Miss Katie, concerned by the commotion, called for a five-minute water break. Emily immediately ran to her mother.

"Was that Daddy?" Emily asked, her eyes wide with confusion.

Sam forced a smile. "It's okay, Em. He's gone now."

Emily frowned, unconvinced. "He waved at me."

Coffey crouched down to Emily's level. "Hi there. You must be Emily. I'm Dan, a friend of your mom's from work."

Emily studied him cautiously. "Do you catch bad guys?"

"I try to," Coffey said with a wink. "Your mom helps me a lot."

This seemed to please Emily, driving away her concerns about Colten and drawing a radiant smile.

When Miss Katie called the girls back to their positions, Coffey took the seat Colten had vacated.

"I didn't know if you'd understand the text," Sam whispered, her voice still unsteady.

Coffey let out a gruff laugh. "They don't call me a detective for nothing, kid." He turned to look at her and his voice softened. "Also, I worked domestic violence cases, long time ago."

"Those FBI agents did this. Ventura and Glover. If I don't deliver what they want, who knows where this ends? Shared custody? I can't let that happen."

Coffey nodded. When he spoke, his voice was gentle but firm. "You need to fix this, Sam."

"I don't know how." She hated the desperation in her voice.

Coffey was quiet for a moment. His gaze followed hers to Emily, her small body moving through dance steps with determined concentration.

"You remember that old saying about the enemy of my enemy?"

"Being my friend?" Sam frowned. "What are you saying?"

"I'm saying maybe it's time to consider unorthodox alliances." He nodded toward the window, where the sun was starting to set over Philadelphia. "Say what you will about the Nolans. They're resourceful. Especially when they're backed into a corner."

Sam stared at him. "You're suggesting I ask the defense attorneys I'm currently facing in court for help?"

"Desperate times." Coffey stood up. "Desperate measures."

41

HAL SAT on the edge of the conference table in their Old City office. The late afternoon sun filtered through the half-closed blinds, casting prison-bar shadows across the floor. Kristina looked at her phone for the hundredth time in the last hour.

"Maybe this was a mistake," she said.

"I'm sure she'll check in when she can."

"Assuming Medrano hasn't already realized 'Alexandra' isn't a real jewelry appraiser. Should we call the police? For all we know, he could be torturing her right now."

"If we call the police, Nico's done." They had both seen the jurors' faces when Gabriel Molina testified. The man's dignified grief had resonated, and the jury wanted someone to pay. Unless they found evidence exonerating him soon, that someone would be Nico. "Besides, Lena can handle herself."

"I'll never forgive myself if something happens to her. My stomach is in knots, Hal."

"She's a Marine. She can wipe the floor with a scumbag like Medrano." He tried to sound more confident than he felt.

"Maybe."

Kristina's reply was cut short by a harsh knock from the door.

Hal went to the window and peered onto the cobblestone street outside their office. Samantha Klein stood at their door.

"It's Sam Klein."

"As if this day couldn't get any worse." Kristina joined him at the window. "Probably wants to ransack the place again."

"I doubt it." Hal watched as Klein knocked again, more insistently this time. She looked harried, her hair disheveled and her suit jacket askew. "She looks upset."

"Klein's emotions are the least of my concerns right now."

But watching her from the window, there was something in Sam's expression that gave Hal pause. He recognized that hunted look from clients who'd run out of options—and more recently, his own reflection in the mirror.

"I'm going to let her in."

"Hal, no."

But he was already moving to the door, unlocking it with a decisive click. Sam pushed her way inside as soon as the lock turned.

"We need to talk," Sam said.

"Okay...." Hal relocked the door behind her.

"No we don't," Kristina said. "You're prosecuting our client. We have nothing to discuss without Judge Harding present."

"This isn't about the case," Sam said. "Not directly."

She crossed her arms. "Then why are you here?"

"Ventura and Glover."

Those names hung in the air like a bad smell. Hal thought of the FBI agents' sabotage of the previous night's press conference, and of the bold promise he and Kristina had made to Brantley—that they could bring the FBI agents down. "What about them?" he asked guardedly.

"My ex showed up at my daughter's dance lesson today."

"And this concerns us how?" Kristina asked.

"Do you know what it took to get that restraining order? Three emergency room visits before anyone would take me seriously."

Hal exchanged a quick glance with Kristina, then focused on Sam. "We have a plan for Ventura and Glover. Soon they'll be facing their own trials instead of interfering with ours, and you can get the restraining order back in place."

"When is *soon*?" Sam paced the small office, her steps quick and agitated. "Colten's going to try again. What if he goes to Emily's school next time? Or my apartment?"

Hal watched Sam carefully. The prosecutor's distress seemed genuine, but that didn't mean she didn't have an additional agenda. She'd manipulated him before. "Why come to us?"

"Someone I trust reminded me that the enemy of my enemy is my friend."

"We're not friends," Kristina said sharply.

"Yeah, that's what I told him." Sam offered a wry smile, then ran a hand through her hair. "Look, I don't like you and you don't like me. But Ventura and Glover are using *all of us* as pawns in their game."

Hal glanced at Kristina, whose expression remained stony. He could read her thoughts as clearly as if she'd spoken them. *Don't trust her. This is a trap.*

Maybe it was. But it might also be an opportunity.

"What are you suggesting?" he said.

"An alliance. Temporary, obviously. Against them."

"And Nico?" Kristina said. "Where does our client fit into this alliance? Are you offering to drop the charges?"

Sam hesitated. "I can't tank my own case."

"Then we have nothing to discuss." Kristina moved toward the door, clearly ready to show Sam out.

"Wait." Sam held up her hands. "If we can expose Ventura's

and Glover's interference with the trial, Judge Harding would have to declare a mistrial."

"Which just means we do this all over again," Kristina said. "Only now, you've had a preview of our defense strategy. No thanks."

"What defense strategy, Kristina? Pretending you have irritable bowel syndrome?"

Kristina's face flushed red and she looked like she might slap the prosecutor. Hal stepped between them. "Sam has a point. We haven't started presenting the defense's case yet, so she hasn't seen much."

"You're taking her side, Hal? Again? Really?"

"A mistrial might even help us. I wouldn't mind a new jury."

Kristina frowned, but Hal could see the shift in her eyes from outright rejection to tactical assessment. Her brain was already working the angles, even if she might not admit it. "We would need to record them somehow. Trick them into admitting what they're doing."

"Oh, is that all?" Sam said.

"We invite them here," Hal said, ignoring Sam's sarcasm. "Tonight. Tell them we want to make a deal."

Sam still looked skeptical. "They're FBI agents. They're not going to just confess to misconduct."

"No, but the subject could come up naturally, if we're negotiating a deal," Hal said.

"And how do you plan to record them? With your phone?"

"Actually," Hal said, "I was thinking your cop friend could handle that."

Sam scoffed. "You want to drag Coffey into this? What about your investigator?"

"Lena's ... occupied with something else tonight." Hal felt Kristina's gaze on him. He tried to keep his face neutral despite his growing concern for Lena's safety.

"Coffey would never go for it," Sam said, shaking her head. "There are protocols, jurisdictional issues. His career would be over if anyone found out."

"Oh, come on, Sam." Hal gave her a knowing look. "We've seen how ruthless you can be when you want something. You claim your daughter's safety is at risk. You can't persuade one cop?"

Sam was quiet. "Maybe," she admitted. "But we still need an excuse to get the Feds here. Even if Nico decided to take a plea deal, we'd handle that officially, at the FBI building or the DA's Office."

"Tell them you had to sweeten the deal for us," Kristina said.

Hal turned to her, surprised by the suggestion.

Kristina met his gaze and shrugged. "We're sleazy, bottom-feeding lawyers, right? We'll get Nico to cooperate, but only if we get something in return."

"I think their offer is to not destroy you," Sam said.

Hal laughed. "Not getting destroyed is table stakes. They need to do better." He thought about it. "We could demand that they feed us clients. Anyone gets arrested by the FBI in Philadelphia who isn't already lawyered up? We get a call."

Kristina nodded. "With our reputation, they'll believe we'd ask for that."

"Hell, I wouldn't mind if it was true," Hal admitted. Kristina gave him a sidelong glance, but he could tell she knew he was joking.

Sam nodded slowly. "This could work." She pulled out her phone. "Let me talk to Coffey."

As Sam stepped out into the hallway to make her call, Kristina turned to Hal, lowering her voice. "Please tell me you don't actually trust her."

"Not even a little bit. But this is our best shot at taking down Ventura and Glover. We fulfill our promise to Brantley and we get a mistrial, all in one swoop. And if Sam refiles charges, we'll nail her with the security footage implicating Medrano."

"Assuming Lena *gets* the footage." Kristina moved closer to him, her voice barely above a whisper. "This could go wrong in so many ways."

"At this point, we may as well put that on our letterhead."

She laughed, and he felt some of the tension from earlier dissolve. "We have adopted a looser risk tolerance."

"It's practically our business model," he said, squeezing her hand.

Sam returned. "Coffey's in. He's bringing the recording equipment. I'll tell Ventura and Glover I've convinced you to consider a deal and that we need to meet tonight since court resumes tomorrow."

Hal smiled. "Let's show these Feds how we handle business in Philly."

42

———

"THESE ARE DEPARTMENT-ISSUE," Coffey said, glaring into Hal's eyes. "So if this all goes to shit, I'm completely fucked."

Despite his close-to-retirement age, the detective loomed over Hal with the springy posture of a professional boxer. Hal swallowed.

"It won't go to shit."

"I'll be listening from my vehicle, down the street. Don't make me bust in here guns blazing."

Sam appeared at Coffey's side and squeezed his arm. "One rescue today was plenty. Just make sure we're recording, okay? The rest is on us."

Something moved in Coffey's face. "Don't forget what's at stake."

"I know, Dan."

"So where are these bugs?" Hal said, looking around the office.

Coffey broke eye-contact with Sam and pointed around the room. "There are three. One in the base of the desk lamp. One in the frame on that diploma. And one in that hideous fake plant. Should cover the whole space."

"I picked out that plant," Kristina said.

Coffey shrugged. Kristina pressed her lips together, face darkening as she bit back whatever she was about to say.

"You need them to explicitly mention interfering with Sam's restraining order," Coffey went on. "Or pressuring you to make the plea deal using illegal methods of coercion. Without that, they're assholes but not criminal assholes."

"We know how to do this," Hal said. Not that he'd ever tried to entrap FBI agents before. The thought of what might happen if they failed twisted his gut.

Kristina checked the time. "They'll be here in fifteen minutes."

Coffey gathered his equipment bag. "Then I'm out." He headed for the door, pausing to look back at Sam. "Be careful, kid."

"I will," she said quietly.

When the door closed behind him, Hal turned to the two women. "So now we wait."

His phone vibrated in his pocket—a text from Lena.

I'm in.

Caught up in orchestrating tonight's trap, he'd almost forgotten about her mission and the danger she might be in. Now a mix of relief and apprehension flooded through him. But he didn't respond. Didn't want to distract Kristina or tip their hand to Sam.

He just hoped she was safe.

Lena adjusted her cleavage—what little she had of it—by unfastening another button on her fitted top. She'd rolled the waistband of her skirt twice to show more leg than usual, a trick she'd seen friends do back in high school.

But compared to the barely-clothed dancers in this place, she might as well be wearing a burka.

He already likes you, she reminded herself. *Or Alexandra anyway, the elegant jewelry appraiser. Not Lena Randall, who'd once disassembled her service rifle blindfolded in under thirty seconds.*

Alexandra Lloyd. Alexandra Lloyd.

She repeated the fake name in her head until it felt almost natural.

The weeknight crowd at Heartbreakers was sparse, a few businessmen nursing overpriced drinks while dancers on stage gyrated to bass-heavy songs she didn't recognize. She moved deeper into the cavernous, dark environment, scanning the space.

Finally, near the end of the bar where the lights were dimmest, she spotted Marcus Medrano talking to a bald, tattooed bartender. His teeth caught the light as he smiled at some joke.

Lena took a deep breath. Time to put Alexandra Lloyd to work.

He straightened as she approached, eyes traveling down her body before returning to her face.

"Already finished the appraisal?" He smiled, leaning back against the bar. "Didn't think you'd deliver the results in person."

Lena leaned in closer than necessary, letting her perfume reach him. "The appraisal's not ready yet, but...." She lowered her voice. "I couldn't stop thinking about you."

She watched his expression change. "I've been thinking about you, too." His eyes dropped to her body again.

"Is there somewhere more private we can talk?"

"Private?"

"Maybe your office?"

When he hesitated, she bit her lip.

"Sure, that works."

He placed a hand on the small of her back, low enough for his fingertips to tease the waist of her skirt. She suppressed her instinct to break his wrist and forced herself to lean into the touch as he guided her through the club.

She took note of their surroundings, mentally marking the exits. She'd spent enough time around dangerous men to recognize the predator in Marcus's movements. The way he carried himself, the controlled power, the casual ownership of the space around him.

This was a man who had hurt people. She had no doubt.

His office was at the back of the club, down a dingy hallway past the dressing rooms. As he bent to unlock the door to his office in the dim light, she fired off a quick text to Hal. *I'm in.*

The office was smaller than she'd expected. A desk cluttered with paperwork sat beneath a bank of monitors.

"So, Alexandra." As he closed the door, he rolled her name around his mouth in a way that somehow made it sound lewd. Then he moved close, pressing his hips to hers. "I'm guessing you're not here to talk about jewelry."

Lena ran her tongue along her lower lip, hoping she wasn't pushing the act too far even as she saw his pupils widen. She touched his arm, willing herself to stay in character. "I'm not here to talk at all."

———

"THEY'RE HERE," Sam said, glancing at her phone.

Hal tugged at his tie, fingers clumsy with nerves. Kristina stepped close and adjusted the knot for him, her touch against his chest steadying him just as the sharp knock came at the door.

The door opened without waiting for an invitation.

Agents Ventura and Glover entered the office with the air of slumming tourists visiting a third-world country. Ventura's lip curled as she surveyed the space. "Quite the comedown from your Center City office—all that glass and marble. Before the cyberattack, of course."

Glover ran a finger along the wall, examining the dust with a smirk. "How the mighty have fallen."

Hal gritted his teeth. "We're more interested in the future than the past."

"Of course," Ventura said, her voice smooth. "And we're so pleased to hear about your client's change of heart."

"He's exploring his options. So are we."

"Better late than never," Glover said. His gaze moved across every surface, lingering a half-second too long on the desk lamp.

Hal felt a cold trickle of sweat down his back. "Nico might be willing to provide information about Brantley," Hal said, "but we're going to need to know what you're offering in exchange."

Ventura's thin lips curved in what might technically qualify as a smile. "Of course. Reduced charges. Possibly witness protection, depending on the nature of his testimony. We'll make sure your client receives *special* treatment."

"I'm talking about adjustments to *our* situation," Hal clarified.

Come on, take the bait.

"Adjustments?" Ventura raised an eyebrow. "I'm not sure I follow."

"After the things you said to us, we need to know that we're safe."

"It's the job of the FBI to keep all Americans safe," Ventura said blandly. "But I'm sure you'll feel more secure once the Ramirez trial is behind you."

Hal clenched his jaw. Exchanged a quick glance with Kristina. If the Feds were going to dodge his attempts to get them to explicitly mention what they'd done, he would need to take a risk and be more direct.

"Let's cut the bullshit," he said. "The threats you made in that parking lot outside Heartbreakers—that needs to stop. And what you did to Sam's restraining order? That ends now, or there's no deal."

Ventura's expression didn't change. "Mr. Nolan, I have no idea what you're talking about. Family court matters are entirely outside our jurisdiction." She paused meaningfully. "That said, things have a way of working out when people cooperate."

Kristina shot him a worried look. Ventura was too smooth, too subtle. They were being outplayed. And time was running out.

———

Lena stepped into Medrano's personal space, placing her hand on his chest with what she hoped looked like genuine interest. "This place is so different from my work environment," she murmured, letting her fingers brush against his shirt.

Marcus's breathing deepened as she leaned closer. "Like what you see?"

"It's sexy," she said, looking up at him through her lashes. She let her gaze drift to the monitors. "You watch all those? Seems like a lot of responsibility."

"The club has cameras everywhere," Marcus said with pride, his voice slightly rougher as he turned toward his desk. "Nothing happens in this place without me knowing about it."

"That's so impressive," she said, moving to sit on the edge of his desk. "Do you keep recordings for long?"

"Ninety days of backup footage," he said, leaning against the desk next to her. "Boss insists on it." His expression shifted slightly, eyes narrowing with caution. "Why are you interested in that?"

She let her hand drift to his arm, squeezing gently. "Just making small talk. I'm a little ... nervous. Maybe a drink would help."

Marcus's suspicion was replaced by a predatory grin. "I've got just the thing." He moved to a cabinet in the corner and came back with an expensive looking bottle of bourbon.

"Actually," she said, touching his arm to stop him before he could pour, "I'd really love a martini. Do you think you could get me one from the bar?"

He snorted. "We don't exactly hire the best bartenders here. Hunter drinks more than he serves."

"I'm not picky," she said, placing her hand on his chest again. "Please?" She bit her lip. "It will relax me."

He studied her for a moment, then made his decision. He set the bourbon bottle on the edge of his desk. "Don't go anywhere."

"I'm right where I want to be."

"Good. Because we're just getting started."

The promise in his tone made her skin crawl, but she smiled. "Can't wait."

He stepped out, closing the door behind him. Lena held her breath, listening until his footsteps faded down the hallway, then exploded into motion. She slid into his chair and faced the glowing monitors. The security system was password-protected, but the session was still active. Marcus hadn't logged out.

Rookie.

She navigated to the archived footage, knowing she had maybe minutes before he returned. The date range loaded—one week before the murder. Time-stamped files filled the screen. One of these files would show the argument. Now she just needed to find it.

———

"We need more than vague assurances," Hal pressed, feeling like he was pushing against a brick wall.

"Such as?" Ventura said smoothly.

"Stop dancing around it," Sam said. Her frustration was evident in her voice, and Hal knew she wasn't faking it. "Once Nico cooperates, the restraining order against Colten needs to be reinstated. Immediately."

"Ms. Klein, I'm not sure what connection you're trying to draw here—"

"You know exactly what connection."

"Come on," Hal cut in. "This isn't a game. You're endangering a child's safety."

"Are you suggesting federal agents tampered with state court orders?" Ventura's eyebrow arched in what looked like genuine amusement.

Kristina tried next. "You've made it clear what happens to people who don't cooperate with you."

"Such dramatic language for a plea deal." Ventura's expression hardened slightly, but her voice remained even. "I thought we were all professionals here."

Glover had moved to the window, casually examining the blinds. "People are always blowing things out of proportion."

Hal felt his frustration building. Every accusation was met with denial or deflection. These people were experts at avoiding explicit statements. He could imagine Coffey sitting in his car down the street, shaking his head as he listened to this fiasco.

Beside him, Kristina tensed slightly. He followed her gaze to see Glover picking up the fake plant, examining it with sudden interest.

Oh Shit.

THE FOOTAGE WAS ORGANIZED by camera and date. Lena quickly scanned through the feeds from the main floor, looking for Natalia—or "Sapphire," as she'd been known here.

Finally, she found what she was looking for. A timestamp from eight days before the murder. The back hallway camera. Natalia, still in her dancer outfit, arguing with a man.

Lena leaned closer, squinting at the footage. The man's back was to the camera, but she could see Natalia's face clearly—angry, frightened.

The man turned slightly, his profile almost visible in the dim light, but not quite. Was it Marcus?

The footage showed him grabbing Natalia's arm, her pulling away. Their body language spoke of a heated argument, though there was no audio. At one point, the man raised a hand as if to strike her, then caught himself.

Turn around, she willed him. *Show your face.*

The office door swung open behind her.

"What the hell are you doing?" Marcus demanded. He carried her drink, the clear liquid sloshing over the rim of the martini glass.

Lena forced a seductive smile as she stood from the chair. "Nothing. I was bored waiting."

Marcus set the martini on the desk, then closed the door behind him. "Bullshit."

"Marcus—"

"You're not a fucking jewelry appraiser."

She saw his hand moving toward his waistband—reaching for a weapon. She had seconds.

She grabbed the martini and threw the alcohol into his face. He recoiled with a shriek as gin burned his eyes, stumbling backward and clawing at his face. *Guess Hal isn't the only one who can weaponize a drink*, she thought.

Then she drove her knee hard into his groin.

Marcus doubled over with a strangled wheeze, and she followed with an elbow strike to his jaw, the impact jarring up through her arm.

He staggered but didn't go down. Instead, he lunged forward, his face furious, and slammed her against the desk. Pain shot through her back as the edge dug in. His hands closed around her throat, cutting off her air, his thumbs pressed viciously into her windpipe.

"Fucking bitch!"

Lena drove her knee upward again, missing his groin this time but catching his thigh. His grip loosened enough for her to twist sideways, breaking his hold.

She stumbled back, trying to put distance between them, but lost her balance on the slick floor. As she fell, Marcus lunged forward, grabbing her ankle before she could scramble away. He yanked hard, dragging her across the floor.

They grappled on the ground, Marcus using his weight advantage to pin her.

"Who the fuck are you?" he growled, his face inches from hers.

Lena didn't waste breath answering. Instead, she headbutted him hard enough to make her own vision blur. His nose cracked, blood spraying.

While he reeled from the headbutt, she squirmed free and scrambled to her feet. She scanned the room frantically. The bourbon bottle he'd pulled from the cabinet earlier—there, still on the desk where he'd left it after she'd asked for a martini instead. Her fingers closed around the neck just as Marcus lunged for her again. She swung it against his temple with all her strength. The glass shattered on impact, making a sickening crunch as bourbon and glass exploded against his skull.

He dropped like a stone.

Gasping, Lena pulled herself up. Marcus lay motionless on the floor, his face a bloody mess.

Shit, shit, shit. Had she killed him? She checked his pulse—still there, thank God.

She grabbed a power cord from the desk and quickly bound his wrists, then used his own belt to secure his ankles.

She needed to move fast. Back to the computer, she sped through the rest of the footage.

The man appeared to be yelling at Natalia. Suddenly, she slapped him across the face. They both stopped, as if her action was a shock to both of them.

Then the man turned away, pulling something from his pocket—a handkerchief. He wiped his face where she'd struck him.

As he did, his face caught the hallway light for just a moment.

Lena's blood ran cold.

It wasn't Marcus Medrano's face.

"THIS IS A NICE PLANT," Glover said, rotating the fake fern. "Looks almost real."

Kristina snorted. "Actually, we've been informed it's cheap crap."

Ventura was watching them with narrowed eyes. "You seem nervous, Mr. Nolan."

"Just anxious to get this deal settled," Hal said. "We *are* here to make a deal, right?"

"That's a good question." Ventura's head tilted slightly.

Glover had moved to the desk lamp now. "I'm not so sure anymore."

Glover removed the lampshade first, then examined the base. His eyes met Ventura's, and something unspoken passed between them.

Without a word, Ventura stood and began methodically examining the room. She moved to the diploma on the wall, running her fingers along the frame's edge until she found what she was hunting for.

"Police issue," she said, removing the tiny listening device and placing it on the table. "Someone's in a lot of trouble."

"We have no idea what you're talking about," Hal said, trying to maintain the pretense. But his voice lacked conviction.

Ventura's bemused half-smile was chilling. "Did you really think this would work?"

Glover snorted. "Amateur hour."

Ventura's voice hardened. "Attempting to record federal agents without consent is a serious offense."

Hal felt the situation spiraling out of control. "Look, we can still work something out—"

He was interrupted by Kristina's phone ringing. She glanced at the screen, then at Hal, her eyes wide.

"I need to take this," she said.

"Stay where you are," Ventura ordered.

"It's my cousin," Kristina said. "Shoot me if you want to. I'm answering it." She turned away despite Ventura's incredulous glare. "Lena?"

Hal couldn't hear Lena's response, but he saw Kristina's face pale.

"What? *Gabriel Molina?*"

At that moment, the lights went out, plunging the office into total darkness.

43

—————

HAL's first thought when the lights went out: *Did we pay the electric bill?*

Then a shotgun blast blew their door to splinters, spinning the room into a light show of muzzle flash and flying wood.

Someone screamed. Special Agent Glover lay curled on the floor, a jagged piece of wood jutting from his leg. "What the hell?" His voice keened. "What the...."

Where their door had been, a figure crouched in the threshold, silhouetted by the faint streetlight behind him. Hal blinked, struggling to process what he was seeing. It looked like Gabriel Molina, but not the dignified father who'd taken the witness stand, not the composed man who'd broken up the fight at Habeas Corkus. This man's salt-and-pepper hair was wild, his face contorted with rage. A gold chain glinted at his throat, its crucifix catching the light.

What the hell indeed.

"Molina?" Hal said. "Why—"

Another blast and the conference room table exploded. The noise hammered Hal's eardrums, left them screaming with feedback, a high-pitched ringing flooding his skull. When the smoke cleared, Hal felt Molina's hateful stare lock onto him—along with the barrels of the shotgun.

The sight of those dark holes threatened to paralyze him. Ever since that day in the courtroom, when Oscar Hazenberg had ripped the pistol from a deputy sheriff's holster and shot him—guns had caused a panic response he could barely control. Now he felt his legs turn watery. All that kept him upright was the knowledge that his body was the only shield between the shotgun and Kristina.

"You couldn't leave it alone, could you, Nolan? My daughter is dead and buried, and you have to parade her sins for all to see!"

"Her sins?" Hal took a wobbly step forward, placing his body more squarely in front of Kristina. "That's not ... that's not what this is about, Gabriel. It's about exposing Natalia's killer."

"Hal." Kristina's whisper behind him was sharp and urgent. "Hal, he *is* her killer."

Hal froze. "What now?"

"Lena found the security footage. The man who argued with Natalia at Heartbreakers wasn't Marcus Medrano. It was Gabriel Molina."

Hal's body went cold.

"Did you think I was stupid?" Molina's voice boomed. "Did you think I wouldn't watch your press conference?"

The press conference in which Hal had promised the world he would unmask Natalia's real killer in court.

All his life, people had warned Hal his big mouth would be the death of him. Apparently, there had been some sense in their advice.

"If I'm going down," Molina said, "I'm taking all of you with me."

Molina leveled the shotgun at Hal's chest.

"Drop it! Police!" Coffey's voice rang out from the doorway.

Thank God. Hal had almost forgotten the detective, sitting in his car down the street, listening.

Molina swung around, aiming the shotgun at Coffey. Hal took advantage of the distraction, grabbing Kristina and diving with her to the floor. Together, they crawled behind the wreckage of the conference table. Not the best cover, but better than nothing.

"Put down the shotgun," Coffey said.

Molina shook his head slowly. "No."

SAM PRESSED her back to the wall, dislodging one of the diplomas. Her heart pounded so hard she thought it might crack her ribs. She'd understood on a rational level that her career might entail danger, but she'd never experienced an actual threat before. Certainly nothing like this.

Did I kiss Emily goodbye?

The thought paralyzed her, wrapped around her mind like a boa constrictor. She couldn't remember. She'd been rushing again—always rushing. Focused on Colten, on the Ramirez trial, on these goddamn FBI agents. Had she kissed her daughter goodbye? The possibility that she might never get another chance squeezed the air from her lungs.

She had to survive this. For Emily. Because leaving her orphaned, with only Colten to claim custody? Not an option.

The shrapnel from the first shotgun blast had lifted Special Agent Glover off his feet. He sprawled against the wall to her right, bleeding from his leg where a jagged length of wood had impaled his calf. He moaned now, eyes rolling back in his head.

Something clattered to the floor at his side. *His gun.*

Slowly, Sam lowered herself to the floor. She crawled toward the agent, ignoring glass that bit into her knees. Her fingers closed around the grip of the fallen weapon, its weight reassuringly solid.

Glover caught her gaze and shook his head urgently. He tried to lift his hand, but loss of blood must have weakened him, because all he could do was gawk at her. "No. He'll ... kill you." The agent struggled to speak. "Don't be a hero."

Sam almost laughed. "Never intended to be."

She turned away from him, looking around the smoke-filled office. Special Agent Lilliana Ventura stood near the window, silhouetted by the dim light from the street.

Sam raised the gun until the barrel aligned with Ventura's head.

Her finger found the trigger, cold iron against her skin.

With one squeeze, she could end the threats, the manipulation, the danger to Emily.

Her daughter's face flashed in her mind—laughing, crying, calling her "Mommy." Sam would do anything to protect her. *Anything.*

Her breath stilled as her finger began to squeeze.

"Don't." Kristina appeared at her side. "Sam, this is too far," she whispered. "Even for you."

Sam didn't take her eyes off her target, but her voice came through clenched teeth. "Even for me?" The contempt beneath Kristina's words infuriated her.

"You know what I mean."

"Yeah, I do know." The gun trembled in her hands, adrenaline making her fingers tingle. "You know why you hate me so much, Kristina? Because you're just like me, but you're too full of yourself to admit it."

"Maybe," Kristina admitted after a beat. "But right now, I'm thinking straight, and you're not." Then, almost as an afterthought: "And I don't hate you. It's more like ... a very strong, visceral dislike."

The unexpected humor cracked through Sam's tunnel vision. She almost laughed. But she kept the gun sighted on Ventura.

"Maybe you're right that we're not so different," Kristina whispered. "But there are boundaries, even for people like … like us."

Sam let out a ragged breath and allowed Kristina's hand to push the barrel of the gun down. "Hal must find you so annoying."

"We've found a way to love each other in spite of our faults."

Sam did laugh then, a quiet tension-breaking sound. As she did, she watched Ventura spring forward, making a run for the door. "What the hell is she—"

Ventura collided with Coffey in the office's doorway, knocking the detective aside so that she could make her escape. It was all the opportunity Gabriel Molina needed to whirl back to his original target.

Hal's mouth opened in a scream.

———

HAL SAW the shotgun swing back toward him, those twin black holes promising death. His muscles locked in place, useless, as if his body had forgotten how to move. Time seemed to slow. The light from the street bathed Molina's face in harsh illumination. His eyes were empty of everything except rage.

So this is how it ends, Hal thought, his mind strangely amused despite the hammering of his heart. At the hands of a man who won third place cosplaying a space solider in a glittery cape. He sincerely hoped Kristina would be able to keep that detail out of his obituary.

Kristina.

He tore his gaze from the shotgun's barrels, turning to look at her one last time.

The crack of a gunshot split the air, and Hal flinched, expecting pain that never came.

Instead, it was Molina who cried out, spinning, crashing into the wall. The shotgun clattered to the floor. He clutched his shoulder. Blood seeped between his fingers, darkening his shirt.

Sam Klein stood from where she'd crouched on the floor, a nine-millimeter still raised in her hands, a thin wisp of smoke curling from the barrel.

Coffey was there in the next instant, diving forward to kick the fallen shotgun across the floor. He pinned Molina against the wall and snapped handcuffs around his wrists, ignoring the man's cries of pain.

"Gabriel Molina, you are under arrest," Coffey said, his voice ragged. "You have the right to remain silent. Anything you say can and will be used against you in a court of law."

As Coffey continued the *Miranda* warning, Hal's legs finally gave out. He sank to his knees, the adrenaline that had kept him upright now abandoning him in a rush.

Kristina was beside him instantly, her arms around his shoulders. "Are you okay?"

"Fine." He nodded, barely able to form the word, his throat tight with emotion.

"I raised her in the church. I taught her to respect herself." Molina glared at Coffey, then at Hal. He spat out the words as if they tasted foul. "When I saw her in that ... place. Dancing like a whore. Taking off her clothes for money." His voice broke. "I tried to save her and she laughed at me. Said she liked it better than nursing school. That she made more in one night than I made in a week." His voice trembled. "She slapped me. Like a slut."

The word triggered Hal's memory. "The arguments the

neighbors heard in her apartment building," he said. "That was you. Not Nico."

"I tried to make her see what she was doing to herself, to our family."

"And when she didn't see, you killed her," Hal said, the words flat.

"You strangled her with your chain," Kristina said. "The one you're wearing right now. And then you planted the USB cable to frame Nico."

Molina's silence was confirmation enough.

From his spot against the wall, Glover let out a pained laugh. "You've got to be kidding me. All along, it was this guy?"

A wail of sirens grew louder outside. Red and blue lights flashed through the window, painting alternating colors over the wreckage of their office.

Moments later, officers streamed in through the broken doorway, paramedics right behind them. The office transformed into a crime scene. Two EMTs rushed to Glover, who had gone alarmingly pale, while another examined Molina's shoulder wound with considerably less urgency.

People gathered on the street outside, a few of them raising their phones to capture the carnage.

"This is definitely going viral," Hal mused. "I'd like to see Ricky Sawyer get this kind of publicity."

Kristina grinned at him. "You know, most lawyers just buy better suits when they're feeling competitive."

"I already have the best suits."

They held onto each other in the center of the ruined office, surrounded by glass and splintered wood, while Gabriel Molina, head bowed in defeat, was led away in handcuffs.

44

HAL WATCHED **Sam Klein** straighten her shoulders as she rose to address the court. Her suit was wrinkled, she had dark circles under her eyes, and there was a brown stain on the sleeve of her suit jacket—barely potable coffee, courtesy of the Philly PD. She hadn't gone home last night.

None of them had.

They'd endured hours of questioning, given their statements multiple times, and explained—very carefully—what had happened in the office of The Nolan Law Firm.

"Your Honor, the Commonwealth moves to dismiss all charges against the defendant, Nico Ramirez."

Her voice was steady but strained, impressively professional given the exhaustion she must be feeling.

The courtroom shifted in collective anticipation. The reporters—who'd been scribbling furiously since the moment they'd entered, trying to connect last night's shootout to today's proceedings—exchanged glances. They'd expected drama, but perhaps not this. Judge Harding stiffened. The poor guy looked like he'd aged two decades since this trial had begun.

Nico Ramirez trembled beside Hal, his breath coming in short, quick bursts.

"Easy," Hal murmured. "This is good news."

But Nico looked like a man who'd stopped believing in good news.

"We're entering a nolle prosequi in the interests of justice," Sam continued, sliding a document toward the clerk.

"Approach the bench please, counselors," Harding said, his tone dangerously level.

Hal and Kristina rose to join Sam at the bench.

"I assume this has something to do with last night's breaking news?" the judge said.

"Yes, Your Honor," Sam said, voice pitched low. "Evidence, uh, came to light that completely exonerates Mr. Ramirez and implicates another individual—Gabriel Molina, the victim's father—in Natalia Ramirez's murder. Mr. Molina made what amounts to an admission of guilt during his apprehension last night."

Harding's eyes narrowed. "His apprehension in the offices of The Nolan Law Firm, where you—an assistant district attorney—Detective Dan Coffey, and two FBI agents also just happened to be present."

"Your Honor—" Hal started.

"No." Harding silenced him with a raised hand. "I want to hear this from the Commonwealth." He glared at Sam. "Where exactly was this new evidence discovered, Ms. Klein?"

Sam hesitated, exchanged a quick look with Hal. "Security footage obtained by the defense last night, from the victim's place of employment, shows Mr. Molina engaged in a heated argument with his daughter days before her death. This footage, combined with Mr. Molina's subsequent actions and statements, convinced the Commonwealth that we cannot in good conscience continue prosecuting Mr. Ramirez."

Harding was shaking his head. "And by 'subsequent actions and statements' you mean attempting to murder you?"

"Your Honor—" Hal tried again.

"No." Harding kept his gaze on Sam. "How did you come to be present at the law offices of defense counsel at"—he consulted a sheet of paper—"9:40 PM last night?"

Sam's throat worked as she swallowed.

"Your Honor—"

"Mr. Nolan, I'll be honest. I am just not ready to hear your voice today."

Hal nodded and pressed his lips together. "Not the first time I've heard that, Your Honor."

"If I may," Kristina interjected, "Ms. Klein was at our office to discuss a potential resolution to this case. Given that federal investigations overlapped with our client's case, we were exploring whether a plea arrangement might serve all parties' interests. That's why Detective Coffey and Special Agents Ventura and Glover were also present."

"To discuss a plea deal." Harding's voice dripped skepticism.

Sure, let's go with that, Hal thought. *Sounds a lot better than trying to entrap corrupt FBI agents with illegally placed recording devices while our investigator honey-trapped a strip club's head of security.*

"The matter was time-sensitive, Your Honor," Sam said. "And required privacy that—"

"You know what?" Harding stared at them for a long moment. "I know I'm not getting the complete story here. But I'm going to let that go—for now—because my primary concern is that an innocent man is sitting in my courtroom facing first-degree murder charges."

"Yes, Your Honor," Sam said. "Which is why the Commonwealth moves to dismiss those charges immediately."

Harding nodded grimly. "Motion granted. Step back."

They returned to their respective tables. Harding cleared his throat and addressed the courtroom.

"The charges against Nico Ramirez are hereby dismissed with prejudice." Harding turned to the jury box, where twelve bewildered faces stared back at him. "Ladies and gentlemen, thank you for your service in what has been, I'm certain, an unusual experience. You are dismissed." He gathered his papers with an air of weary resignation. "Mr. Ramirez, you are free to go. This court is adjourned."

Nico sat frozen, staring straight ahead.

"It's over," Hal told him. "You can go home."

"Just like that?" Nico's voice was barely audible over the commotion of the emptying courtroom.

"Just like that." Kristina squeezed his shoulder. "Dismissed with prejudice. Just as good as a not-guilty verdict."

"Brantley will be relieved," Hal said. "Saved him the expense of the full dog-and-pony show."

Nico didn't even smile at the joke, and watching him, Hal felt a strange hollowness where triumph should be.

"What happens now?"

"Paperwork, mostly. But we'll handle that. You go back to your life."

Nico snorted a miserable laugh. "What life?"

Outside the courthouse, they found Sam Klein in the hallway, staring at her phone. Her shoulders were hunched, her face tight.

"Hey," Hal said. "Smile. You did a good thing in there. Not to mention, you know, saving my life last night."

"Yeah." Sam pocketed her phone. "Consider that a professional courtesy." She sighed. "I'd better get back to the office. Burke's already called three times."

"Burke." Hal knew the head of the Homicide Unit despised him. Some people's egos just couldn't handle a good courtroom thrashing. "Let me guess. He found out we were the defense attorneys and demanded a conviction at any cost."

"And I just pulled the plug on the entire prosecution." Sam's bitter laugh echoed in the hallway. "Time to face the firing squad."

Kristina exchanged a quick glance with Hal, her expression softening slightly. As Sam turned to leave, Kristina caught her arm. "Maybe we can help with that."

45

———

Sam had always imagined career death would feel more dramatic, but sitting in Burke's office—with its grimy window, diplomas hung slightly crooked on the wall, and lingering smell of old coffee—was just depressingly bureaucratic.

Burke didn't look up from the paperwork in front of him when she entered. His bulky frame dominated the chair, his bushy eyebrows furrowed over what she assumed was her personnel file.

"Sit."

Sam remained standing.

Burke looked up, irritation flashing in his eyes. The seconds stretched between them. Finally, Burke closed the file and leaned back in his chair.

"I gave you a first-degree murder case, and you let the Nolans outmaneuver you."

Sam almost laughed at *gave*. But semantics were the least of her problems now.

"I wasn't outmaneuvered. New evidence—"

"Don't." He raised a hand, not unlike how Judge Harding had raised a hand to silence Hal in the courtroom. She closed her mouth. "The Nolans are courtroom con artists. They don't try cases. They undermine them. And you just stood there and watched them do it."

"They found the real killer."

"Sleight-of-hand." Burke waved a hand dismissively. "This is exactly why I tried to keep you off major cases. Some people just don't have what it takes to be prosecutors."

Sam lifted her chin. "I did the right thing."

"The right thing?" Burke's laugh was dry and cutting. "First, you deliberately hid that the Nolans took over the case—knowing I'd pull you. Then you ran a death penalty prosecution with zero supervision. And last night? What exactly were you doing in their office during a shooting? I can only guess." He leaned across his desk, voice dropping to a cruel whisper. "Now you have the audacity to stand there with that self-righteous look? You didn't do the right thing, Sam. You embarrassed yourself. Again."

Sam felt her shoulders tighten, the strain at the base of her neck that had become a constant companion since the *Orozco* case.

She'd worked her ass off these past three years to come back from that mistake. Ramirez had been her shot. She'd done the right thing this time—for the most part.

And the result was the same.

She shifted from one leg to the other, suddenly feeling exposed in her wrinkled suit—the same one she'd been wearing since yesterday. Burke seeming to enjoy watching her squirm.

"HR is drawing up your termination paperwork. Clean out your desk."

Sam had expected it, but the words still hit her like a physical blow.

Her legal career, over. The salary that covered Emily's dance classes and their shitty health insurance, gone. The apartment, now a countdown to eviction. And the legal battle with Colten? She didn't even want to think about that.

In the suffocating silence that followed, Burke watched her with barely disguised satisfaction. She willed herself not to cry, even as she felt wetness gather in her eyes.

His intercom buzzed, the grating sound cutting through the tension. "Mr. Burke?"

"Not now."

The sound of his assistant awkwardly clearing her throat crackled through the speaker. "Um, the DA is giving a press conference. You might want to turn on your TV."

Burke scowled. "I said not—"

"It's about the Ramirez case."

Burke's head whipped toward the screen mounted on his wall. He grabbed a remote from his desk and turned on the TV. District Attorney Jessica Black stood behind the podium of the DA pressroom, her black hair gleaming under the lights.

"...want to commend ADA Samantha Klein for her handling of the Ramirez case," Black was saying. "Ms. Klein exemplifies the kind of prosecutor this office seeks to cultivate—one who pursues justice rather than convictions for their own sake."

Burke's face flushed crimson, the veins in his forehead pulsing. Sam felt like she'd been dropped into some alternate universe.

"What the hell?" His whisper mirrored her own thoughts.

Black continued. "When new evidence emerged suggesting the defendant's innocence, ADA Klein didn't hesitate to do the right thing, despite significant pressure. That's the kind of moral courage and sound judgment we expect from our top homicide prosecutors."

Top homicide prosecutors? As far as Sam knew, Jessica Black had never noticed her existence in her entire tenure at the DA's Office.

"I'm impressed by ADA Klein's ethical handling of a complex situation. This office stands behind her decision one-hundred percent."

Black fielded a few more questions about the case, making it clear that the DA's Office considered the matter closed and justice served. When the press conference ended, Burke's office fell into stunned silence. He fumbled for the remote and shut off the TV.

"How...?" Burke's face darkened. "*Nolan.*"

Sam's mind raced. The Nolans had orchestrated this? She'd heard whispers about their connection to Black, but getting the DA to paint Sam as some paragon of prosecutorial virtue? A reluctant smile tugged at the corner of her mouth before she could press her lips together to suppress it.

"Looks like you're the one who was outmaneuvered."

"You think this is funny?" Burke sputtered, actual spit flying from his lips as his hands trembled over her file. "Black may have been fooled by whatever line the Nolans fed her, but not me. I know you. I know what you're capable of. Believe me, Sam, this is far from over."

"You're right, Aldo," she said, turning toward the door. "I'm just getting started."

She was grinning as she walked out of Burke's office. She felt lighter than she had in years.

46

COLTEN ROTH TOOK another swig from the Bud Light he'd cleverly poured into a travel mug. His Charger's headlights carved through Lincoln Drive's tree-choked darkness.

The locals called this stretch Dead Man's Gulch. *Pussies.*

He cranked up the audio and fed the Charger more gas, ignoring the 25 MPH speed limit and sending the aftermarket V8 into a throaty growl. The speedometer climbed past seventy. Past eighty.

He'd spent the last six years trying to forget about Samantha Klein. But now that some judge had randomly lifted the restraining order, he couldn't seem to get Sam—or their daughter—out of his mind.

He still remembered vividly that day she'd stood up in court and told a judge he abused her. As if it was *his* fault she bruised easily. And she'd taken away his little girl.

Blood of his blood.

A child who *should* love him unconditionally—and would, if Sam hadn't poisoned the girl's mind against him.

Bitch.

Well, things were going to be different now. He was going to be part of Emily's life whether Sam liked it or not.

Part of Sam's life, too.

He adjusted his pants at the thought.

The Charger bottomed out on a dip, and he had to wrestle the wheel for control. After a brief scare, he was cruising again, cliff on one side, Wissahickon Creek on the other.

Then blue and red lights lit up his rearview mirror. A short little bleep of siren.

"Fuck me." Colten eased his foot off the accelerator and yanked the wheel right, tires chewing earth as he pulled onto the narrow shoulder.

He shoved the travel mug under his seat. *Better safe than sorry.*

The police car parked directly behind him. It was one of those unmarked cars—he could tell that even with the spotlight flooding his vision. He checked his reflection. Bloodshot eyes stared back. *Good enough.*

The cop's door opened. Colten rolled his shoulders, took a deep breath. A man approached his door. Knocked twice on the window.

Colten hit the button. The window descended with a whine, letting in the scent of dirt and dead leaves and the creek.

"How's your night, Mr. Roth?"

Colten startled. "What?"

Detective Dan Coffey leaned into view, his weathered face lit by the police car's headlights.

Colten's mouth opened. Nothing came out.

"Step out of the car," Coffey said.

Not a suggestion. Not a request.

"Now."

47

THE WILLIAM J. Green Jr. Federal Building loomed over downtown Philly, ten stories of beige bureaucracy housing multiple federal agencies, including the FBI's Philadelphia field office. Hal and Kristina rode the elevator in silence, both dreading the purpose of Agent Cooley's vague summons.

"Perfect timing," Cooley said when they reached his doorway. "You can help me carry these boxes to my car."

Hal froze, staring at the half-empty bookshelves and the desk stripped of personal items. Three cardboard boxes sat on the floor, packed with what looked like years' worth of personal belongings—framed certificates, coffee mugs, desk accessories. A framed photo—some kind of graduation ceremony—peeked out from beneath a tangle of charging cables.

Hal's stomach dropped. "Tell me this isn't what it looks like."

"Wish I could." Cooley wrapped a picture frame in a sheet of newspaper. Hal glimpsed a smiling woman and two teenage boys before the image disappeared. "I was 'offered' the opportunity to resign. Apparently, I've been struggling with procedural compliance for some time—at least according to recent amendments to my file."

"Ventura and Glover," Kristina said.

Cooley's silence was answer enough. He gestured to the two chairs facing his desk. "Sit. We don't have much time."

"Charles—"

Cooley's gaze was firm. He pointed again at the chairs. "Building security has been instructed to escort me out by six."

Hal exchanged a quick glance with Kristina. As they seated themselves, guilt coiled in his chest. Cooley had warned them, but they'd charged ahead anyway, convinced of their ability to handle a couple of dirty agents. Instead, Ventura and Glover had handled them. And now a good man was paying the price.

Collateral damage. It was becoming an uncomfortably familiar pattern.

"I'm sorry," Hal said. The words felt grossly inadequate.

Cooley waved away the apology. "Don't be. I knew what I was doing when I met with you in Reading Terminal Market." He continued emptying his desk drawers. "I made my choices just like you made yours."

"There has to be something we can do," Kristina said. "An appeal, a whistleblower complaint—"

"After what they did—" Hal began.

"What did they do exactly?" Cooley set down a stapler with more force than necessary. "There's no recording. Your bugs were discovered and destroyed."

"We will fix this," Hal said, the words tasting hollow even as he spoke them.

Cooley actually laughed at that, a short, harsh sound. "How? With your extensive connections at the FBI? Your influence with the federal judiciary? It would be the word of two infamously tricky defense lawyers against two FBI agents with spotless records and friends in the Director's office." Cooley shook his head. "I appreciate the offer, but it would only make things worse. The Bureau takes care of its own. Usually that's a good thing. Sometimes it's not."

He methodically wrapped another photo frame.

A wave of frustrated helplessness washed over Hal. "We'll find a way."

"No, you won't," Cooley said, the bluntness of his tone silencing Hal's protests. "My career is over. And you two have your own problems to worry about."

"Olivia Hazenberg," Kristina said.

Cooley nodded. "That's why I called you here. I felt you should hear it directly from me."

Hal felt a knot of dread tighten in his stomach. "Hear what?"

"The investigation into the cyberattacks on your firm was officially closed this morning, all surveillance details reassigned. Less than an hour later, Olivia Hazenberg disappeared. She's gone off the grid. And I strongly doubt she's forgotten her vendetta against you."

Hal stared at the FBI agent. The room felt smaller, closing in on him. The woman who'd decimated their law practice with ransomware, who'd emptied their bank accounts and tried to destroy their lives, was now in the wild?

"They can't just—" Hal started. But he knew they could, they had.

Cooley sealed a box with packing tape, the ripping sound harsh. "I'm sorry, Hal."

"They're letting a cyber terrorist walk free just to punish us?" Hal said.

"What about the secure bank account you set up for us?" Kristina said. "Is that compromised too?"

Cooley looked up from his packing. His expression was grim. "That account was Bureau-monitored. With the investigation closed, that protection ends. You'll want to move whatever funds you have left as soon as possible, though I can't guarantee any financial institution will be safe if she targets you again."

Kristina's voice rose, incredulous. "All this because we did our jobs?"

"From their perspective, you interfered with a RICO case. A case they've been building for years."

"Nico was innocent," Kristina said.

"And?" Cooley said. "You cost them their best shot at Brantley. I warned you not to mess with Ventura and Glover."

"They have to be stopped," Hal said.

"That's a problem for another day." Cooley closed the final box, sealing it with deliberate care. "And when that day comes...." He met Hal's gaze meaningfully. "I have a feeling you'll know exactly what to do."

"Count on it."

"For now, keep your focus on Hazenberg. She's unstable, brilliant, and motivated. Angry and completely off our radar. If she surfaces, don't try to handle it yourselves. Call the police. Assume she's capable of violence."

He lifted a box from the floor and placed it on his now-empty desk. The other two boxes followed, stacked neatly. A career reduced to three cardboard containers.

"Let me help with those," Hal said, rising to grab one of the boxes.

"I've got it." Cooley hefted two boxes, stacking them easily.

Hal reached for the third box anyway. They made their way through the office in silence, past cubicles where agents studiously avoided eye contact. The elevator ride to the lobby was interminable, the silence broken only by the mechanical hum of the descending car. When they reached Cooley's sedan in a nearby parking garage, he popped the trunk and they loaded the boxes.

Cooley extended his hand first to Kristina, then to Hal. His grip was firm, final.

"Good luck," he said. "I mean that."

Hal felt the weight of those words settle in his chest. "And I meant what I said, too. We will fix this."

"Fix it?" Cooley slid into the driver's seat and started the engine. "I hope you survive it."

He closed the door and put the car in drive. They watched as he navigated through the garage and disappeared up the exit ramp, leaving them alone in the dim fluorescent lighting.

48

THEY WERE SUPPOSED to be celebrating, but no one ordered champagne.

Cheerful chatter rose from the tables around them, accompanied by the clink of silverware and the sizzle from the open kitchen. But their table was quiet.

The leather booth squeaked as Hal shifted uncomfortably. Even a week after the attack on his office, his body was sore in places he didn't know could ache. Nico pushed a piece of medium-rare ribeye around his plate, even though the steak should have been a revelation after a month of prison food. Kristina folded and refolded her napkin. Lena examined her knuckles, swollen and scabbed from her fight with Marcus Medrano.

Some celebration.

"Food okay?" Kristina asked Nico, breaking the silence that had settled over their table.

"Yeah." Nico nodded mechanically. "Yeah, it's great. Thank you."

His gratitude made Hal's insides twist. They'd saved him from a murder charge, but his wife was still dead. And even worse, his marriage, and the future he'd imagined with Natalia, had all been exposed as a lie. The bruises from his prison beating might have faded weeks ago, but the deeper wounds? Those would never heal.

Kristina squeezed Hal's knee under the table. Probably thinking the same thing.

He took a long pull of wine. What could he say? *Sorry your wife lived a double life? Sorry we saved you from death row only to leave you with nothing?*

"She was probably trying to protect you," Kristina offered gently.

"From what? The truth?" Nico pushed his plate away. "I worked all those hours to pay for her tuition. Came home exhausted every night, proud that I was helping her become a nurse. And the whole time, she was lying to me."

Welcome to marriage, kid.

Hal caught himself before the cynical thought escaped. His own marriage had its share of deceptions lately—mostly his, to be fair. But compared to the Ramirez family, the Nolans were an image of marital bliss.

Hal's gaze drifted to the bar, where the evening news played silently on the mounted television, closed captions scrolling across the screen.

FINANCIAL FUGITIVE: BRANTLEY DISAPPEARS AMID FEDERAL PROBE.

"You gotta be kidding me."

The others turned to look. A photo of Gavin Brantley appeared beside the anchor's face.

"Could you please turn up the volume?" Kristina called to the bartender.

"—sources close to the investigation report that Brantley was last seen boarding his private jet at Philadelphia International Airport yesterday evening," the anchor was saying. "The flight plan indicated the Cayman Islands as the destination, but the aircraft never arrived. Federal authorities are now investigating whether Brantley, who is the subject of ongoing FBI and SEC investigations, has fled the country with an estimated seventy million dollars in client funds."

"Seventy million?" Lena whistled.

The four of them watched in silence. *Seventy million dollars.* Imagine the billable hours had Brantley retained them to defend him in court. It would have put them back at the top of the Philadelphia criminal bar—made them legal superstars.

There goes our retirement fund.

Pulling his gaze from the TV, he found Kristina watching him with a sympathetic expression. "It wasn't meant to be, Hal."

"Yeah, guess I'll have to cancel that order for the yacht."

She didn't smile. "I'm serious."

"We were so close."

"He made us think that. Strung us along, just like all the clients he bilked. But we never really had a chance because he never intended to face a jury. Guys like Brantley always run."

Hal nodded. He knew she was right. And instead of feeling the loss of all that money and publicity, he was surprised to feel something else instead.

Relief.

"Good riddance," he said.

The news moved on to other stories. Nico pushed his plate away, the steak barely touched. "I should get going," he said abruptly.

"You okay?" Hal asked.

Nico's gaze was distant. "I keep thinking about time. All those hours working to help pay for nursing classes that never happened. Then weeks in jail for a crime I didn't commit." He shook his head slowly. "Life's too short. I don't want to waste another minute of it sitting here."

"I'm gonna try not to be offended by that," Hal said with a grin.

"Actually, I think it's a great toast." Lena raised her water glass. "To not wasting any more time with lawyers."

"Hilarious," Hal said. But he raised his own glass and touched it to hers. After a moment, Nico and Kristina brought their glasses to the table's center, too.

"To moving forward, without looking back," Kristina said. Her eyes met Hal's.

The waiter approached, seeming to sense a shift. "Will there be anything else?"

"Just the check, please," Hal said.

"So what will you do now?" Kristina asked Nico. "Really?"

Hal watched uncertainty flicker across his client's face. "Might travel for a while," Nico said. "Clear my head."

Running, just like Brantley. Hal didn't point out the irony. Besides, who was he to judge?

The waiter returned with the check in a leather folder. Hal's heart rate spiked as he reached for his wallet, images of their disaster at Bistro Cannata flashing through his mind. Cooley had warned them they could no longer count on the protection of their magical government bank account.

He slid his card into the folder and handed it back, forcing a casual smile.

The waiter returned quickly—too quickly? Hal searched his face for any hint of that apologetic expression that would precede awkward news. But the man only said, "Thank you," as he placed the folder on the table.

Hal's shoulders didn't fully relax until he opened the leather cover and saw the neatly printed receipt. He exhaled slowly, catching Kristina's eye.

"Guess we live to fight another day," he whispered.

Outside the restaurant, the evening had turned cool. They

stood on the sidewalk, the city's sounds washing over them—
pedestrians talking, distant sirens, car horns. Hal flagged down a
taxi for Nico. As the car pulled up, their client seemed to
hesitate.

"I know I'm not acting grateful, but...." He shook Hal's hand,
then Kristina's. "I am."

Hal nodded. "Take care of yourself, Nico."

They watched his taxi disappear into traffic. Lena stretched,
wincing slightly.

"You heading home too?" Hal asked her.

She nodded. "Early morning surveillance job. You're not my
only clients, you know."

"Just your most fun, right? Who else sends you to game
shops and strip clubs?"

"Only you." She gave Hal a quick hug, then Kristina a longer
one. "Call me if you need me," she told her cousin.

"I will."

When Lena was gone, he and Kristina walked in silence
toward their apartment. The night air carried a hint of rain and
he breathed in the scent of wet asphalt as the first drops darkened the pavement of Walnut Street. Their shoulders bumped.
A police cruiser rolled slowly past them, the officer doing a
double-take as he recognized them. His mouth tightened into a
thin line of disgust.

Well, at least we still have our reputations.

"Another solid win for The Nolan Law Firm," Kristina said
softly.

Hal let out a laugh. "What was your favorite part? The utter
devastation of our client's soul? The destruction of an honest
FBI agent's career? Brantley escaping justice to live out his retirement in some tropical paradise?"

"The part where we saved an innocent man's life was pretty
great."

"Yeah." He found himself smiling despite everything. "We're good at that, aren't we?"

She slipped her hand into his, their fingers intertwining. "No one's better."

Their shoulders bumped again, this time deliberately. Hal stopped walking, pulling her gently toward him. They stood face to face in the light drizzle, raindrops catching in her eyelashes. "Let's go home and do something else we're good at."

Her lips curved into a smile. "Finally a strategy I can fully endorse."

At their apartment, Hal fumbled with his keys before getting the door open. He reached for the light switch.

His fingers immediately tensed. Something was wrong. The air smelled different—a faint hint of perfume he didn't recognize.

Before he could warn Kristina, she stepped past him into the living room and stopped abruptly.

"Hal," she said, her voice tight with alarm.

A woman sat on their couch. Relaxed, casual, a small laptop lazily balanced on her knees. Dark hair fell past her shoulders. When she smiled, there was no warmth in her expression. Her eyes, behind stylish glasses, were cold and clinical and contemptuous.

Just like her brother's.

"Hope you don't mind," Olivia Hazenberg said. "I let myself in."

THE END

Thank you for reading **Deal Breaker!**

If you enjoyed the book, please post a review on Amazon and let everyone know. Your opinion will directly influence the success of the book. It doesn't need to be an in-depth report—

just a few sentences helps a lot. If you could take a few minutes to help spread the word, I would greatly appreciate it.

The next book in the Hal and Kristina Nolan Legal Thriller Series is called *Original Sin*. I hope you check it out.

—Larry A. Winters

Want to find out what happens next?
Pre-order the next book in the *Hal and Kristina Nolan Legal Thrillers* series, **Original Sin!**

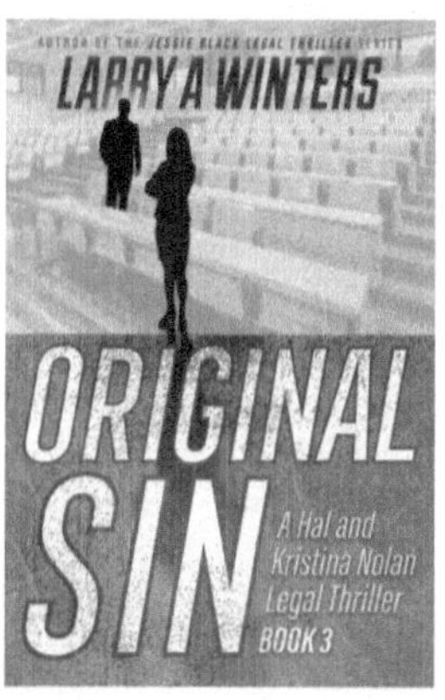

Coming soon - pre-order today!

BOOKS BY LARRY A. WINTERS

The Hal and Kristina Nolan Legal Thriller Series
The Legal Limit
Deal Breaker
Original Sin *(coming soon)*

The Jessie Black Legal Thriller Series
Grave Testimony (prequel)
Burnout
Informant
Deadly Evidence
Fatal Defense
False Justice
Silenced Witness
Lethal Innocence
Conviction
Murder Charge
Return of the Prosecutor
Last Stand
Blood Oath

Also Featuring Jessie Black
Web of Lies
Witness Hunt

Other Books
Hardcore

ABOUT THE AUTHOR

Larry A. Winters's stories feature a rogue's gallery of brilliant lawyers, determined cops, and vicious bad guys of all sorts. When not writing, he can be found living a life of excitement. Not really, but he does know a good time when he sees one: reading a book by the fireplace on a cold evening, catching a rare movie night with his wife (when a friend or family member can be coerced into babysitting duty), smart TV dramas (and dumb TV comedies), vacations (those that involve reading on the beach, a lot of eating, and not a lot else), cardio (generally beginning upon his return from said vacations, and quickly tapering off), video games (even though he stinks at them), and stockpiling gadgets (with a particular weakness for tablets and ereaders).

www.larryawinters.com